Dear Reader,

You can't believe all the stories you've heard about me. Sure, I've been called "America's Favorite Heartthrob" and "Playboy of the Western World." Sure, I've done some things to earn my reputation. But I do have *some* morals. I was trying to behave myself in this tiny Wisconsin town—and doing such a good job that my "I'm just a regular guy" routine backfired.

Now, it's a pleasure trying to persuade Olivia James that I'm not really just the boy next door. But while I'm playing the parts of attentive suitor and passionate lover, I'm slowly being groomed by a brood of cunning children for the role of ready-made father.

For the first time ever, the thought of being a parent doesn't sound bad at all. And if I could get their irritating, intriguing mother as part of the bargain, I might even be willing to make a deal!

Joe Harrington

1. ALABAMA
Full House • Jackie Weger
2. ALASKA
Borrowed Dreams • Debbie Macomber
3. ARIZONA
Call It Destiny • Jayne Ann Krentz
4. ARKANSAS
Another Kind of Love • Mary Lynn Baxter
5. CALIFORNIA
Deceptions • Annette Broadrick
6. COLORADO
Stormwalker • Dallas Schulze
7. CONNECTICUT
Straight from the Heart • Barbara Delinsky
8. DELAWARE
Author's Choice • Elizabeth August
9. FLORIDA
Dream Come True • Ann Major
10. GEORGIA
Way of the Willow • Linda Shaw
11. HAWAII
Tangled Lies • Anne Stuart
12. IDAHO
Rogue's Valley • Kathleen Creighton
13. ILLINOIS
Love by Proxy • Diana Palmer
14. INDIANA
Possibles • Lass Small
15. IOWA
Kiss Yesterday Goodbye • Leigh Michaels
16. KANSAS
A Time To Keep • Curtiss Ann Matlock
17. KENTUCKY
One Pale, Fawn Glove • Linda Shaw
18. LOUISIANA
Bayou Midnight • Emilie Richards
19. MAINE
Rocky Road • Anne Stuart
20. MARYLAND
The Love Thing • Dixie Browning
21. MASSACHUSETTS
Pros and Cons • Bethany Campbell
22. MICHIGAN
To Tame a Wolf • Anne McAllister
23. MINNESOTA
Winter Lady • Janet Joyce
24. MISSISSIPPI
After the Storm • Rebecca Flanders
25. MISSOURI
Choices • Annette Broadrick
26. MONTANA
Part of the Bargain • Linda Lael Miller
27. NEBRASKA
Secrets of Tyrone • Regan Forest
28. NEVADA
Nobody's Baby • Barbara Bretton
29. NEW HAMPSHIRE
Natural Attraction • Marisa Carroll
30. NEW JERSEY
Moments Harsh, Moments Gentle • Joan Hohl
31. NEW MEXICO
Within Reach • Marilyn Pappano
32. NEW YORK
In Good Faith • Judith McWilliams
33. NORTH CAROLINA
The Security Man • Dixie Browning
34. NORTH DAKOTA
A Class Act • Kathleen Eagle
35. OHIO
Too Near the Fire • Lindsay McKenna
36. OKLAHOMA
A Time and a Season • Curtiss Ann Matlock
37. OREGON
Uneasy Alliance • Jayne Ann Krentz
38. PENNSYLVANIA
The Wrong Man • Ann Major
39. RHODE ISLAND
The Bargain • Patricia Coughlin
40. SOUTH CAROLINA
The Last Frontier • Rebecca Flanders
41. SOUTH DAKOTA
For Old Times' Sake • Kathleen Eagle
42. TENNESSEE
To Love a Dreamer • Ruth Langan
43. TEXAS
For the Love of Mike • Candace Schuler
44. UTAH
To Tame the Hunter • Stephanie James
45. VERMONT
Finders Keepers • Carla Neggers
46. VIRGINIA
The Devlin Dare • Cathy Gillen Thacker
47. WASHINGTON
The Waiting Game • Jayne Ann Krentz
48. WEST VIRGINIA
All in the Family • Heather Graham Pozzessere
49. WISCONSIN
Starstruck • Anne McAllister
50. WYOMING
Special Touches • Sharon Brondos

ANNE McALLISTER

Starstruck

Harlequin Books

TORONTO • NEW YORK • LONDON
AMSTERDAM • PARIS • SYDNEY • HAMBURG
STOCKHOLM • ATHENS • TOKYO • MILAN
MADRID • WARSAW • BUDAPEST • AUCKLAND

For Peter always,
and this time,
especially, for Susan

HARLEQUIN ENTERPRISES LTD.
225 Duncan Mill Road, Don Mills,
Ontario, Canada M3B 3K9

STARSTRUCK

ISBN: 0-373-45199-7

Published Harlequin Enterprises, Ltd. 1985, 1993

Printed in the U.S.A.

Chapter One

"Me? Interview Joe Harrington? You must be out of your mind!" Liv James stared across her messy desk with a mixture of exasperation and incredulity at her fellow reporter who had just ruined a perfectly lovely, sunny May afternoon by offering this astonishing rumor. "I'd rather cover the Kennel Club finals," she added with the distaste of a woman allergic to dogs.

"You may well get to if you don't show a little more enthusiasm for one of the world's more famous actor-directors," Frances Slade cautioned her, excitement wreathing her usually imperturbable, grandmotherly face. "Me, I'd interview him in a minute. Who knows where it might lead?" she went on dreamily.

"To bed," Liv said flatly. "With Joe Harrington, I hear that's where it always leads."

"Ah, but what a night," Frances sighed with a gleeful chuckle.

"Whatever would George say?" Liv teased. George and Frances had been married well over thirty years, which Liv was beginning to think was some kind of record in this day and age.

"That could be a problem," Frances agreed. "And you're more his type, anyway. He seems to go for tall, slender blondes. You see him with them all the time." She eyed Liv's upswept ash-blond hair and slim figure as if she were actually assessing their potential.

"You see Joe Harrington with anything in skirts," Liv retorted.

"Besides," Frances went on as if she hadn't heard, "you're uncommitted."

"And damned well going to stay that way."

"Touchy, touchy," Frances chided her. "I thought you were well over Tom."

"I am. And I have no intention of interviewing Joe Harrington because he's just another Tom James to the nth degree. It's men like him who give idiots like Tom their ideas." Her dentist ex-husband had decided after ten years of marriage that he needed to "feel free." Currently he was experiencing that freedom in the arms of a twenty-four-year-old graduate student who had come to him for a root canal and had stayed to help him "fulfill" himself. Her name was Trudy, but there had been Janice and Patty and Di and several others before her, and Liv was not impressed. Except by the irresponsibility of it all.

"I'm not sure it's quite fair to blame Joe Harrington for all of Tom's sins," Frances objected. "After all, Joe wasn't ever married with five kids."

"Maybe not," Liv admitted grudgingly, "but he is certainly a source of inspiration." She began straightening her desk, lining up pencils, sorting paper clips, anything to take her mind off the irritation she felt at Frances's even having suggested such an outrageous idea. "Anyway," she said as an afterthought, "I'm off early today. Marv's given me a break because it's my birthday."

"Maybe that's why you get to do the interview," Frances laughed. "Mmmmmm, what a present!"

"Cut that out," Liv said, grinning in spite of herself. "What I am getting for my birthday is a casserole I made on the weekend, if Noel remembers to put it in the oven, and a cake that Ben, Stephen and Theo are baking with a little help from their friends and an original watercolor by Jennifer. All far superior gifts to an interview with the playboy of the western world."

"Don't be surprised if you get that, too," Frances said and jerked her head in the direction of the editor making his way across the busy newspaper office toward them. "Here comes Marv."

"Have I got a job for you!" Marv Ketchum boomed with the same heartiness that he once used when he sent Liv off to write a story on ice fishing. She was glad it was not December.

"Oh?" Liv looked up, the hairs on the back of her neck standing up as she anticipated the ax about to fall.

"Story of the year," he went on jovially, "and *you* get to cover it. What do you say to that?"

"That I hope it's tomorrow, because I'm leaving at three-thirty today."

Marv sighed, losing his heartiness. "I was afraid of that."

"It isn't?"

"No." Then, apparently deciding that his best tactic was a strong offense, he said abruptly, "I want you to be at the Sheraton at five o'clock to interview Joe Harrington."

Frances beamed, her existence justified. Liv's teeth snapped together so hard they hurt.

"He's agreed to an interview—" Marv began.

"Bully for him," Liv muttered. "Why me? I thought the national desk guys would cover him. I mean, he's in Madison to speak for that world peace organization, isn't he? That's their area, not mine."

"Well," Marv said, ticking them off on his fingers, "Fitz went to Chicago for a story, Daly is in Minneapolis, Holt has the flu...."

"Fitz went to Chicago? But I saw him twenty minutes ago."

"Leaving," Marv said with satisfaction. "So that means you're it. Have it on my desk by ten o'clock tomorrow morning."

"Wait a minute," Liv said as he moved away. "What about Frances? Can't Frances do it?" Surely George wouldn't really mind if she sacrificed his wife on the altar of America's favorite heartthrob.

Marv shook his head. "Come along to my office," he said and nearly dragged her with him, shutting the door behind her. "Sit," he commanded.

"I'll stand."

"Look, be reasonable," he said, trying to moderate his tone and not wholly succeeding. "Think how many women would like to be in your shoes. How many would give everything they own to interview Joe Harrington?"

"They're welcome," Liv said tartly, gray eyes flashing. "All I want is a nice, hectic evening alone with my kids."

"You like your job, don't you?" Marv said silkily, suddenly looking every inch the tough boss.

Liv stared. "You wouldn't?" she gasped. He knew how much she needed this job. He had given it to her on very slim reasons and very great faith when she was newly divorced three years before and had presented him with a resume that said, "Twenty-nine years old, five children, no experience." Surely he wouldn't snatch it away now—not because of someone like Joe Harrington!

"I probably wouldn't," Marv said heavily as he lit a cigar and took several short puffs. "But I need to impress you with how very much I want this interview. Joe Harrington gives damned few of them. And if he's suddenly willing to talk to *Madison Times'* feature writer, Olivia James, you're going to listen!"

"But why me?" Liv demanded again. "Surely you could send someone else."

"I could," Marv agreed. "But he won't talk to anyone else. It's you he wants."

"Me?" She was incredulous. "He doesn't even know me!"

Marv shrugged. "He must know *of* you then. His secretary, some guy named Gates, called me this afternoon and said Harrington would talk to you. No one else."

"That's absurd." Liv turned and put her hand on the doorknob.

"Olivia." Marv's voice was like steel. "I wrote Harrington's agent about an interview weeks ago when we first knew he was coming to Madison to give this speech. 'No interviews,' the agent said. 'Everything he wants to say he'll say in his speech.' Fitz contacted him again about a week ago on the off-chance he'd changed his mind. He hadn't. Then today I get a call from Harrington's secretary and he says, 'You have a reporter named Olivia James, right?' and I say, 'Right,' and he says, 'Mr. Harrington says if you still want the interview, he'll talk to her.'" Marv lifted his shoulders eloquently. "Think what you like," he told her. "Just be there at five o'clock."

"And if I'm not?" Liv didn't like the sound of this one bit. Joe Harrington sounded even worse than she had imagined.

"You will be, Liv," Marv said softly, cigar smoke puffing out of his lips like smoke from a fire-breathing dragon. "Because you know how much an interview like this would mean to the paper. To me. To you. You're a professional, Liv. You don't have to like him, for heaven's sake. You've only got to listen!"

Liv sagged against the door frame, seeing mortgage payments and outgrown shoes. Weighed against them, a personal dislike of men like Joe Harrington seemed petty indeed. She was thirty-two years old and the mother of five children ranging in age from twelve to five. Surely she could put her personal feelings aside and be professional enough to handle a simple interview. Marv was right. Besides, after Tom she ought to have plenty of natural immunity to the type. "All right," she said. "You win."

"That's my girl." Marv beamed at her, and Liv gave him a wry smile as she went out.

"Are you going to do it, then?" Frances pounced on her the moment she returned to her desk.

Liv made a face. "What do you think? Now all I've got to do is figure out how to fit him in. If I stop by the vet's for the rabbit *before* I go to the cleaners, and then I—"

"I almost forgot," Frances interrupted. "Noel just called and said he had baseball practice, so he can't put in the casserole. And the nurse at Ben's school phoned and said he cut his lip. I asked her if it needed stitches and she said no, so I told her you'd wait to see it till he got home." Frances's children were grown, but she hadn't forgotten what it was like.

"Wonderful," Liv said absently, mentally calculating how long it would take her to dash home and put the casserole in the oven before she got the rabbit, picked up the cleaning and arrived at the Sheraton. Darn Joe Harrington anyway. And, oh, hell, Stephen had a cello lesson. She would have to call Tom to take him to that. "If I leave now," she told Frances, glancing at her watch, "I just might make it."

"Give 'im a kiss for me." Frances grinned, making smacking sounds with her lips.

Liv rolled her eyes. "A punch in the nose is more like it."

"NOT TONIGHT, sweetheart. No. Tomorrow at the earliest." Joe Harrington ran a hand through his thick brown hair, which needed cutting, and rued its tendency to curl. Scowling he rubbed his eyes wearily. "Yeah, yeah. I miss you, too," he mumbled. It was a lie—he could scarcely remember what she looked like. Luscious. Buxom, no doubt. They all were. Brain like a pea. He slipped off his shirt and tossed it onto the bed, rummaging through his suitcase and pulling out a pair of faded jeans and a gray sweatshirt that had seen better days. He felt as though his entire body had seen better days. Of course one glance in the full-length mirror against the closet door showed that he was still trim and fit. Who, at thirty-six, wouldn't be if he spent days riding elephants and swinging through trees, chasing bandits and diamond smugglers through God's and Hollywood's best obstacle courses?

"But, Joe, I don't want to go to the party without you," the sexily husky voice on the other end of the line nagged him.

"Linda, if you don't want to go, don't go," he snapped, stepping out of his slacks and pulling on the jeans, the phone tucked under his ear. "I gotta run. Talk to you later."

"You'll call first thing when you get back, won't you?" she begged.

"Sure, sure." Joe dropped the receiver on the bed as her voice went on whiningly and tugged the sweatshirt over his head. Then he picked the receiver up and said, "Bye," hanging up before she could continue. A little Linda Lucas went a long way. How had she known where he was staying, anyway? He wadded up his shirt and slacks and stuffed them into the suitcase, slamming it shut. Then he collapsed onto the bed with a groan. Maybe he could catch forty winks before he had to be on the road again.

A breakfast speech in St. Louis, a luncheon speech in Chicago and a meeting with the cardinal, another speech in Milwaukee just finished, and now two hours in a car before he would give his last speech of the day in Madison. "Why do you do it?" Linda had railed at him when she wasn't cooing and batting her eyelashes. Joe grimaced. Why indeed? Except that he had a conscience; he felt obliged to speak out for the things that he believed in such as a need for world peace and communications between nations—and, oddly enough, people seemed willing to listen. "Because the name Joe Harrington commands respect," his agent told him. But, Joe thought grimly, at least he wasn't quite fool enough to believe that. They came because he was a sex symbol, a turn-on. A slight smile touched his face at the thought. Would he turn *her* on tonight? Olivia, Tim had said her name was.

"You have an interview with her at five o'clock," Tim had told him. "Are you sure you know what you're doing? I mean, she's not exactly your type."

"I didn't know I had a type." Joe grinned and demonstrated his best leer.

Tim shrugged, still dubious. "You know what I mean. Small town girls are not quite your speed."

"Oh, but you're wrong," Joe replied. "Madison is a veritable metropolis compared to the Sioux City of my youth." He raised his shoulders indolently. "Besides, a fresh face is what I need right now."

"Whatever you say," Tim agreed, and did as he was told. Anyway, the interview was set up, although Tim's tone implied that he still thought Joe was slightly mad to want it.

Obviously he hadn't felt what Joe had when he'd seen that grainy newspaper photo from the *Madison Times* that someone handed him. He didn't exactly know what he felt either—a quickening, a sense of recognition, an instant attraction to the slender woman with the fair hair and wide eyes, who was caught in the act of backing down a zoning commissioner in a nose-to-nose shouting match. The caption had said simply, "Local reporter battles official," and Joe had stared at it all the way from St. Louis to Chicago. In Chicago he had told Tim Gates he would consider an interview with this reporter if Tim could track her down.

"Interview?" Tim's brows had lifted skeptically.

Joe had grinned. "And all that that entails." He shut his eyes now, anticipating it.

The phone shrilled again. Joe's eyes snapped open. How long had he been lying there? He was probably already late. Fumbling, he grabbed for the receiver. "'Lo?" His voice was husky with sleep.

"Napping? Joe Harrington? I don't believe it," came a pert, female voice.

"I have to sleep sometime, Ellie." Joe sat up, raking a hand through his hair and grinning. "How did you find me?" His sister was a vast improvement over the variety of female he usually found on the other end of the line.

"Bribery, love. Even your Mrs. Thomas—and there a dragon of a housekeeper—isn't immune to a little bribe under the table."

"So what's up? Need help with a plot?"

"I wouldn't ask *you* if I did," his sister retorted. "What do you know about happily ever after, for heaven's sake?" Ellie wrote plays, phenomenally successful comedies about love and romance and the foibles of human nature. On more than one occasion she had borrowed more than a bit of her brother and had blithely married him off at the end. Compensating, he supposed, for his complete lack of cooperation in real life.

"Not a thing," he replied genially. "Now, what can I do for you?"

"It's Dad's seventieth birthday tomorrow," Ellie reminded him. "Mike and I are flying to Omaha tonight and driving up to Sioux City tomorrow. Any messages? You don't, by chance, want to come?"

"Cripes, I forgot!" Joe's head dropped back on the pillow. "No, I can't come. Wouldn't if I could, and you know it. Until he puts away his blueprint for my life, he's not going to find me walking through his front door. But yes, give him a message. Tell him happy birthday. Tell him I love him in spite of.... Tell him I wish.... Oh, never mind. I'll call him and tell him myself." The old man would never waste a phone call arguing. He valued the dollar far too much—even those of his son who had plenty.

"I hoped you would," Ellie said smugly.

"Very clever," Joe said. "And what were you going to do if I had said to tell him to go to hell and take his bank vice presidency and his homecoming queen and the 2.5 kids with him?"

"Tell him that you wished him a happy birthday," Ellie said promptly. "I'm quite at home with fiction. But in this case, I am glad I don't have to. Are you mellowing, perhaps?"

"Sure," Joe said sarcastically. "By this time next year he'll be welcoming me home as the prodigal son. Only instead of coming back a beggar, I'll come with a wife and half a dozen kids! Think that'd make him happy?"

"Would it make *you* happy, Joe?" Ellie asked softly. "That's the question."

Joe laughed and stood up, sliding his feet into a pair of tattered running shoes, his eye catching the photo of "local reporter" Olivia James, tonight's entertainment. And tomorrow, who knew? "Would that make me happy, Ellie?" he sounded incredulous. "What do you think?" Still chuckling, he hung up.

JOE HARRINGTON might be handsome, charming, seductive, intriguing and passionate, Liv thought irritably as she paced the length of the Sheraton's lobby for the fiftieth time, but he was also late. It was twenty minutes to six, for heaven's sake! She should have got Jennifer from the babysitter's ten minutes ago. And Tom would be dropping Stephen off at home a little past six, and if she wasn't there by then she would be treated to Tom's lecture on her responsibility to the children. She ground her teeth and brushed an errant lock of hair away from her ear, annoyed just thinking about that. Where was *his* responsibility to the children? She had had the very devil of a time getting him to agree to drop Stephen off at his cello lesson in the first place.

"That's your responsibility, Olivia," he had said when she finally got through to his receptionist. "You have custody."

"Yes. But if you want them to eat this month, you had better take him to cello because I'll lose my job if I don't get this interview," she snapped. "Or perhaps you'd like to pay a bit more child support?" He had fought long and hard against paying as much as he did, so she thought she was safe there.

"Interview with whom?" he asked.

"Joe Harrington."

"*You're* interviewing Joe Harrington?" He sounded as if his saliva ejector had just sucked all the air right out of him. No doubt he thought that the plain, jean-clad, pony-tailed Olivia James whom he had known and left wasn't fit to interview the sex symbol whom all American women lusted after.

"Yes," she said. "Little old me. But don't worry. It's not by choice."

"I didn't suppose it would be," he said more calmly. "You never were the passionate sort."

The temptation to slam the receiver in his ear was almost overwhelming. "Will you take Stephen or not?" she bit out.

Evidently sensing her contained fury, Tom backed off a little. "All right. Tell him to meet me in front of your place. I'll run him home after, too. But he can't dawdle around. I'm driving to Chicago tonight." The last was a calculated barb to prove that this negotiation was not going to go all her way. Liv had loved going to Chicago, and when she and Tom were married, they got there twice a year at the most. From what she heard from the kids, he was now busy "finding himself," with Trudy's help, in the Windy City almost every weekend.

"Thank you." She had hung up thinking that Marv had had no idea what he had asked of her when he sent her to do this interview. It wasn't just Joe Harrington who was involved; it was the kids, it was Tom, it was her whole life. But she had done it, arriving at the Sheraton promptly at five o'clock—and now he wasn't even showing up.

"Excuse me," she said to the man at the desk. "Are you sure he didn't just sneak past?"

"Joe Harrington?" His voice implied that Joe Harrington, like the royal family, couldn't possibly sneak anywhere.

"Well..." She couldn't wait much longer. She had hurried home, popped the casserole in the oven, picked up the cleaning, fetched the rabbit from the vet's—and it was hopping around the back of her VW bus this very moment. It might last an hour or so in there without dying of heat prostration, but it had been there almost that long now. And the casserole would burn... and Jennifer was waiting....

"Look!" the desk clerk sounded triumphant. "Here he comes now!"

Liv turned, not knowing exactly what to expect. But whatever it had been, it wasn't what she got. All the news photos and publicity shots she'd ever seen of Joe Harrington had made him appear suave, debonair, sexy and totally in command. But that hadn't even begun to capture the sheer magnetism of the man now approaching the desk. Even dressed in the wholly unexpected gray sweatshirt, much-laundered jeans and running shoes without socks, and carrying a suitcase that looked as though it had seen him through ten years at summer camp, Joe Harrington was a force to be reckoned with. His lithe but well-muscled body was apparent despite the disreputable clothes. He looked disgustingly attractive for a man who, by rights, ought to be showing signs of dissipation, Liv thought with annoyance. His brown hair was thick and shiny, the tendency to curl giving him a boyish look at odds with the sense of full-adult masculinity that emanated from him. She could see how he would inspire men like Tom, but they would never achieve the same effect in a million years. She swallowed hard. *Darn it, Olivia,* she told herself firmly, *shape up. He's got every woman in the world falling at his feet. He doesn't need you, too.*

She wiped her hands furtively on the sides of her rust-colored linen skirt and then walked briskly toward him, extending her hand. "Mr. Harrington, I'm Olivia James with the *Madison Times.* Your Mr. Gates said you would speak with me this afternoon." She focused on the potted palm somewhere just past his left ear. One look at his green gaze, even diminished by the horn-rimmed glasses perched on the end of his nose, had unnerved her so badly that her hand shook.

"Miss James," he drawled. "Yes, Tim mentioned it to me while I was in Milwaukee." He was holding her hand far longer than it should have taken for a perfunctory handshake. His hand was warm and slightly rough to the touch. Liv tugged hers away, but he hung on, apparently unwilling to let her go. What did he mean, "mentioned it," for heaven's sake? It was *his* idea.

Her gaze flickered back to meet his. "If you'll let go, Mr. Harrington," she said, grateful that her usual asperity hadn't entirely deserted her, "we could sit down over there and get this over with."

His eyes widened momentarily at her words and tone, but then a slow grin appeared on his face. A seductive grin, Liv decided, wishing she had a suit of armor. "Joe," he corrected easily. "Call me Joe. And you're Olivia?"

Ms. James, she wanted to say. Or *Mrs.*—which would be more to the point. But she nodded, trapped, managing only a croaking, "People call me Liv." What was wrong with her? Surely she'd seen a handsome man before!

"Well, Liv," he said, still not relinquishing her hand, "I'm delighted to talk to you. But we're running a little late and...."

No kidding, Liv thought. "I won't take much of your time, Mr. Harr—Joe," she amended quickly, seeing his frown.

"I have an idea," he said, the slow smile beginning again at the corners of his mouth, spreading to reveal the famous boyish grin tooth by tooth. How does he do that, Liv wondered. "I've got to get cleaned up before this speech tonight. You come on up to my room with me and we'll talk while I shower and shave."

Liv's mouth flew open. No wonder he went to bed with half the women in the world. He certainly didn't waste any time on preliminaries! "I think not, Mr. Harrington," she said, ice dripping from her voice. "I conduct interviews in lobbies, not hotel bedrooms. Or bathrooms. And this interview isn't likely to be conducted at all!" The nerve of the man!

"Hold on..."

"No, you hold on, Mr. Harrington. I didn't want to do this interview with you in the first place! I had enough complications in my life today without adding God's gift to women—"

"Miss James—"

"Don't Miss James me, Mr. Harrington," she exploded. "I have a casserole in the oven about to burn, a child at the baby-sitter's whom I should have picked up twenty minutes ago and a rabbit about to die of heat prostration in the back of my bus! I can damned well do without you! Now, if you'll excuse me, I'm sure your speech tonight will tell me everything I want to know." And if Marv didn't like it, she thought, he could have her job—and the shower-and-shave interview that went with it, too! She spun on her heel and strode toward the main entrance of the lobby. She had almost reached it when a hand shot out and grabbed her arm.

"What kind of casserole?"

Liv stared at him. "Chicken and rice," she said finally.

"Room for one more?"

"What?"

He looked slightly sheepish. "You've got the wrong idea," he said. "I didn't mean.... Oh well, maybe I did, I don't know. But a chicken-and-rice casserole sounds better right now. Is there enough?"

"Yes, but...."

The grin nearly split his face. "I'll pick up my key later," he said to the stunned desk clerk who had watched the whole exchange. "Let's go. I want no burned casseroles, mad baby-sitters or dead rabbits on my conscience."

"You aren't serious," Liv protested. But evidently he was, for he was propelling her out the door so quickly that she nearly lost her footing.

"Of course I am. Do you know that last time I had a real, home-cooked meal?"

"No," she faltered. This couldn't be happening.

"Neither do I. But I'll trade you. An interview for some chicken-and-rice casserole. Sound fair?" he flashed her a disarming grin. "And safer?" he added, and she saw a teasing light in his eyes.

She wasn't so sure about that. "I guess, but—"

"Which car?"

"The green VW bus." She pointed to it and then had to scurry to keep up with his long strides. "But what about your shower and shave?" she remembered.

"You have running water in your house, I presume?" he drawled, and she thought that *safe* wasn't a word she'd have used at all.

Lord save me, Liv thought and unlocked the door. "Throw your suitcase in the back, then," she told him, momentarily resigned to the fate that had sent her life spinning out of control. "And be careful not to hit the rabbit."

Chapter Two

"So, tell me about yourself," Joe said, settling easily into the passenger seat of the VW bus and turning sideways to watch Liv start the engine.

"That's my line, I believe," she snapped irritably. "You're the one who's supposed to answer the questions."

"All in good time," he promised. "Over dinner, I think. But now it's your turn." He was smiling at her, the sort of smile that they always did close-ups of in his movies, the ones in which he was trying to find out what made the heroine tick so he could use the right line to get her into bed with him. Liv clenched her teeth and concentrated on backing out of the hotel lot without sideswiping the Buick next to her. "Well," he prompted when nothing but silence was forthcoming.

"You're not interested in me," Liv said firmly, wishing he'd stop looking at her that way. "I'm not a very interesting person."

The dark brows drew together in a frown. "Not interesting? Hardly. You're the first woman I've ever met with a rabbit running loose in her car."

"Something that doesn't happen every day, I assure you," she said. Nor did taking Joe Harrington home for dinner, she thought grimly.

"Well then, we've determined that you're fond of rabbits and casseroles," he went on relentlessly. "And you have a child, I presume. It is your child we're picking up at the baby-sitter's?"

"Yes." They were in the throes of rush-hour traffic speeding along the shore of Lake Monona, and Liv was trying to pay attention to the road.

"But you don't have a husband." It wasn't a question.

"What?" She nearly veered into a passing hog truck.

"No ring," he said smoothly.

"I suppose that's the first thing you look for in a woman," Liv said acidly.

"Not quite." He grinned, and she knew he was watching the color rise in her cheeks and was amused by it. "But I don't fool around with married women, if that's what you mean."

"I'm glad to know you draw the line somewhere," she said, slipping the bus neatly between two trucks and signaling to turn. "And here I was thinking you had no morals whatsoever." She really didn't care what she said to him now. If he was going to take offense he'd have done so in the lobby when she'd blown up. If he was simply going to invite himself along for dinner he deserved everything he got.

Joe ran his tongue over his lips. "You're not going to be an easy interview, are you?" he asked shortly.

"I hope not," Liv said. She turned into the tree-lined street where Jennifer's baby-sitter lived. "As I told you, this wasn't my idea. And if you'd said no, I could've gone to Marv and said you'd changed your mind. Inasmuch as you apparently haven't, I intend to get a good ten-inch story."

"And a pound of flesh, obviously," Joe said with a hint of grimness.

Liv gave him a sharp look as she turned into the driveway, but Joe was looking around the van curiously, not watching her.

"Who plays baseball?" he asked, fingering the glove he had picked up off the floorboards.

"That's Ben's," Liv said.

"Who's Ben? Your lover?"

Liv cut the engine and turned to glare at him. "Don't judge us all by your standards, Mr. Harrington. Ben is my ten-year-old son." She opened the door and began to step out.

"And the other one?" he asked, jerking his head toward the larger, more worn glove on the middle seat.

"Noel's."

"Another son?" He looked as though he didn't believe a word of it.

"Clever of you. You're getting the idea," she said, turning away toward the five-year-old bundle of energy who was hurtling across the yard. "Hi, Jenn," she called. "Tell Marge I'm sorry I'm late."

Joe muttered, *"Three?"* He looked at her narrowly, the green eyes glinting behind the lenses of his glasses. "Are you pulling my leg, Olivia James?" he demanded.

Liv gave him a prime smile, the one she saved for all the men she'd met in the last three years who thought that five children constituted a flaw in her character. "Why no, kind sir. Why don't you ask if there are any more like them at home?"

It was Joe's turn to stare. "Are there?" His voice was hollow, as it was in his movies when the bad guy had a gun leveled on him.

"Two," Liv said demurely, as she moved away to talk to Jennifer's baby-sitter who had come out onto the porch. She couldn't resist tossing him a backward glance as she did so. It was always worth it to see their faces when she told them. Some of them counted on their fingers. Joe Harrington was no exception. He looked as if he'd been poleaxed. Then, much to her amazement, he burst out laughing. She had just reached the porch when he leaned out the window and yelled at her, "Now I understand your predilection for rabbits!"

"Who's that?" Margie Cunningham asked, peering around Liv's shoulder to try to catch a glimpse of the man sitting in the van.

"A friend," Liv mumbled, mortified, hoping that he wouldn't do anything that would identify himself. Having friends who yelled things like that would be bad enough. Hearing it from one of America's foremost sex symbols was too much all together.

"Happy birthday," Marge said. "Doing anything special?"

If only she knew, Liv thought. "No, covering a story," she said. "Sorry I was a bit late. I got a short-notice interview."

"No problem," Marge assured her. "Say, did you hear that Joe Harrington's speaking at the university tonight?"

"Yes. On international communications, I think," Liv said. "Celebrities for Peace or some crazy thing." She shrugged. "The peace idea isn't crazy, but why should some actors know more about it than anyone else?"

"Who cares?" Margie said, the same dreamy look in her eyes that Liv had seen earlier in Frances's. "He's so gorgeous, I wouldn't care if he was talking about grafting apple trees. I'd go to hear him anyway."

And another one bites the dust, Liv thought. Pity he had decided to waste his time on her when conquests were his for the asking all over town. He must really want that chicken and rice a lot, she thought wryly. "So long," she said to Margie, and fairly sprinted to reach the car by the time Jennifer did. Jennifer didn't know who Joe Harrington was—there was no need to worry about her being overawed by his presence or anything like that. The worry was what she would say to him, no matter who he was. Jennifer, Liv knew from five years experience, did not know the meaning of the word discretion.

"Who're you?" Jennifer asked as she climbed in over the driver's seat and regarded the man slouching across the way with calm speculation.

"I'm Joe," he said easily. "Who are you?"

"Jennifer Alison James," she told him. "I'm five. How old are you?"

Take that, Liv thought, starting the engine and backing out of the drive with a smile on her face. Joe slanted her a grin.

"Another reporter in the family, huh?" he asked. "I'm thirty-six," he told Jennifer.

"That's older than Mommy, isn't it?" Jennifer asked. "She's thirty-two."

Joe shot Liv a smug smile. "Is she, now?" He stretched his legs and smirked at her. He looks just like a cat, she thought. A very large, dangerous cat. A tiger. Did tigers have such startling green eyes?

"Yes. Are you coming to our house for dinner?"

"Uh huh."

"Good." Jennifer bounced up and down on the middle seat, her golden hair swinging in a halo around her head. Like a cherub, Liv thought, downshifting as she went around a corner. "Are you going to be Mommy's boyfriend?"

"Jennifer!" So much for cherubim.

"It's a thought," Joe said lazily, not at all discomfitted. "Does Mommy need a boyfriend?"

"No, Mommy doesn't!" Liv snapped, trying to control a desperate urge to drive directly into Lake Monona. "Jennifer, I bet you can't hold your breath until I count to thirty. And you—" she shot Joe a quelling glance that would have been more effective if he hadn't already been almost doubled over laughing "—you hold yours for five minutes!"

"Yes, ma'am, whatever you say, ma'am," he mocked, wiping the grin off his face with his hand though his eyes continued to laugh at her.

The silence that ensued was almost worse than the conversation. No job is worth this, Liv thought. But it was too late to get rid of him now. If she dumped him out, he would probably just follow her home, or call up Marv and complain. Why didn't he at least stop staring at her? It wasn't so much that he seemed to be looking at her as if she were a bug under glass. That wasn't the feeling at all. Rather, she got the idea that she was being savored, like a very tasty looking mouse on a tiger's dinner plate. Just before he opened his mouth. It was a relief to pull into her own driveway next to the story-and-a-half frame house she had been lucky enough to find within her budget when Tom left them and their other house was sold.

"I took it out, Ma! It was burning!"

"Here, look at my lip!"

"Theo ripped his new cords!"

"I did not! Tony ripped 'em!"

"Slow down," Liv said to the swarm of boys clustering around her as she got out of the car. "One at a time." But she was only half-aware of sorting out the nearly burned dinner, the torn pants and the split lip. A part of her was tuned solely to the man still seated in the VW, and a prickling on her neck made her aware that he had got out and was coming to stand beside her.

"Nice lip," he said to Ben.

The ten-year-old grinned, flipping a strand of brown hair out of his eyes. "You shoulda seen the other guy."

"A fight?"

"Naw. A misunderstanding. If you call it a fight, old Grish makes you stay after school."

"I see." Joe's tongue traced a circle inside his cheek. "You must be Ben."

"Yeah. Who're you?"

Not something he was asked every day, Liv was sure. Thank heavens she didn't have movie addicts among her children. Only Noel had seen *Hills of Thunder,* Joe's latest box office smash.

"This is Joe Harrington," she said. "He's giving a speech tonight that I have to cover. And you have to baby-sit," she turned to say to Noel who, at any other time, would have looked pained. At the moment, however, her tall, blond twelve-year-old son was staring in awe at the man before him.

"Steve Scott," he murmured, slack-jawed at being face-to-face with the hero Joe had played in his last two movies.

Joe made a wry face. "Among other things," he said, offering Noel a handshake. "Joe Harrington, really. Steve Scott is a lot of things that I'm not."

A ladies' man not being one of them, Liv recalled, remembering the bevy of gorgeous women chasing after the playboy adventurer Joe had been in the film. She had forgotten how enthralled Noel had been with that film.

"This is Noel," she said quickly, putting her arm around the boy, who was almost as tall as she was. "My oldest," she added. "He's twelve. And this toothless urchin is Theo, who's seven." She hugged the brown-haired, gap-toothed boy leaning against her. "We're missing Stephen, my eight-year-old. He's at a cello lesson."

Joe courteously shook hands with them all, and Liv, surprisingly, found herself relaxing a bit. After the initial moment of awe when Noel recognized him as a movie star, Joe seemed to fit right in. Better, in fact, than some of her occasional, few-and-far-between dates had. They had stood around looking as though they were trying to formulate their position on birth control, whereas Joe immediately organized the kids, sending Theo out to the car to rescue the rabbit and Noel after the cleaning, and telling Ben, "Let's you and I set the table, and maybe your mother will feed us before I starve to death."

It was easy to see why he was also a successful director, Liv thought. He seemed born to take charge, even in places where he had absolutely no business running anything! But it was hard to feel completely irritated with him when he was giving her five seconds to herself for a change. She couldn't remember the last time that had happened to her.

"Thanks," she told him grudgingly when she returned from the bedroom to find him moving around the table busily laying out forks and knives.

"Pure self-interest," he said. "I haven't eaten since St. Louis at seven this morning. Everyone else had chicken à la king during the speech in Chicago at noon."

"What about you?" Liv asked, tearing up lettuce for a salad, but finding her attention drifting to the man behind her.

"I gave the speech."

"Poor thing." Liv smiled at him. "Such a rough life," she teased. But privately she was beginning to think it wasn't such a bed of roses after all. He was every bit as handsome as his pictures, but there was a weariness about the man that she wouldn't have predicted. And he was obviously as hungry as he said he was. As soon as they sat down, he piled his plate with casserole, lettuce, and a large helping of her Jell-O salad, shoveling it in without a word, while the children chattered on around him.

"About the interview," Liv said to him when the chatter abated momentarily.

"What interview?" he asked through a mouthful of Jell-O.

"The one you're here for," she reminded him archly. "You're not getting out of it that easily."

He grinned, unabashed. "Can't blame a guy for trying."

"I can if my job depends on it," she said, feeling annoyed. The grin was provoking all sorts of flutters and unbusinesslike feelings in the pit of her stomach. "And for heaven's sake, take some peas," she snapped at him. "How can I get Theo to eat them if you don't?"

"I hate peas," Joe confessed, looking sheepish. Four pairs of eyes looked up with interest.

Liv glared.

Joe groaned. "Pass the peas," he said to Theo, who grinned and handed him the bowl. He took three quick bites from the helping he put on his plate, made an agonized face, and swallowed. "There," he said to Liv, as if he had just thwarted the vilest villain.

"Hooray! Cake time!" Jennifer cheered.

"Whose birthday?" Joe asked when Ben produced a cake, rather lopsided but definitely made with love, and began poking five candles into it. "Jennifer's?"

"Nope," Noel said as he carried the lighted cake to the table and set it in front of Liv. "The three is in the tens column."

Joe looked baffled for a moment.

"C'mon," Liv said, laughing. "That's not even new math!"

"It's Mommy's," Jennifer announced, "and she gets thirty-two spanks, because on my birthday I got five."

"No." Liv shook her head quickly. "Kisses. Mothers get kisses."

"Thirty-two is an awful lot of kisses," Ben said with distaste.

"You do one each," Joe said quickly. "I'll take care of the rest."

"What?" Liv felt herself go crimson.

"Come on," Joe said to the kids. "Line up." They got up, giggling, and marched around her chair, each administering a self-conscious peck, except of course Jennifer who literally threw herself into it, bestowing a wet, smacking kiss on Liv's red cheek. She ducked her head, unable to take her eyes off her hands in her lap.

"My turn," Joe said softly. He got up and walked down the length of the table so that he stood perilously close, almost touching her. "Happy birthday," he murmured, and with an entranced audience of young Jameses looking on, he bent down and captured Liv's chin in his hand, lifting her face so that he could brush his lips very lightly across hers. Almost unconsciously Liv leaned into the feather-light caress, and his lips returned, firmer, lingering, tantalizing. Then almost reluctantly he lifted his head, and she saw a smile on his face that sent shivers clear to her toes.

"Whoooo-eeee!" Noel yelled. "How about that?"

"Wait till I tell 'em at school!" Theo chimed in, his eyes like saucers.

"But even if you save one for Stephen to give her," Ben, the ever-practical, said to Joe, "You've still got to give her twenty-six more."

"Don't worry," Joe said, laugh lines appearing at the corners of his eyes. "I can manage it."

My goodness, Liv thought, no wonder legions of women fall at his feet. He can charm the socks off anyone without even trying! Twenty-six kisses, indeed!

"Blow out the candles!" Jennifer urged.

"Make a wish!" Ben's eyes were alive with excitement.

Liv looked across the candles, down the table at Joe. His gaze was unfathomable, and for the first time she wondered what the real Joe Harrington was like, the man behind the movie star. What was he besides a talented actor and director and a clever playboy who was notoriously good in bed? *I wish I knew,* she thought and, closing her eyes, she took a deep breath. Sighing, she blew out every candle.

JOE DUCKED HIS HEAD under the shower letting the icy water drum mercilessly on his skull. He didn't have much time. "Fifteen minutes," Liv had said, "or we'll be late." But the shower was a necessity, as much to purify his mind as to cleanse his body of the grime of a long day's travels.

Five kids! How could she have five kids? Not even *he,* Joe Harrington, had ever put the make on a woman with *five* kids!

Yet, a stubborn little inner voice mocked him. He tried to silence it but it persisted. *You want her,* it taunted him. *No matter that she's up to her ears in children, thinks you crawled out from under a rock somewhere and obviously wishes you'd vanish back under one as quickly as possible, you still want her.* He scrubbed himself viciously with a frayed orange washcloth, as though doing so might somehow eradicate this absurd desire. It didn't work.

"So much for fresh faces," he muttered. She was hardly the sort to fancy being next in line after Linda Lucas! His mouth quirked in a reluctant grin. He could well imagine her throwing the casserole at him if he tried a pass like the first one again. A momentary recollection of her nose-to-nose with the zoning commissioner flickered in his mind. No doubt now who won that altercation, he thought. She was definitely a force to be reckoned with.

She'd have to be, he acknowledged, to have managed to survive with those five kids. It would take a strong woman just to cope. He wondered what her ex-husband was like, other than being a fool for letting such a woman go. All he knew was that the man still lived nearby—"Dad's bringing Stephen home," Ben had told him when he asked where the other boy was. He would have liked to have asked about this "dad," but Ben had gone on to tell his mother that his father had called and had said he would be bringing Stephen after dinner, not to wait for him, and Joe couldn't see himself bringing up the subject of her ex-husband with Liv. Approachable she wasn't. Except when he had kissed her. Then there had been an electricity between them that had nearly knocked him off his feet, and he suspected that she felt it too. It wasn't his run-of-the-mill reaction to a kiss, that was for sure, and he thanked heaven he had the option of giving her twenty-six more of them. He was going to use every one!

"Joe, Mom says hurry up!" A voice hollered at him over the noise of the shower. Whose voice? Noel's? Ben's? Theo's? He felt suddenly out of his depth. What did he know about kids, anyway? *Eat your dinner, give your speech and run, fella,* he told himself. *That's what you ought to do.* Then he thought, run to what? Linda Lucas? Hardly. Theirs wasn't a relationship so much as it had been a mutual-usefulness pact, however possessive she might want to act at times. She was seen at all the right parties on the arm of the famous Joe Harrington, and in return she granted him certain favors he didn't want to think about right now. It was as simple and meaningless as that.

And there was no doubt that Olivia James knew it. What had she called him? "God's gift to women?" That and probably a few other things behind his back. Well, she was honest about what she thought, at any rate. And not far from wrong, he reflected. At least up to this point. The question was, what now?

He shut off the shower and pulled back the shower curtain, dripping his way across the bathroom floor as he tried unsuccessfully to discover a towel. It was a far cry from the Sheraton, he thought in amusement—half a dozen toothbrushes in a rack on the wall, a pair of moldy sneakers peering out from beneath the sink, a racquet ball in the soap dish, and not a towel to be found.

"Hell," he muttered. He poked his head out the door, hoping to see a stray child who might fetch him one. No luck. He retreated to the bathroom and peered out the window. Craning his neck he could see Liv standing in the driveway talking to a tall, dark-haired man who was leaning against the door of a late-model car. "Dad" most likely. Joe squinted, but he couldn't make out much at this distance and without his glasses. Besides, his gaze seemed to want to linger stubbornly on Liv.

She had changed out of the rust-colored skirt and paisley blouse and was now wearing a dressier light blue jersey dress that was cinched by a belt at the waist, so that it accentuated the curve of her hips. Jeez, so much for cold showers. He groaned, feeling the tightening in his loins, and dragged his eyes away. No help that way, that was for sure. He opened the door again. Theo had looked like a sympathetic sort. Besides, Theo owed him one for the peas. Theo it would be.

"Theo!" he bellowed. "Theo! Come here!"

IF TOM DIDN'T get into that car and drive away in five seconds, Liv thought she might scream. Of all the days that he should feel inclined to stand and talk, especially after his nagging her about having to get off to Chicago, this was the one she needed the least. She couldn't even bring herself to look at him. She felt sure he would see Joe Harrington's lips imprinted on hers. Besides that, the longer he stayed and the more he said, the angrier she got.

"I just *can't* take them that weekend," Tom was saying, looking far more like a harried father than she thought he had any right to. "Surely you can understand that!"

"What I understand," Liv said, trying to hang on to the last shreds of her temper, "is that you never seem to want your children anymore."

"That's not true. I just have plans for next Saturday."

"You had plans with the kids first."

"So that's what I'm telling you. I want to change it."

They had been through this before countless times. It was as though once he had divorced her, he had divorced the kids too. Looking at him now, it was hard to imagine what she had ever seen in him. Certainly he didn't have the magnetism of Joe Harrington. But, at nineteen, he had swept her off her feet, and they had struggled together to get him through college and dental school, while she earned her degree and raised the kids. It hadn't seemed terribly burdensome at the time—at least not to her. She had figured that the time they devoted to child-rearing early on they could make up for later. After all, to her way of thinking, they had agreed to stick together forever. But Tom had other ideas. He had, he said much later, never been really satisfied with their relationship. But he hadn't actually come out and said it until ten years later when it was more socially acceptable to admit that marriage and a family "cramped his style." Then, when he did say it, he told Liv that he wanted "breathing space" and an "open marriage." Liv, having learned about Trudy by that time, told him that what he really wanted was a divorce. And that was what he got. Now she just wished he'd go away. If he didn't, Joe Harrington was going to walk out the kitchen door and create a situation that Liv had no desire to deal with tonight. Or any other night, for that matter.

"Mom." Theo appeared to tug at her arm.

"Say goodbye to your father," she said, mentally urging Tom into his car.

"Goodbye," Theo said. "Mom...."

"Hi, Theo, how's it going?" Tom ruffled his son's dark hair.

"Okay. Mom...."

"What?"

"Joe needs a towel."

Oh, no, thought Liv.

"What?" Tom demanded, straightening up.

"Can I give him one of the new yellow ones?" Theo went on.

"Anything. Whatever you want," Liv said. "All right," she told Tom, "I'll take them next weekend." Anything, she thought frantically, just leave.

"Joe who?"

"Then you can take them the following weekend."

"Not Joe Harrington?" Tom looked stunned as the possibility occurred to him.

"I told you I had to interview him when I asked you to take Stephen to cello," she reminded him, trying for a casual indifference she was far from feeling.

"An interview is one thing; a towel is something else!"

"What's it to you?" she demanded, suddenly incensed by the proprietary attitude in his remarks. "You forfeited your right to all concern about my life a long time ago. Surely someone who can move from Janice to Patty to Di to Trudy to who knows how many others has no call to question me about anything!"

"Not in front of my children," Tom retorted hotly.

"Oh really? An ounce of discretion makes it all right, then?"

Tom's face was as red as Jennifer's kickball. "Joe Harrington, for heaven's sake!" he fumed, scuffing the dirt in the flower bed with his toe.

"Oh, have a bit of sense, can't you?" Liv hissed. "Do you honestly think that I'm going to run out and jump into bed with America's number one heartthrob in the very house where all my children are eating dinner? Tom, we were married for ten years. Didn't you learn anything about me? You said earlier that I wasn't the passionate sort."

"You sound passionate right now," Tom said, staring at her as though she'd grown another head.

"I'm angry. I'm also going to be late for this speech I've got to cover. And as the speaker is riding with me, I hope you'll excuse me now."

Liv turned on her heel and strode into the house, not quickly enough to miss Jennifer throwing herself on her father and asking, "Did you meet Joe? He's going to be Mommy's boyfriend. Isn't that neat?"

She was, fortunately, out of earshot before Tom could reply. It was sufficient to hear the tires squeal on the asphalt as the car peeled away.

"ABOUT OUR INTERVIEW," Liv said in her most businesslike tones once they were under way.

"I was born in Sioux City, Iowa thirty-six years ago. I have two older sisters, two very nice if a bit conservative parents. My father is an accountant and my mother bakes blue-ribbon pumpkin pie. When I was in third grade I had a dog named Goofy. I flunked economics in high school and dated the prom queen. I wasn't the king, by the way. I went to Iowa State for one year to pacify my father, then left home to join a repertory company outside Chicago. A year later I went to New York. Then Hollywood. After three years I hit it big with films, and now I'm everybody's fair-haired boy. The story of my life in a nutshell." He blurted it all in a rush, then slumped back against the seat and looked at her assessingly. "Okay?"

Liv clicked her tongue against her teeth. "Well, I'm not going to be able to get ten inches out of it, that's for sure." She glanced at him out of the corner of her eye. He was dressed fit to kill now—the charcoal gray suit beautifully tailored, worn with a blue oxford cloth long-sleeve shirt and a navy-and-maroon striped tie. His overly-long hair had been substantially tamed with a comb, but it still flopped engagingly across his forehead in strands still damp from the shower. She could smell his distinctive, woodsy after-shave blowing in her direction because of the draft from his open window, and she inhaled deeply, knowing that she would remember the scent forever. *Forget it, Liv,* she told herself. *Get to the job at hand.*

"Tell me about your movie roles," she probed. "There are rumors that you'll be doing another Steve Scott film." This, of course, was from Frances, who had seen the last one five times.

"Not if I can help it," Joe replied, his features creasing into a scowl.

"You don't like adventure films?"

He shrugged. "They're not bad. It's just that no one ever sees beyond them. I did ten pictures before Steve Scott came along. I've played everything from a Chicago mobster to a down-and-out athlete to a defrocked priest. I like the variety. Now I'm just 'Steve Scott' and everyone expects me to shoot first and talk later, to wrestle the tiger and woo the girl."

Or wrestle the girl, Liv thought. That was certainly the impression he gave. At first glance, anyway. She was grateful for the stoplight impeding their progress. It gave her a chance to study him. He was raking his hand through his hair irritably and muttering, "There's more to me than that."

Was there, she wondered. Scant moments ago he had tried to give her an interview that amounted to an encapsulated brush-off. Now he was saying things about his career that she didn't ever remember reading about him before. She could well imagine that being known as Steve Scott would have its drawbacks as well as its compensations, but she hadn't expected a man like Joe Harrington to appreciate that. Perhaps he was right. Perhaps she ought to take another look. A careful one. "Are you planning other roles, then? New films that will demand more of you?" she asked as the light turned green and they started up again.

He sighed. "I don't know. I've had plenty of offers. Nothing really touches me though. There are other things I'd like to try." He stopped abruptly, staring down at his fingers, laced between his knees.

"Such as?"

He lifted his eyes to stare out at the lakefront as they passed. "More directing projects," he said finally. "This peace thing. Some writing. I want to get out from in front of the camera now. But I haven't decided exactly how yet."

The auditorium where he was to speak loomed just ahead of them. Damn, just when things were getting interesting. "How about if we continue the interview after your speech?" she suggested.

He cocked his head and grinned at her. "Is that a proposition?"

"No, it's not!" Darn him! The moment she felt the tiniest bit comfortable with him, he said something that sent all her defenses to the fore. "It's common sense, that's all. If we continue now, you'll be late. Not," she added irritably, "that it would be a big loss, I don't suppose."

"What's that supposed to mean?"

"What do actors know about peace, anyway?" Liv asked. "I probably know as much as you do."

"Maybe," he acknowledged, which surprised her. She had been prepared for a giant display of male ego, but Joe just said, "More people would be willing to listen to me though, I bet," and grinned mockingly at her.

"Only because of your beautiful body," Liv retorted. She drove into the parking lot as close as she could to the entrance of the building and said, "You get out here. I'll find a place to park."

Shrugging, Joe opened the door and swung out, stopping after he did so to turn and fix her with a hard stare. "You don't like me much, do you?" he asked.

"No," Liv said, "I don't." But she didn't feel quite the same conviction about her dislike that she had five hours before. After meeting him she couldn't say whether she disliked him or not. He made her feel uncomfortable and incredibly aware, and she knew very well that she didn't like that. She also knew that she didn't want to like him. One unfaithful male was enough in anyone's life. From Tom James to someone like Joe Harrington was only stepping from a badly designed economy version to the top-of-the-line model of the same man.

Still, she reflected guiltily, she didn't have to come right out and say she didn't like him, did she? She opened her mouth to apologize, but Joe had already shut the door and was stalking off, head high, the wind catching his coattail and blowing it back away from his lean frame. She saw the rigid set to his shoulders and bit her lip. Probably she'd made him furious, she thought with a surprising twinge of regret. She would hardly blame him if he were totally fed up with her continual barrage of set-downs and got himself a taxi or a willing-to-please female to take him back to the Sheraton. She couldn't have blamed him if he said to hell with her and the interview all together.

By the time Liv got inside the auditorium where Joe was speaking, there wasn't a seat left. Hordes of women and a surprisingly large number of men, old and young alike, were crowded shoulder to shoulder, jostling and talking, waiting to hear what Joe Harrington had to say. Or to see what he looked like in person, Liv thought, remembering Margie and her talk about grafting apple trees.

She fumbled through her purse for her notebook and pen, hoping that she would catch a few good quotes which, along with the thumbnail sketch of his life which he had rattled off earlier, would add up to a plausible story if she never saw him again.

Suddenly there was a collective sigh and wild applause, and the local director of the organization sponsoring Joe's appearance stepped forward and introduced "America's favorite man." Liv thought she saw Joe wince at the introduction. But it happened so fast that she could have been wrong. What was more obvious to her, though apparently not to the enthusiastic crowd, was how very weary he was. She could see the fatigue even from where she was sitting scrunched against the back wall. She felt a twinge of compassion for him and hoped he would make it through the speech. It wouldn't do for him to fall asleep at the podium, she thought, her pen poised as he began to speak.

Exhausted or not, from somewhere deep within, Joe managed to dredge up enough energy to give a thoughtful, obviously well-researched yet sincerely impassioned speech. Liv was amazed. The pen hung useless from her fingers. The lightweight, shallow-minded playboy she'd been expecting to hear never materialized at all. She was captivated by his words, especially those at the end when he leaned over the podium and thrust his hair back off his forehead, saying bluntly, "You don't have to have kids to want the world to be safe for the next generation. I don't have any kids, but that's no reason for me not to get involved. Until tonight I'd never met a little boy named Theo and a little girl called Jennifer, but the world is a richer place for their being in it. And it will be a richer place for their children being in it too—if we keep the world intact long enough for them to be born to enjoy it!"

The crowd roared approval. Those who had come to see his body and his handsome face stayed to hear what he had to say. Liv could tell from the expressions on their faces, intense, rapt expressions that touched her almost as much as his words. She stayed, too, grinning, shaking, as though she had given the speech herself. It was a side of Joe Harrington that she'd never imagined, the side that the gossip columnists never seemed to write about—maybe didn't even know—but it made Frances seem not so crazy after all.

Liv was pressed up against the door by the stream of people rushing past, ready to mob the refreshment area where Joe would be. Stuffing her notes back into her purse,

Liv stepped into the flow and was swept along into a long, spacious reception area now crowded beyond all recognition with hordes of people.

She saw Joe at the far end of the room, mobbed by autograph seekers and out-of-town reporters, and wondered whether she should wait or vanish without a trace. He might not want to see her at all. Undecided, she hovered just inside the door, glancing from Joe to the nearest exit and back again. He seemed to be searching the crowd for someone, his gaze swiveling over the sea of faces until, at last, it settled on her. Then, with a word to the man at his side, he began to elbow his way through the crowd in her direction, the green eyes never leaving hers.

"Ready?" he asked when he reached her, and slipped an arm around her, drawing her against the hard warmth of his chest.

"Um, yes," Liv stammered. "But don't you have to—I mean, all these people are...."

"Let's go," Joe said, and he plunged through the milling crowd, towing Liv after him, smiling and shaking hands all the way, saying, "Thanks. Thanks for coming," and finally he wrenched open the door that let them out of the noise, glare and cigarette smoke and into the blessed dimness and fresh air of the parking lot. The lake shimmered under the streetlights in the distance, and Joe heaved a long sigh.

"Whew," Liv said, shaking her head in amazement. "Is it always like that?"

"Often enough. Tim gets me out of it, usually. But he flew back to L.A. tonight."

"That's the advance man who set up our interview?" she asked cautiously. They were walking through rows and rows of cars now and he still had his arm around her, so he couldn't still be mad. Perversely she knew she should be wishing he were, instead of holding her against his hip as they walked so that their strides coordinated, their rhythms meshed. She could feel the weariness in his body and wanted to soothe it. A foolish desire, she reminded herself.

"Yeah, that was Tim," he answered her, and sighed. "About that interview...."

"Don't worry about it," she told him. "I have enough. And I wouldn't blame you if you didn't give it to me, anyhow. I was unconscionably rude to you earlier."

Joe laughed. "No, just honest." He gave her a tired grin, which she returned.

"Well, not actually," she said, surprised at her own daring. "I find that you improve on acquaintance. I think I rather do like you after all."

"Despite my rather inept pass as you when we first met?"

"Despite that," Liv agreed, unlocking the door to the bus. The wind lifted her hair and she felt a cooling breeze on her neck. Thank goodness, she thought, feeling entirely too hot otherwise.

"Tell me, how did I redeem myself?"

She considered this. "Well," she began slowly, "once you got over the shock, you didn't turn and run when you found out I had five kids. And you ate your peas and hung up the towel straight in the bathroom. Also, you're trying to keep the world safe and peaceful for my children. Quite a lot, actually," she told him, smiling and feeling ridiculously happy all of a sudden that he hadn't left her to go back to his hotel room alone.

Joe grinned. "Good for me," he said softly. "Can I add something to the list?"

"What's that?" She looked up into the shadows of his face, just scant inches from her own, and felt her breath shorten. Another of the twenty-six kisses, she wondered.

"Can I drive home?"

Liv's eyes widened. "Drive home?" she repeated stupidly.

"It helps me to relax," he explained. "And the rest would probably do you good, too."

Stunned by the turn of events, Liv could do nothing but agree. Drive home? "I guess," she said and immediately wished she didn't sound so ungracious. Then added, "But it's a very temperamental car. It's only used to me."

"I'll use my unbeatable charm," Joe assured her, smiling. "Please?" There was a husky note in his voice that forbade her to deny him anything and she thought, *no wonder he's so successful with women,* but she handed him her keys and he helped her in and shut her door.

"Don't blame me if it stalls," Liv said when he'd come around and got in beside her.

It didn't. Apparently the Harrington charm worked as well on VWs as on women. Once convinced that he was really going to drive, Liv felt herself almost unconsciously relax. In fact she rather enjoyed letting him take over. For one thing she had a chance to watch him unobserved. The tiger qualities she had noticed earlier hadn't completely disappeared, but they didn't seem so threatening now. The harsh lines of his face had gentled, whether from relief or exhaustion she didn't know. But as he drove he seemed less of the tense, prowling jungle cat of early evening and more the domesticated variety, ready to curl up on the hearth rug and go to sleep.

Also, driving her bus made him infinitely more approachable somehow. As though in spite of the vast discrepancy in their worlds of experience, here at least they had something in common.

"You missed the turn-off to your hotel," she said suddenly, noting that they had left the Sheraton far behind.

"I know."

"But—"

"I'm taking you home."

"But—"

"Relax," Joe commanded, flashing her a smile that suddenly, despite her better judgment, made her do just that. It was a long time since someone had taken over her life, even for a moment. For a change—not as a habit—it felt rather nice. She leaned back against the seat and closed her eyes.

"Here we are." Joe pulled into the driveway and cut the engine, turning to look at her again with that knowing glint in his eyes. "Safe and sound."

"Thank you." She smiled back at him, feeling somewhat giddy and silly, as though she'd had too much wine, when in fact she hadn't even touched a drop of the watered-down fruit punch at the reception after his speech.

"Now you say, 'Won't you come in for some coffee,'" Joe prompted.

Liv wet her lips and saw him lean closer. "Won't you...." Her voice trailed off, breathless.

"Thank you. Don't mind if I do." He seemed to jerk himself back and opened the door, going around the bus and helping her out, like a "proper date" her mother would have said. She giggled to herself.

The living room was quiet. Even Noel had gone to bed. His math book lay open on the couch, and a pile of unfolded laundry had made it as far as the overstuffed chair. Liv groaned inwardly, wondering what Joe would make of her "homey" atmosphere. But she needn't have given it a thought, she realized, for he crossed the room to the couch, shoved the math book aside and sank down.

"Are you sure you want coffee?" she asked. He had collapsed completely after pulling off his coat, loosening his tie and unbuttoning the top two buttons of his shirt. Now he sat, head flung back, eyes closed, totally spent.

"Mmm? How about tea? Less caffeine," Joe mumbled without opening his eyes. "Suit you?"

"Sure. I'll put the kettle on." It will give me a chance to collect my wits, she thought, warring with the feelings of warmth and protectiveness that he was evoking in her. She didn't need that. Why did he have to be so...so...so likeable? Liv slipped out of her high heeled shoes and padded into the kitchen in her stockings, relishing the cool feel of the linoleum beneath her feet. It was the one counterpoint to the sultry May evening, and she wriggled her toes gratefully while she puttered about, putting on the kettle, getting the tea out of the cupboard and setting cups and saucers on a tray. She wondered if Joe took milk or sugar and was about to go back into the living room and ask when she decided not to. Being around him was entirely too heady an experience. She could do with a few minutes more space. So she went to check on the kids while the water got hot. Jennifer had fallen asleep in Theo's bed, and Liv hoisted her daughter into her arms, burying her face in Jennifer's blond hair. *Touch,* she thought, *I'm starved for touch.* But as she lay Jennifer in her own bed, Liv admitted that it wasn't entirely that. She wanted, perversely, to feel Joe's touch again, his lips on hers, his arms around her, pressing her close. Stop it, she thought and, hearing the kettle whistle, she hurried back to the kitchen.

"Milk or sugar?" she called now, and getting no answer, she shrugged and put both on the tray and carried it back into the living room. The playboy of the western world was fast asleep on the sofa.

"Joe?" She put his cup on the end table beside him, but he didn't stir. She stood looking at him, a whole school of feelings swimming like fish in her head. Silently then, she moved the laundry onto the floor and sank into the heavy armchair opposite and sipped her tea as she watched him. It was strangely companionable and relaxing, just sitting there with Joe Harrington asleep across the room. Liv smiled, wondering what Frances would think. Surely she wouldn't suspect the gentleness and vulnerability that Liv could see now in him. It wasn't a side he showed to his adoring public. But if millions of women swooned over him wide-awake, she mused with a tiny smile, just think how many would be drooling if they could see him now.

She didn't know how long she sat watching him, but finally she caught herself yawning too. She supposed she ought to call a taxi and bundle him into it and send him back to his hotel.

Oh yes, sure, Liv thought. And how would her reputation look then? "Local reporter sends Romeo home in midnight taxi ride." She could see the headlines now. Well, Marv probably would have mercy, but there were other less scrupulous newspapers around. And it didn't bear thinking about, anyway. Joe didn't look as though he was going to move for the rest of the night. It might be wisest just to let sleeping tigers lie.

She sighed and got up, going to her room for a lightweight blanket, which she dropped on the coffee table. She bent over and unlaced his shoes, slipping them off his feet and easing the tie off his neck.

There were advantages to being five times a mother, she thought wryly, not the least of which was being able to undress children for bed without waking them. But Joe Harrington was not a child, she warned herself. What he would think if he woke now to find her in the process of unbuttoning his shirt did not bear thinking about.

Joe groaned and slid sideways onto the sofa and she eased his shirt off, dropping it beside the blanket. There, that was as far as she dared go. Leaving him in his undershirt, dress pants and socks, she draped the blanket over him, and he rolled toward the back of the sofa, clutching the blanket.

"Mmmmm," he breathed, a half-smile on his face. Liv sighed and brushed a lock of dark hair off his forehead, her hand lingering just for a moment.

"Good night," she whispered and put out the light.

Well, she thought, that's that. Another distinction to add to her uniqueness—a dubious one at that—*I am,* she thought as she slipped into her double bed alone, *the only woman in the world to make Joe Harrington fall asleep.*

Chapter Three

In the morning he was gone.

Liv's alarm went off at six and she sprang out of bed, throwing on the first suitable skirt and blouse that came to hand and brushing her shoulder length hair back and anchoring it with a headband because she didn't want to take the time to pin it up. Not, she told herself, because she looked prettier with her hair down.

It didn't matter whether she did or not, for when she crept out into the living room, expecting to see his lean muscular body curled up on her sofa, she found instead only a folded up blanket and no sign at all of Joe. The whole previous evening might have been nothing more than the very detailed hallucination of a demented, middle-aged mother but for the freshly perked coffee she found in the kitchen and a note scratched on the back of a shopping list that said simply, "Thanks. Joe."

For what? she wondered. Certainly not for what he usually got from the women he spent the night with. But then, he hadn't actually spent the night with her, not really. He had only slept on her couch. She wondered if Frances would believe that if she told her. Not that she was going to tell her. Not after all the carrying-on she had done yesterday about having to do this interview. There was no point in looking a complete fool if she didn't have to. She poured herself a cup of his coffee and contemplated the note, her eyes drifting from it to the unoccupied couch. It was really better that he was gone, she told herself firmly. She couldn't imagine explaining his presence to the kids, and later getting wind of what Tom would say when one of them let it drop that Joe Harrington had spent the night. Her mouth turned up in a smile at that. Imagine his having the time for a Tom James reject! Because, even if he hadn't slept with her, which she didn't really want anyway, he had seemed to like her all right. And that was a bit of an ego boost right there, unless one harped on the fact that he quite frankly seemed to like every woman.

She sighed and got up, padding upstairs to the bathroom which was, fortunately, still unoccupied. One bathroom and six people made for hectic mornings. She glanced around the tiny room critically for the first time since she had resigned herself to it when she had bought the house two years ago. It wasn't much to look at, that was for sure—cracked tile around the shower and toy boats on the floor, towels that looked as though they'd sailed the *Mayflower* if not the Ark. Not exactly the sunken tubs and silver fixtures that she was sure Joe must be used to.

Still, he had showered here. Maybe she could charge admission, create a local landmark—*Joe Harrington Showered Here*—and put the money aside to buy new towels or, better yet, a lock for the bathroom door.

Ah, another sign that she hadn't imagined it all. The crumpled gray sweatshirt and the jeans were still in a heap on the floor. Probably he was used to maids, too, she thought. Or a mother. She picked up his things automatically, just as she picked up Stephen's socks or Noel's shorts, and began to fold them, carrying them back to her room, absently rubbing the soft fabric of the sweatshirt against her cheek. The faint aroma of Joe's woodsy after-shave assailed her, and she dropped the shirt hastily onto the bed.

Shape up, she told herself sternly, *you have five kids to bundle off to school and a story to write. This morning is no different than any other.*

It wasn't, either. Noel couldn't find his math homework without a full-scale search of the entire house; Ben's left sneaker had miraculously disappeared; the oatmeal was lumpy and the tooth fairy had completely forgotten about Theo's latest missing tooth.

"Probably Joe scared him away," Jennifer pronounced solemnly between bites of oatmeal, when Theo appeared disgruntled, holding his tooth accusingly in his hand.

"He left too early, dopey," Theo argued. "You weren't even in bed yet."

"Huh-uh," Jennifer denied, swinging her blond mop in an emphatic negative motion. "He came back. I seed him. He was sleepin' on the couch."

"He was?" All eyes looked up from the oatmeal and focused on Jennifer.

Liv groaned inwardly and said, "Hurry up and eat."

But no one paid any attention. Jennifer was basking in all her glory. "Yup, he was," she want on. The head bobbed positively this time. "I got up to go to the bathroom, and I looked downstairs, and there he was!" Her eyes were wide and starry. "Snorin'," she added.

"Gosh, Steve Scott on our couch," Noel breathed after a moment's silence. He looked at his mother with new respect.

"Wait'll the kids at school hear about that," Stephen marveled. "Why did I have to go to dumb cello yesterday, anyway?"

"The kids aren't going to hear," Liv said firmly. "And cello is not dumb."

"Compared to Steve Scott it is," Stephen said glumly as he dissected another of the oatmeal lumps.

"Nevertheless, what happens in this house is not for public consumption," Liv warned them, glaring.

"What's that mean?" Theo asked.

"It means shut up," Noel explained. "Or else."

Theo looked up at Liv, all innocence. "Does it, Mommy?"

"Yes." The last thing she wanted was a story going around about Joe Harrington spending the night at her house. The sooner it was forgotten the better. By everyone. Especially herself.

TYPING A matter-of-fact story about Joe was just what she needed, Liv decided when she dropped her purse into her desk drawer and faced the reality of another day's work. It would put him into proper perspective and eradicate all those fleeting images of boyish grins and tired eyes and, heaven help her, those warm and teasing lips that had plagued her all the way to work. She sat down and prepared to get to work, to exorcise his ghostly presence and reduce him to a neat ten-inch story.

She had almost succeeded when Frances puffed breathlessly into the office, flung her ever-present knitting onto her desk and demanded, "Tell all, Liv. Is he every bit as gorgeous in person as on the screen?"

"Oh, definitely," Liv said coolly, with much more disinterest than she actually felt. "Here." She ripped the sheet out of the typewriter. "You can be the first on your block to know."

Frances snatched the paper and eased her substantial form into her chair, her eyes never leaving the paper in front of her. When she finished it, she looked up and pushed her glasses higher on her nose. "Very cagey," she said. "Very noncommital. Now, tell me, what's he *really* like?"

"Honestly, Frances," Liv grinned, pleased that she'd done what she had set out to do, which was to say nothing scandalous or titillating at all, "he's really like that." He was, too. She had tried to present his sincerity, his commitment to the cause of peace, and not just concentrate on his sexual escapades or his fabulous body or even his acting and directing ability. She did, however, pay lip service to his charm.

"I'm sure he is," Frances said. " 'Boyish, charming, sincere,'—oh, definitely. But—" she lowered her voice to a conspiratorial whisper— "did he make a pass at you?"

"What?" Trust Frances not to beat around the bush. "Of course not!" she lied. She was certainly not going to mention that humiliating shower-and-shave offer.

"Why not?" Now it was Frances who sounded offended. "You're young and pretty, and he's definitely as sexy as they come."

He was that, Liv thought. "Perhaps I'm just not his type."

Frances looked at her as though she'd forgot her mind when she came to work that morning. "All right," she said on a note of faked injury, "if that's the way you want it, don't tell me, then."

Liv grinned. "Oh, no you don't, you old fraud. You're not going to coerce me into telling you anything that way. You read everything important in my story. Really. We had a nice chat. I drove him to the speech. He spoke. That was that. But I will admit, he was better than I expected." Further than that she was not prepared to go. There was no telling what Frances's busily embroidering mind could make out of their dinner and Joe's night on her couch.

"If you say so," Frances said reluctantly, but she still gave Liv the occasional suspicious glance while she busied herself setting up the weekly TV section.

"I do," Liv told her flatly, and hoped that that was the end of it. She put her story on Marv's desk well before ten and gathered up her things so that she could drive over to the university and do a story on the string quartet which had come to give a recital and conduct a workshop. It was routine and yet pleasurable, moving about, talking to interesting people, getting a little sun in the process. *Soothing,* Liv thought, *just what I need after the tumult of last night's interview.*

"Off again?" Frances queried.

"I'll be over at the music department at the university," Liv said, "if anyone needs me." The kids, she meant.

"Like Joe Harrington?"

Liv rolled her eyes. "Of course," she said airily because Frances had Joe Harrington on the brain. Then a sudden impish grin crossed her face. "If he calls, tell him he still owes me twenty-six more," she told Frances laughing.

Frances's jaw dropped. "Twenty-six what?"

"He'll know," Liv replied, breezing past her out the door. She knew full well that Joe Harrington was a once-in-a-lifetime experience, already a thing of the past, an event to tell her grandchildren about. What on earth would he ever call her for? To get his jeans and sweatshirt back? Hardly. He could certainly afford new ones. But it had been worth saying, just to see the expression on Frances's face.

FRANCES COULD HAVE said the same about her.

"I told him," Frances said the minute Liv walked back in the newsroom door. "And he said to tell you he always pays up. What in heaven's name does he mean?"

"Who?" Liv asked, her mind still full of Paganini and a violinist with a charming Portuguese accent.

"Joe Harrington. Who else?"

"What?" Liv sank into her chair, stunned, the Portuguese violinist abruptly consigned to oblivion. "Joe Harrington called here? Me?" It wasn't possible.

"Well, you said—"

"I was joking," she replied weakly.

"Nevertheless, I'd know that voice anywhere." Frances's eyes went all dreamy again. "Such vibrance. So sexy."

"For God's sake, what did he say?"

"Not much," Frances replied with a shrug. "He wanted to talk to you. I told him you weren't here, and I gave him your message."

Liv went crimson, remembering the message.

"And he said he'd call back later." She gave Liv one of her doting-mother smiles. "I knew you'd make an impression."

Liv shook her head, confused. This couldn't be happening, not when she'd spent all morning putting him out of her mind. "He must've left something in my car," she improvised, then thought, maybe he really did want his clothes back!

"What's up with the quartet?" Marv asked, materializing beside Liv's desk, cigar in place in the corner of his mouth.

"Quartet?" He might as well have been speaking to her in Hungarian.

"Where've you been all morning, then?"

Liv shook her head blearily again, like a drunk come-to to find herself in an unknown neighborhood, then fumbled through her purse, her mind in as great a disarray as her bag.

"Don't mind her," Frances explained. "She just had a call from Joe Harrington."

"No kidding." Marv looked impressed. "Another story?"

"No." Liv was positive about that, then wished she weren't, for what other reason would Marv think he had for calling her?

"Oh." Marv regarded her curiously, chewing on the cigar. "He *did* want more from you than the interview then."

"Marv!" Liv glared at him, mortified. How dare he say such incriminating things in front of Frances?

He spread his hands, looking sheepish and even had the grace to blush. "Sorry," he said, turning to beat a hasty retreat to his office. "Let me have that material on the quartet, if you remember who they are, as soon as you can."

"Sooooo," Frances said, eyeing Liv narrowly. "He didn't make a pass, huh?"

"Oh, you know Joe Harrington," Liv mumbled, still mortified. "He says, 'Pass the peas,' and it sounds like a pass."

"Where in an interview do you say a thing like 'Pass the peas'?" Frances wanted to know.

"That was just an example," Liv retorted irritably. "Don't be so literal. You know what I mean—pass the peas, I need a towel. . . ."

Frances's eyes grew like mushrooms, almost popping out of her head. "This gets more intriguing by the minute."

"Not really," Liv said, ducking her head to rummage through her bag for the quartet notes and to avoid Frances's speculative gaze.

"Well, I think there's hope," Frances said. "Especially if he's calling you."

"Dream on," Liv said. "We've seen the last of him. He went to Portland today. Who knows where he'll be tomorrow. He probably lost his little black book and thinks it might be in my car. He'll probably ask me to send it on."

"We'll see," Frances said. "I, for one, don't think we've heard the last of this. After all, he still has twenty-six somethings that he owes you, doesn't he?"

Liv had forgotten that. *Oh Lord,* she groaned, *me and my big mouth.*

Still, she wasn't completely prepared when she picked up the phone that evening to hear a gruff, sexy voice say, "Hi."

"Who is this?" She knew damned well who it was. There wasn't another voice like his anywhere. But why was he calling her?

"I see you're just as determined to deflate my ego now as you were last night," he said, laughing softly. His laughter sent prickles all the way down to her toes, and she sat down abruptly on the wooden kitchen chair.

"Oh, Mr. Harrington, what can I do for you?"

"Come on, Liv," the voice cajoled. "I thought we were friends. You can't call a guy by his last name after you've undressed him and put him to bed, can you?"

"I did not undress you!"

"Well, not entirely, maybe," he allowed. "Made me more comfortable, let's say."

"Let's not say anything, Mr. Harrington!"

"Sorry, I'm just teasing." She could tell he was grinning. She could see him now in her mind's eye, the quirk of his mouth, the mischievous glint in his tiger's eyes. "I'm just really calling to say thanks. I appreciated the blanket. And your letting me stay."

"I...you...you're welcome," she stammered, disconcerted by his sudden sincerity.

"Did it make things awkward for you?"

She sat up straighter. He cared? "Well, um, no... but—"

"I tried to get out before the kids woke up," he went on. "And none of the neighbors saw me leave. I walked down to a supermarket parking lot and called a taxi from there." He sounded breathless, a bit hesitant and worried. Nothing like the devil-may-care Joe Harrington immortalized in print everywhere. Imagine, a Joe Harrington concerned about the proprieties of a situation. Liv smiled.

"No, it was, um, all right," she told him. No sense in bringing up Frances's thoughts. Those were entirely her own fault after her reference to the twenty-six somethings he owed her. "Well, good bye."

"Hey, hang on," he said quickly, the diffident, nervous Joe suddenly vanishing. "There's a little matter of the twenty-six kisses I still owe you!"

Liv felt the heat leap to her cheeks. Why had she ever said that to Frances? She would never live it down! "Don't be ridiculous," she blurted. "Frances just made some silly remark about you calling me while I was out of the office, and so I said...Frances thinks you're just too...too..." Couldn't she say anything without sticking her foot in her mouth?

"Marvelous for words? Sexy for my own good?" Joe filled in, laughter rich in his voice.

"That's the general idea," Liv agreed dryly. "Anyway, forget it."

"I don't want to forget it," he murmured, his voice velvety in her ear. Goose bumps broke out on her arms. "But," he went on in a more normal tone, "there's nothing much I can do about it right now. Tomorrow I'm flying to Hawaii for two days, and then I have to give a series of talks in Texas and Oklahoma or thereabouts. Then, I think, it's on to the East Coast to sway the Bostonians and New Yorkers with my words of wisdom."

Liv felt a momentary stab of disappointment, which she just as quickly banished, as he outlined his itinerary. Life was complicated enough without wishing she had a man like Joe Harrington in it, even briefly. "Sounds like fun," she said brightly. A change from early Madison eclectic, which was the only thing on her horizon, anyway.

"Oh sure." Joe's tone was ironic. "Once you've seen one airplane, you've seen them all. And one hotel room is pretty much like another." He sighed. "But it's something that I promised myself I would do."

"I'm impressed," Liv told him sincerely, and she was. She had thought he was just a handsome face and a little talent, but there was clearly more to him than that. His commitment to the cause he espoused was very obvious the night he gave his speech in Madison, and he seemed quite willing to put his body where his mouth was for a long while.

"Are you?" he sounded doubtful.

"Yes," she told him, and was prodded by the feeling that she said it as much because she was sure he needed to hear it as because it was, in fact, true. He sounded bone-weary, and she remembered how exhausted he had looked the night before. It was past ten here, which meant it was only eight on the West Coast, but already he sounded equally tired tonight. "Don't you have to give a speech this evening?"

"No. I've given four today already. That's enough of inflicting myself on the public for one day. But," he added, "I must admit, the crowds are good. And if they come to hear me because of Steve Scott and all that rot, at least they seem to leave thinking a bit about the future of the world."

Liv shifted in the chair and thought how amazing it was to be sitting in her kitchen with a pile of jeans to be mended and the evening paper scattered on the table in front of her, and to be talking to America's great heartthrob. Somehow he didn't fit the image, and not because he was less but because he was more. A real, living, breathing man, not some publicist's dummy. She felt herself warming all over as she listened to him talk on, telling her about the places he'd been today, the people he'd seen—the hordes of young women and the ham-handed public officials who'd dogged his steps—with a surprisingly self-deprecating sense of humor that poked as much fun at his own image as at people who let themselves be swayed by it. She grinned when he paused and told him, "It's just that you're so wonderful."

"I know. I could tell how impressed you were yesterday."

"That didn't really have anything to do with you," she told him now, realizing for the first time herself that it really didn't. It wasn't Joe, the person, she was annoyed at, it was the symbol of male freedom that he represented to Tom and men like him.

"Explain," he insisted.

But she couldn't. Not to him, not yet. He made her feel strange, alive, real—and the feelings scared her. She had to think about them, digest them, come to terms with them. Rationalize them, she mocked herself. "I don't think I want to right now," she said because, somehow, she felt that tonight he had given her a taste of who he was as a person, not a sex symbol, and she owed him the same honesty. "But I am sorry I took it out on you. This call must be costing you a fortune."

"Don't you think I can afford it?"

"Probably." He probably could own the phone company if he wanted to. "But I have this whole stack of mending to do and I haven't. . . ." She was babbling now, nervous.

"Okay," he sighed. "I get the picture. Say hi to the kids for me." And he was gone. Liv held the buzzing phone to her ear for a full minute before she replaced it on the hook, and when she did so she felt unaccountably lonely. No, not unaccountably. The reason was obvious—and ridiculous—she was missing Joe.

She drifted through the whole next day, responding absently to Marv's requests and Frances's observations, nearly forgetting to attend Noel's baseball game, and marking all of Stephen's multiplication homework wrong because she thought it was addition.

"Mom!" he howled with an eight-year-old's righteous indignation. "You were just s'posed to look and see how well I knew 'em, not mark all over 'em with your dumb red pencil!"

"Oh?" It barely penetrated the fog that was her brain. It was like being an adolescent all over again—the constant mooning and aching, the I-wonder-what-he's-doing-now syndrome that affected her every waking second. *Lord, I should be locked up,* she thought, shaking her head and trying to act like the sane, sensible mother of five that she had been up until two days ago. *Next thing you know I'll be reading movie magazines,* she thought as she scorched her good ivory blouse and decided that she'd better stop ironing before she burned the house down.

It was a delayed reaction to being exposed to a celebrity, she decided. But that was absurd because she'd met former President Carter, Robert Redford and Mother Teresa of Calcutta in the course of her work, too, and none of them had caused her to forget the sevens multiplication table or burn her blouse.

"Phone, Mom," Ben hollered.

"Is this the old woman in the shoe?" Joe's voice asked when she answered.

"You!"

"You were expecting maybe Warren Beatty?"

"I was expecting the termite exterminator," she said, heart aflutter.

"Disappointed?"

"Not very," she admitted. "He has at least as many children as I do."

"God save us," she heard Joe mutter.

"What do you want?"

"To talk to you."

"About what?"

"That's what I like about you. You're so direct, so straightforward." He was grinning, she could tell. "What did you do today?" he asked.

Burned a blouse, tied my typewriter ribbon in knots, thought of you, ruined Stephen's math homework, spelled "through" five different ways in one seven-inch story, thought of you.... "Not much," she said. "Is that why you called?"

"Partly. And partly to tell you the weather in Hawaii is rotten, the surf stinks, the girls are ugly—"

"And you just wanted me to know that?" Liv felt laughter rising within her.

"Sure," he said simply. "Tell me about Noel's ball game. Did he get a hit?"

She was more than a little surprised that he even knew about it, and said so.

"Of course I know. Remember, we talked about it at dinner, over the chicken-and-rice casserole."

Liv remembered kisses at dinner and little else, but she stammered, "Oh, yes, er, well, his team did win. He got a triple, I think."

"You *think?*" Joe sounded horrified. "Don't you know? Ah, well—" his tone turned philosophical "—my mother never knew how well I did either. Or when I struck out."

Liv thought that Joe Harrington's even *having* a mother was novel. She hadn't considered him as a part of a family, somehow. It made him seem far too human. "So what did you do today?" she asked brightly, keeping such thoughts at bay.

He told her about a marvelous reception at the airport in Oahu and about the fabulous luncheon he had attended.

"I thought you never ate," she said. "I thought you gave the speeches while other people ate."

"I'm learning to survive on flattery and the smell of food alone," he told her. "I'll be nothing but skin and bones by the time you see me again."

With a blonde on your arm, in some weekly gossip magazine, Liv thought with a grimness that surprised even her. "Poor guy," she commiserated. "Want me to send you a care package?"

"Only if you're in it."

"Joe!" But she knew he was only teasing, and anyway, the threat no longer existed. He was thousands of miles away and her chances of seeing him again, other than in two-dimensional black and white or living color, were virtually nil.

"Tim's banging on the door," he said then, and she heard him put his hand over the receiver and shout, "Come in." Then he said. "I have to go. I'll call again." And he was gone.

She never did figure out what the purpose of the call was. But it effectively brightened her mood for the rest of the evening. She hummed her way through folding the laundry and even managed to be pleasant to Tom when he called to say there was absolutely no way he could take Noel and Ben waterskiing that weekend as he had promised.

Joe's calls kept coming. Not always in the evening. At odd moments throughout the day or night the phone would ring and it would be Joe. They would talk for fifteen or twenty minutes—usually just the banter of good friends—sharing what they had done that day, teasing and laughing, and Liv stopped being surprised to discover the call was from him and came to look forward to it.

We're friends, she thought, pleased, and didn't bat an eyelash anymore when Frances put on her knowing leer and asked if Joe Harrington had called back. It was a standing joke between them now. Frances never knew that, in fact, he had, and that the secret admirer she teased Liv about, whose calls always made her smile for the rest of the day, was none other than Joe Harrington.

So Liv had no one to talk to about her feelings when the day came that he didn't call. For over two weeks she had heard from him every single day. And then one Friday no call came. He had been in Miami the night before, and she knew that his schedule would be hectic all that afternoon and evening, so she had expected to hear from him in the morning. Marv sent her to Sauk City to interview a potter and she didn't get back til almost noon, but there were no messages on her desk.

She camped by the phone all afternoon, and while it rang often enough, none of the callers was Joe. Each time it wasn't, her hopes fell a little further, and by the time she dragged herself out to the car that night, she was convinced that she would never hear from him again.

After all, who could expect a busy, influential, sexy man like Joe to call and call and call. He was bound to get bored with her and her mundane existence sooner or later. What else could she expect? But it would have been nice, she thought, if he had had the finesse to say, "It's been nice knowing you," during their last conversation. Something to let her know that their friendship was over. She stared at the phone during dinner and while she and Noel did the dishes, but it didn't ring.

Watched phones never do, she told herself. She decided to paint Jennifer's room that evening and forget him.

She tried. She got Noel to watch the younger kids, and coerced Ben into helping her paint. Between them they had three periwinkle-blue walls by ten o'clock.

"It's getting late," Liv told Ben finally. "You go take a shower and get into bed. I'll finish up."

There was only the one wall left to paint and she wanted—no, needed—to finish it tonight. The kids went to bed and the phone was silent and Liv continued to paint. The night air cooled surprisingly for mid-June, lifting the curtains and chilling Liv as she stood in her T-shirt and jeans and regarded her handiwork. There was a storm coming; she could feel it in the air. She laid the roller carefully on the tray of paint and trekked down to her room to find a warmer shirt.

"Ring, damn it," she muttered to the phone on her bedside table. But she knew it wouldn't. However wonderful it had been having a friend like Joe, she knew it wasn't destined to last. She saw his sweatshirt lying on top of her dresser and her hand reached out to pick it up and rub it gently against her cheek; she still found in it the faint aroma of Joe.

It's warm and I'm cold, she rationalized, *and he's never coming back.* She slipped it over her head, snuggling into its warmth, pierced by a loneliness she wouldn't have thought possible, and squared her shoulders and went back to pain.

She finished by eleven o'clock. The last wall wasn't as neatly done as the first three. She kept jerking the roller every time she thought she heard the phone ring. It never did, though she had run to her bedroom to answer it ten times at least. By the end of the evening all she had to show for her diligence was a bruise on her shin where she had banged against Jennifer's toy chest and lots of periwinkle-blue spatters on Joe's shirt and her own jeans.

Exhausted and depressed she dragged herself to bed. Stop it, she commanded. But she didn't. Her eyes ached, her mind ached and she felt absolutely empty. Flicking off the overhead light she kicked her jeans into a heap on the floor and fell into bed. It's a virus, she told herself. *I'm coming down with something.* She didn't want to think about what.

"SHHHHHHH."

Giggle. Creak. Shuffle.

"Hush."

Clink.

"Is she *still* asleep?"

"Stuff it, I said."

Liv squeezed her eyes shut against the sunlight. "Go 'way," she mumbled.

"See, she is, too, awake."

"Barely." The voice was dry, amused, and very masculine.

Liv's eyes flew open.

Joe stood at the foot of her bed holding a breakfast tray complete with pancakes, bacon and a bouquet of daisies. He was surrounded by a horde of grinning children. Liv dragged the covers up under her chin, stunned and staring. Only the smell of the bacon and the chirp of the flicker in the tree outside the window convinced her that she was really seeing him.

"Wha... what?" she croaked.

"Sit up and feast, Sleeping Beauty." Joe carried the tray around to the side of the bed and stood over her, tall and devastatingly attractive.

What a dream, Liv thought. It must be possible to smell bacon and hear birds in one's dreams. *Don't let me wake up,* she prayed, but then, in the same moment, realized with dismay that she had.

"Sit up and eat, Mommy," Jennifer commanded. "Joe and us made you pancakes and bacon."

"They were swell. We ate most of 'em," Stephen piped up.

Liv looked from Joe to the kids and back to Joe, feeling rather like a rabbit caught in a trap. He had his tiger's eyes again. "How long..." she began. "Where did you...."

There seemed to be so many questions. Mainly, of course, what was he doing here? He looked tired, despite the grin on his face. He was wearing a pale blue and white-striped open-neck sport shirt and a pair of jeans even more faded and disreputable than the ones he'd left on her bathroom floor. And—oh dear, she remembered she was wearing his sweatshirt! She scrunched even further under the covers till only her nose, eyes and tousled blond hair were showing.

"Just let me get dressed and I'll come into the kitchen to eat," she mumbled beneath the blanket.

Joe shook his head. "Humor us. We shouldn't have to go to all this trouble to give you breakfast in bed for nothing. I mean how often do you have breakfast in bed?" His eyes were mesmerizing her, drowning her in the deep green sea of his gaze. It terrified her. Joe Harrington at two or five thousand miles was a wonderful friend—at two feet he was capable of inspiring only panic. But he wasn't going away, and neither were the five other pairs of eyes that were fastened on her, waiting for her to sit up and eat her breakfast. Slowly, nervously, feeling as if she were disrobing in front of him, she did.

"Very good," she mumbled around her first mouthful of pancake, awash in syrup, and six smiles beamed back at her. Then five of them vanished in a flurry because it was really rather boring to sit there and watch their mother eat. The sixth, unfortunately, didn't move an inch.

"What a surprise," she said stiltedly into the silence that enveloped them. "Thank you." She could have been eating file cards for all she knew.

"You're welcome." He looked excessively pleased with himself, and Liv recalled the misery she'd felt when he hadn't phoned last night.

"What *are* you doing here?" She demanded. "Really?"

"Would you believe that I came for my jeans and sweatshirt?"

Liv's hand went to her breasts; her face flamed.

"But I've changed my mind." He grinned. "The shirt looks far better on you than it ever did on me."

"I—"

"Anyhow, that's not really why I came." He stuffed his hands into his back pockets and wandered over to stare out the window, away from her. His back was to her and she traced the line of his shoulders, then let her eyes drop lower to the elbows jutting out behind him and the narrow line of his hips. "I came to find me a house," he said.

Chapter Four

"To do what? What did you say?" Liv looked stunned.

"A house." Joe wiped damp palms on the sides of his jeans and continued to gaze blankly out the window, hoping that the famous Harrington acting ability wouldn't desert him now. He hadn't felt like such a nervous, fumbling, moonstruck schoolboy in years.

"Why on earth are you looking for a house?" Liv sat up and set the tray aside on the table, wrapping her arms around her knees like a young girl. He darted a glance at her, taking in the rumpled, defenseless gentleness, and the ache in his insides sharpened perceptibly. He couldn't even look at her without wanting her. And on that bed! In *his* sweatshirt! It didn't bear thinking about.

He flung himself across the room to the other window and stood leaning against the frame, looking out into the garden, taking deep, slow breaths that some drama coach had once told him would calm him. He hoped so. He needed a bit of calm now. He'd been strung up since he'd met her.

"I like it here," he said to the garden. "I want some peace and quiet to work on a screenplay that I'm interested in. I'm fed up with emphasizing acting." Not bad, he thought. His tone was carefully nonchalant, controlled. He managed a slight, self-mocking smile and turned so that she could see his profile. "And there are other advantages in the immediate neighborhood." He allowed himself a quick, leering glance in her direction, the sort that Steve Scott would have sent his leading lady to let her know she interested him. He only wished he felt as confident of Liv as Steve Scott felt of his lady-loves.

You'd have thought he was trying to get up the courage to ask a girl out for the first time, he thought. He almost snorted with impatience at his own ineptitude. Liv was looking at him, obviously flustered, the color high in her cheeks. At least he seemed to have put her off balance with his statement as badly as he was off balance himself. Quite likely she didn't know what to make of him, either. Superstar playboys must be as foreign to her as lovely, normal, sane women were to him. Neither one of them seemed to know how to act.

"Well," she said, with the spunk that he had found so appealing the first time he was here, "you had better clear out of my room, then. I'm certainly not getting up and dressing while you're here."

"Why not?" Joe smiled, feeling immediately more confident. This kind of light, sexual bantering came all too easy.

"I need to think of my children," she said softly, not bantering at all.

Joe felt as though she had knocked the breath right out of him. He felt certain she must see the dull red he knew was creeping above his collar. But if she did, at least she was kind enough not to comment on it. It was bad enough that he felt his remark was cheap.

"I'll wait in the kitchen," he mumbled, backing toward the door. "There're plenty of dishes to do." He couldn't get out of the room fast enough, not even when a part of him truly wanted to stay. *Scruples?* he chided himself. *At your age?* He shook his head in disbelief and started clearing the dishes off the kitchen table, scraping the plates and stacking them in the sink. But he couldn't deny it. Something about her made him want to clean up his act. He hadn't wanted to be caught leaving her house early that morning when he had spent the night, and he didn't want to embarrass her in front of her kids. He wanted their friendship to be aboveboard, clean, not a gossip monger's delight. He turned on the water and stared out the window above the sink at Theo and Jennifer, who were playing in the yard. Nice kids. He liked them. He didn't want to feel embarrassed or awkward in front of them, either, he realized. And that was an alien feeling, too.

Joe hadn't cared what anyone else said about his sexual escapades or relationships in years. And now he was worrying about the reputation of a thirty-two-year-old divorcée and her near half-dozen kids! What a switch, he thought with a savage humor, attacking with unnecessary vigor some dried egg yolk in a mixing bowl.

What was he doing here, anyway? He should be in Vic Truro's hot tub in L.A. musing over Vic's new screenplay, or swimming laps in his own pool, or—he glanced at his watch—still sleeping in his water bed, one arm slung over Linda Lucas or Paulette or Candi or Sherry....

"Hell!" The knife skidded down the side of the bowl and sliced into his thumb. He dropped the bowl and sucked on his thumb, the warm, metallic taste of the blood touching his tongue.

"What have you done?" Liv's voice came from behind him, and he spun around to see her come briskly into the room, all her earlier comfortable dishevelment gone. In formfitting, wheat-colored jeans and a bright orange halter, her hair pulled up into a tight knot on the back of her head, she looked every bit as brisk and efficient as the reporter he had first encountered. He knew very well, then, what he was doing here. His heart began racing again in his chest.

"I cut it," he mumbled, his words garbled because his thumb was still in his mouth. Steve Scott never did things like this, he knew with unerring certainty, annoyed that she should see him do something so dumb.

"Let me see it." She reached for his hand, and he took one last lick, hoping that that would stem the flow of blood, but it didn't. The blood ran down his hand and dripped on her jeans.

"Put it under the water," she commanded, thrusting his hand into the sink and filling a bowl with cold water. "It's pretty deep. How did you—"

"The knife slipped," Joe said, looking away. The water was turning red and his stomach lurched. Liv flung open a cabinet door and rummaged around while he waited, then returned before he could worry about how long it would take for him to bleed to death on her kitchen floor. She removed his hand from the water and probed the cut, then deftly bandaged it.

"I think it'll be okay without stitches," she offered. "But I'll take you to the hospital if you want."

"No." Not only did he not want stitches, he did not want the publicity that would come with it. And, he thought, neither would she. Some gossipy person would report that Joe Harrington was seen arriving in the early morning with reporter Olivia James, with whom he had obviously spent the night. No, Liv definitely did not need that!

What she needed, he had decided over the past two weeks, was somebody to be there for her, to make her life a bit easier, a bit more enjoyable, not someone complicating it or making it worse. And ever since he had met her, ever since she had flung his pass back in his face and had fed him birthday cake and chicken and rice, he had wanted to be that person. He wanted to share things with her—hence, the phone calls, and when they weren't enough any more, he had had to come in person.

Now he stood silently watching her as she gently continued to wipe the blood from his hand. The cut didn't hurt, yet, but her careful ministrations touched him to the core.

It was, he realized, the first time she had touched him that he could remember. When she had practically undressed him, he hadn't known a thing—damn it. But his imagination had worked overtime since, picturing her touching him. He may have taken Linda to his bed in L.A., but it wasn't

Linda he saw in his mind, nor Linda's hands moving over him, caressing, teasing, exciting. His hand lurched violently.

"Does it hurt a lot?" Liv asked sympathetically.

It wasn't his hand that hurt. "No, not very much," he managed, trying in vain to steady his voice. The flames in his loins were consuming him; surely she could tell. But he didn't dare glance at her to know. Instead he forced his mind away from her, looking intently out past the curtains toward the sandbox where Theo and Jennifer and a neighbor boy were playing with some Matchbox cars and trucks. They were arguing about some road construction they had embarked upon, and if he strained he could make out what they were saying. So he strained, and didn't look at Liv again until she released his hand and said, "I think you'll live."

"Thanks."

"Don't mention it. It's all part of the job description."

"As?"

"Mother."

"Not mine." He laughed, and was gratified when she blushed. But then, just as quickly, she was all business again.

"Tell me about this house you want and why."

"I just don't like living in L.A. all year," he said, finding it easier to talk to her now that she wasn't half-dressed and in bed. "And I like my privacy, as I'm sure you've heard. So I thought that Madison would be a good place to get away to for a while. All the Hollywood hype can get to a guy, you know?" He grimaced at the eyebrow she arched at him. "I know I ask for a lot of it, but just the same, I do like a respite," he admitted, and was glad when she offered him a small smile.

"So you decided that this was as far into the back of the beyond as you could get?" Liv questioned, cocking her head and looking at him with a certain tolerant amusement.

"Partly. And I like being around water. Madison's got a lot of that. I'd like to find a place on the water if I can. Isolated, if at all possible."

"Ah, Joe Harrington, hermit," she teased.

"No. Just Joe Harrington, exhausted. Joe Harrington in need of some space."

"I'd like some of that too," she said suddenly, and then stopped abruptly, as though the words had popped out unbidden, which, in fact, he guessed they had.

"I bet you would," he said softly. "It must get to be a lot, five kids on your own."

"I'm not complaining," she said fiercely, looking like a mother tiger defending her cubs.

"I wasn't implying that," Joe said mildly, knowing instinctively that it was a sore point. "I just think you've got a hard job. You do it very well."

"Thanks." She smiled at him nervously, brushing a hand against her hair as though trying to make sure her mask was in place. "I—I guess I'm a bit defensive about it. Single parent and all that."

Liv was looking at him with wide, gray eyes, like a stormy sea capped with a sunburst of blond hair. "Not defensive," he said, scarcely above a whisper, drowning in her eyes. Her lips were soft, inviting, trembling slightly just inches below his own. Joe Harrington, superstar stud, wouldn't have hesitated an instant, but Joe Harrington, scrupulous schoolboy with sweating palms, didn't know if he dared.

She didn't move, just stood immobile under his gaze until he could stand the temptation of her parted lips no longer, and bent his head, capturing her mouth with his own.

It was like riding a bicycle without brakes—helpless, frantic, out of control. How on earth could he stop, he wondered desperately. Every fiber of his being wanted to crush her against him, molding her body to his and never letting her go. Reluctantly, gasping for breath, he tore his mouth away, clenching his fists against his sides and praying for self-control. He knew the kiss wasn't going to be enough to satisfy. He knew, too, that if he wanted to see her again, there wasn't going to be what he considered "enough" for a long time. The ache in him was definitely going to get worse before it got better.

Like a diver come to the surface after a long and arduous dive, he slowly reoriented himself, steadying his breathing and his heart, and opening his eyes. Wide gray eyes stared into his. My God, had she watched his whole struggle? Likely. She didn't look flustered at all. Just indifferent. Or stunned.

But he doubted the latter, especially when she straightened up and said matter-of-factly, "Only twenty-five more. I'll call George Slade about a house for you."

Joe hardly heard the second part of the statement; he was still reeling from the first. Was that all she thought it was? One of those birthday kisses he'd purloined from her children? He stared at her, unable to disguise the hurt. Not even *he* was that good an actor. She looked back at him from where she was dialing the telephone and suddenly set it back on the hook.

"I'm sorry," she said awkwardly, a wistful smile touching her lips. "That wasn't a nice thing to say."

She looked genuinely sorry, which surprised him. None of the other women in his life, other than his mother and sisters, had ever cared much one way or another how he felt beyond how it affected what he could do for them. And they certainly never bothered to apologize, either, unless it was in their own best interests. But Liv seemed genuinely concerned that she had hurt him. And he wasn't above agreeing with her. "No," he said, "it wasn't."

She looked away in apparent confusion.

"Did you mean it?"

"What?" She looked really confused now.

"Is that all you really thought it was," he persisted, needing to know. "Number twenty-five?"

"I don't know what to think," she snapped, like a kitten trapped in a corner. "I don't know what you're doing in my life, anyway!" It was almost a wail, and he could commiserate completely.

I could say the same thing about you, Joe thought ruefully. "I don't know, either," he said softly. "I don't know." He reached out and touched her cheek tentatively, needing some sort of contact and hoping that she wouldn't draw away. He almost collapsed with relief when, instead, she turned her lips to caress his palm. "I want to find out, don't you?" he asked.

Her lips moved against his hand. "Yes," they said. "Heaven help me, yes."

SHE MUST BE out of her mind, Liv thought as they sped through tree-lined residential streets toward the shore of Lake Monona. How could she ever seriously consider getting involved with a man like Joe Harrington? It was one thing to allow herself to enjoy long-distance phone calls and entertain harmless fantasies about the man. It was quite another to be going house hunting with him on a Saturday in June.

She darted a quick glance at the man who was driving her car with such ease and familiarity. He was concentrating on driving, humming something indistinct but decidedly cheerful, the rugged lines of his face relaxed, giving him an air of content that she hadn't seen on him earlier that morning. She looked away again almost instantly. Contemplating Joe Harrington was dangerous to her emotional health. As much as his movie-star image epitomized everything she despised about some men in general and her ex-husband in particular, Joe, the living, breathing man alongside her, was something else again. And she knew, against her better judgment, that she didn't despise him at all. It would be infinitely safer if she did.

"Next street, I think," he was saying now.

Ben, Theo, Stephen and Jennifer were bouncing on the back seats chanting, "There! No, there! Maybe there!" Liv would have throttled all of them if she had been driving, but Joe seemed oblivious to the noise. He seemed to know exactly what he was looking for, and noise, distractions, and other suggestions didn't faze him in the least.

They had driven right past George Slade's first recommendation without even stopping. "Not enough privacy," Joe had said, scarcely giving the two-story white frame house a glance. "And I thought I mentioned water."

There's imperiousness for you, Liv thought. "George said it had a lake view," she explained, but she was just as glad he hadn't stopped. She didn't care for the house either. "Turn here," she said now, and felt a prickle of excitement when they turned onto a narrow street that ran along the edge of a creek that flowed through a heavily wooded park into the lake.

"Neato!" Stephen exclaimed. "Could I ever get lost in there!"

"Explorers!" Ben breathed. "We could be explorers!"

"Like Henry and Angus," Theo chimed in, recalling his favorite story.

Liv turned to hush them, when she caught a glimpse of the same starry-eyed enthusiasm on Joe's face. He looks as young as they do, she thought suddenly. And when she saw the house almost at the water's edge, she breathed, "That's it," before she could stop herself.

Joe didn't say anything, but he stopped the car immediately and bounded out even faster than the kids. It wasn't a pretentious house by Madison's standards, certainly not the majestic modern glass palace that Liv would have associated with a movie star who liked privacy, or one of the gingerbread Victorians that abounded hereabouts. Low-slung and rambling, it sprawled beneath the trees like a contented cat. Rough, weathered wood and a huge stone chimney allowed it to blend into the surrounding forest. Liv had heard about houses designed to fit in with their surroundings, but a lifetime of tract houses and unimaginative boxes designed for the most mechanical of human existences had left her unprepared for this.

"Joe!" Theo yelled from halfway across the yard, "Look, here's a boathouse! Joe!"

"Can we go see, Joe?" Jennifer asked, halfway between the boys, who were racing for the water's edge, and her mother, who was standing by the car, feeling that if she took one step into that house she would be lost forever.

"Go ahead," Joe hollered back from the front porch. He fumbled with the key in his hand, then inserted it into the lock, but before he turned it he stopped and looked over his shoulder.

"Liv?" he said, an almost imperceptible roughness in his voice. "Coming?"

He held out his hand, waiting, and Liv thought helplessly, *I can't.*

It was more than a house, it was a dream house. The one she had envisioned in her fantasies since she was a child. She hadn't actually seen this one specifically, but it had everything she'd ever wanted—a fireplace, pine trees, homey warmth. How could she go in and walk around saying politely, "How nice," and then go home to her bland box, leaving Joe Harrington in possession of her dreams? She glanced up at him.

He wasn't waiting by the door anymore, but had walked back across the yard, stopping beside her, so close she could touch him. "What's wrong?" His voice was low and curiously gentle for a man who had been consumed by enthusiasm moments before.

"N-nothing," she stammered, unable to look at him. It's envy, idiot, she told herself disgustedly. If it were going to be yours, you'd be running in, too.

"I know you like it," he said. "So do I."

Of course he did. That was another part of the problem. Knowing that he shared her dreams was making her even more vulnerable to him. And she couldn't tell him that. Nor could she say how much she envied him. How childish that would seem. Grow up, she told herself sharply, the way she might snap at Noel for whining about something far beneath him, and dredged up a wavering smile. "Let's go."

The inside was all she had hoped—and feared—it would be. Natural oak woodwork, room-sized braided rugs and comfortable, slightly lumpy furniture about two generations out of date. It had been the home of an architect and was now in the hands of his estate; hence its completely furnished rental state, George had told her when she had called to say she had a friend looking for a house for a few months.

Joe led her from room to room as proudly as though he were the architect himself or a magician who had conjured the house up out of thin air, as well he might have, Liv thought, for she had never had an inkling that such a perfect house existed, especially near here.

"I think," Joe said, when they had done the whole tour through the four bedrooms, the spacious living-dining room, the den and the recently modernized kitchen, "that we'll take it, don't you?"

It was a slip of the tongue, Liv thought, moistening her lips. He meant "I", not "we", but he was looking at her as though he expected her response.

"Yes," she croaked, and felt her cheeks burn at his smile.

"Good. Then will you call this Slade guy from your place and tell him I'm moving in today?"

"Today?"

Joe grinned. "Why not?" He leaned against the gleaming yellow kitchen counter and regarded her with mischief in his eyes. "Or were you planning to offer me space in your bed tonight?"

He was teasing, Liv knew, but she wished he wouldn't. It made it even harder to keep thinking of him as a "friend." And there was no sense in thinking of him as anything else. Joe would not be in Madison for long, she was sure, and he wasn't the type who made commitments. Just as she wasn't given to having affairs, no matter how brief or wonderful they might be.

"No answer to that?" Joe teased when she looked at the floor without responding. His hand reached out and loosened the knot of her hair, letting it cascade around her shoulders, and she looked up at him with wide, nervous eyes. He's just a friend, she reminded herself again.

"I like it up," she said, trying to brush his hand away.

He wound his fingers in her hair. "So do I," he confided with a gleam in his eyes. "But I like it down better. I like to wrap my fingers in it." He moved closer till their bodies were almost touching. His breath was fanning her cheek, moving the strands of hair on her neck, and she shivered. "And I'd like to—" He broke off suddenly and stepped back, his hand dropping to his side. "Oh, Liv," he murmured, his mouth twisting. He jammed his hands into his jeans' pockets and stared at the toes of his shoes.

Liv, taken aback, stared helplessly at him. What kind of line was this? Expecting to be swept off her feet by the experienced man-about-town, she couldn't make sense of these advance-and-retreat tactics. Keep 'em off balance, she thought wryly. Maybe that's how he does it. Whatever he was doing, she acknowledged, it worked. If he had come on strong with her, like the playboy everyone said he was, she could have resisted him easily. But this... how could she resist this?

"Mommy! Come an' see the beach Joe's got!" Theo burst into the kitchen and skidded to a stop. "C'mon!" He grabbed Liv's hand and she allowed him to pull her outside. Saved by a child, she thought, letting Theo drag her to where the grass gave way to sand near the water's edge.

"Now this is what I meant by water," Joe said, coming to stand behind her. "Want to wade?"

"Now?"

He shrugged. "Why not?"

A giggle swept up inside her. "Why not?"

"Really, can we?" Ben asked and let out a whoop of joy when he saw his mother kick off her sandals and join Joe, who had already rolled up his pant legs and was walking through the water.

Wading, of course, was not where it ended, as Liv suspected it would not. First Stephen splashed Ben, who retaliated and in the process soaked Joe.

"Like that, is it?" Joe laughed and clapped his hands together in the water sending a geyser of water over everyone. Especially Liv.

Her halter clung wetly to her breasts and she felt his gaze on her, warmer than the sun and burning, and scooping up a double handful of water, she poured it down the front of his shirt. "That'll cool you off," she promised, chortling until he came after her. "No! Joe, stop! No!"

But there was no stopping Joe until he had grabbed her and lifted her high in the air, then waded out waist deep where he promptly sank, submerging them both.

"Joe!" she spluttered, hair streaming in her face.

"Cooled you off too, didn't I?" he smirked.

But he was still holding her against him and she could feel the hardness of his body through the wet jeans and see the unquenched passion in his face. "Not really," she said honestly. He went suddenly still, his breathing rapid as he studied her assessingly, and Liv wondered if she should have been so forthright. Then he set her down about six inches from him so the water lapped between them, and he took a deep breath.

"No, not really," he agreed. "But there's not much I can do about it here and now." He shot a significant glance at the kids lined up on shore like spectators at a swimming match. "The audience wouldn't approve."

"Nor would I," Liv said shakily, shifting her gaze away from his bare chest where rivulets of water coursed through dark, glistening hair.

"Oh?"

"No." She wouldn't let herself, *couldn't* let herself. They were just friends, nothing more. She waded briskly toward the shore. "Come on, gang. Time to go home."

"Can we come back tomorrow?" Ben questioned.

"I don't think—" Liv began, but Joe cut her off.

"Of course. Ride over on your bikes. It's not much more than a mile."

"I don't want them to be a bother," Liv protested.

"No bother. I don't invite people I don't want."

His words were terse. It wasn't possible to construe them as mere politeness. He meant it; she could see it in his eyes, hear it in his tone. He was looking at her intently. *Not* the way one friend looks at another. She could still feel the imprint of his body against her own. Gulping, she looked away, wondering what in the world she was letting herself in for.

"YOU MEAN THEY'RE all gone?" Joe could hardly believe it. He was the last one out of the shower, and when he emerged and glanced around the living room with its definite signs of youthful habitation, he couldn't see any youths at all.

"They've gone out with their father," Liv told him from where she sat on the arm of the chair, surveying the wreckage. "Every Saturday that I can manage it, Tom takes them. Even if it's only for dinner."

"What do you mean, if *you* can manage it?" He was tempted to go over and pull her off the chair and take her into his arms. But sanity prevailed, and he sank down instead on the couch and picked up a Frisbee, spinning it idly on his finger.

"When we were together, Tom and I," she said quickly, as though the memories were distasteful or painful, "I never minded having the kids around all the time. There was enough of me to go around. Or so I thought." She laughed somewhat bitterly at that, and Joe ached just hearing her. "Apparently Tom didn't, but that's not the point. Anyway, now that I am the sole parent in residence, I find that I need a break. If only for a while." She gave him a tentative smile. "I'm sorry. This must be boring for you."

"Not at all." And amazingly enough, it wasn't. He didn't care the slightest bit about the domestic tribulations of anyone else, but Liv was different. He wanted to know everything about her, what made her happy, sad, silly, depressed. She intrigued him, tantalized him. He didn't even know why. Because she seemed indifferent to his fame, his reputation? Perhaps. Because she didn't fall into bed with him at the first hint of a pass? Maybe. Whatever it was, he wanted more. And with no kids in sight, he stood a better chance of getting it. "I like the idea of being alone with you for a change," he said, regarding her over the top of the spinning Frisbee.

She started when she heard that. The realization that the kids' going with Tom had left her not just free but alone with Joe Harrington apparently just hit her. "Er, would you like me to drive you back to your new house?" she asked, bouncing to her feet as thought he were a salesman just begging to be shown to the door.

"What I would like is to have dinner with you. Just the two of us."

"I know a nice little Greek place that has—"

"No Greek place."

"Mexican? La Golondrina is—"

"Not Mexican either."

"Well, there is McDonald's, but...." Liv faltered.

A grin split Joe's features. "Your place or mine?" he invited.

"I...I...."

He sprang lithely to his feet and crossed the room to stand in front of her, wanting to make himself clear. "This is not a proposition," he explained. "Not exactly," he added. As much as he would have liked to drag her off to his lair and ravish her, he found that he wanted more than that. Linda Lucas wasn't a scintillating companion. Liv was. He didn't only want to go to bed with her. He wanted to talk with her, tease her, listen to her, touch her.

"What is it, then," she asked, "if it's not a proposition?" She wet her lips nervously.

"A simple request for your company at dinner. At your place or mine, because I don't like the notoriety of going out. That may sound conceited—it probably is conceited—but I can't ever seem to get a meal in a restaurant without giving autographs or having some starstruck waitress drop soup in my lap. And, well, I'd just like to be alone with you." He gave her one of his famous grins, but it didn't seem faked. Rather it seemed spontaneous, special, just for her. As if he'd never smiled at another woman. *And if you believe that, he'll sell you the Brooklyn Bridge,* she thought. But it didn't stop her giving in.

"Your place," she told him, more daring than she would have thought possible. "It'll be a nice change from mine."

"Terrific. I'll cook. You relax." He was bundling her out the door as if he thought she'd change her mind, reaching behind him long enough only to grab his battered suitcase, which she had avoided mentioning ever since she'd seen it in her living room that morning. *Good,* she thought now, relieved, *at least he isn't intending to spend the night in my bed.* Fears quieted, however temporarily, she started to relax.

"You go in," Joe told her as he drove them to the supermarket parking lot. She looked at him, puzzled, and he gave an embarrassed shrug. "I'd probably cause a riot," he explained, red-faced.

He might, too, she realized as she pushed her cart up to the check-out counter and saw his face staring at her from one of the weekly magazines. What would the checker think if Joe Harrington himself plunked down two steaks, potatoes, lettuce, peppers and tomatoes in front of her? Liv picked up the magazine and flipped through it.

There he was with his arm around lovely starlet Linda Lucas at some Beverly Hills party. And there was another shot of him with producer Luther Nelson, who was trying to get him to agree to star in another film as adventurer hero, Steve Scott. On the next page she saw a helicopter view of his "hideaway" above Malibu. Lord, Liv thought, staring at it, what does he need a place here for? She scanned the article as the checker rang up her purchases. It didn't tell her anything about Joe Harrington that she didn't already know, being only a rehash of earlier articles set up with a few new photos. Only the last sentence hung in her mind: "Harrington's a man of mystery, a very private man whose public antics on and off screen have led millions to think they know him well, when, in fact, they don't know him at all."

True, true, true, Liv thought, gathering up her purchases and stepping back into the heat of the lovely June evening. How many millions would guess that at this moment the famous Mr. Harrington was sitting in a rusty VW bus, nose buried in a three-month-old *Soccer Digest,* waiting for nobody-reporter and mother of five, Olivia James, so he could take her down to his rented house and cook her dinner?

"Hi. Took you long enough." He looked up giving her a warm, friendly smile that made her glow.

She handed him the bags and climbed in. "I know. But not as long as you would have taken. Nobody asked for my autograph."

"True." He peered into the sacks. "What're we having?"

"Steak, potatoes, salad. Can you manage that?"

"Definitely. I'm a whiz. Especially good at hash browns. I hope you don't want baked." He looked at her as Theo did when he was trying to convince her that rocky road ice cream was far better than vanilla.

"Hash browns would be great."

He looked pleased, starting up the engine and waiting patiently for a break in the traffic. Liv watched him, liking the way he handled her car, liking the way his glasses perched on his nose, making him look scholarly as well as sexy, liking the way his jeans hugged the contours of his thighs. She removed her gaze from his pants and watched him shift gears. He had strong hands, capable ones with long, slender fingers sprinkled with dark hairs. She glanced at the man driving the car next to them. He was laughing at something the woman in the car with him had said. They looked like a happily married couple. Like us, she thought suddenly, and blushed.

How fanciful that is, she chided herself. Joe Harrington was not any old married man, nor was he likely to become one. Especially not with her. Just because he looked ordinary enough didn't mean she ought to be getting ideas about him. This man raked in millions yearly making movies and providing hot copy for all the latest personality magazines.

"I saw what you meant," she told him as they wound their way back to Joe's new house on the lake. "You were all over the covers of the magazines I saw."

Joe groaned audibly. "And don't believe a word you read of it. It's all 'JOE HARRINGTON WAS MY LOVER—AGING STARLET TELLS ALL,' or 'JOE HARRINGTON—IS HE REALLY LIKE STEVE SCOTT?' or 'JOE HARRINGTON'S BIGGEST SECRET.'" He shook his head wearily. "It makes me sick. Which one did you see?"

"It wasn't too awful. Just a rehash of your early interviews." Then she felt the color creep into her cheeks as she realized that she had admitted to having read all his early interviews. "And pictures. Lots of pictures," she added quickly.

"I can imagine," Joe said dryly.

"You and Luther Nelson."

"Yeah. He's not a bad guy, except when he wants something from you."

"You and Linda Lucas," Liv went on, hating the catch in her voice.

"Hmm," Joe replied, whatever that meant. It certainly wasn't a denial of involvement with her. Liv knew she could hardly expect one. Joe had never been a saint. Still, she would have liked to know if he was still seeing her. Or anyone else. He was probably an expert at dangling four or five women at a time. *Damn,* she thought fiercely, *why do I even care? Why am I letting myself be one of them?*

The answer to that was increasingly obvious. She couldn't seem to help herself. No willpower, she thought glumly. No self-discipline. A living example of the expression "putty in his hands." If only he weren't Joe Harrington she would feel a lot better about the way he attracted her. Joe Harrington's biggest secret, she thought wryly, was how he could make normally sane, intelligent women forget their common sense and fall for him even against their better judgment.

"What are you thinking about?" he asked. "You should see the expressions on your face."

"About Joe Harrington's biggest secret." She grinned.

He laughed softly, then his eyes grew serious though he still smiled. "We'll have to talk about that," he promised. "Later." And her heart quickened in response. "Right now I'm starving. And I bet you are, too."

True to his word, the moment they arrived at his house, Joe settled her into a leather-covered armchair, propped her feet on the hassock and handed her a glass of wine, saying, "Now, relax and enjoy it and watch the master chef at work."

"Those are daring words," Liv countered. "Especially from someone who's never cooked in this kitchen and doesn't know if there's a frying pan to be found."

There was. And Joe proceeded to amaze her with his ease in the kitchen. Another side of the man to like, damn it, she thought as she sipped her wine and watched him move about humming to himself. She was getting in deeper and deeper, sinking fast, and she couldn't seem to help herself. The wine made her ears warm and her mind slightly muzzy, and she lay her head back and closed her eyes wondering if it were all a dream.

"Did you think to pick up some salad dressing?" Joe asked, glancing at her across the polished wood bar that separated her armchair from the kitchen.

"Sorry, no. But I can make some Olivia James's Secret Salad Dressing if you can find some oil, vinegar and spices," she offered, hating to get up, but looking forward to working alongside him in the kitchen.

"I'll see what I can do," he said. "My expertise doesn't run to salad dressing. Never took a class in that."

"You learned to cook in a class?" That didn't seem to fit his character at all.

"Naw. My mother thought I ought to know how to cook. She said it wasn't just girls who needed to get around in a kitchen. My father didn't agree, but she won out. Now he complains that my independence in the kitchen has contributed to the fact that he doesn't have a daughter-in-law." He was grinning, but she heard a hard edge to his voice.

"And is that the truth of the matter?" she asked from her kneeling position in front of one of the cabinets.

"Could be." He chopped the potatoes quickly and plunked them into the sizzling skillet, stirring them with a fork.

"That's a story," she laughed. "JOE HARRINGTON COOKS—DOESN'T NEED A WIFE."

"I'll suggest it next time a reporter is looking for an angle on a story." He poured some more wine in her glass. "Here, drink up."

"Are you trying to get me drunk?"

He lifted his eyebrows. "Would it help?"

She considered the matter seriously, studying the way the soft blue denim creased at his knees. "I think it might," she said slowly.

He dumped her wine in the sink.

"What are you doing?" she yelped, grabbing his hand.

He set the glass back on the counter and resumed stirring the potatoes. "I want you to know what you're doing," he said, eyes intent on the frying pan.

Liv's expression was bemused. "You mean you're not going to ply me with liquor and drag me off to the bedroom?" she asked, expressing both her greatest fear and a disappointment she wished she didn't feel.

Joe shook his head, his mouth crooked.

"Why not?"

Joe stared, fork in midair. "What did you say?"

"I said, why not?"

"I don't know," he said after a long moment during which she was wishing she hadn't asked. Oh, why was she so fuzzy-minded all of a sudden? "Pour me another glass of wine, will you?" he muttered.

She did, still amused that he wouldn't let her have any, and even more so when she saw him lift the glass and drain it in one long swallow. He shoved the glass toward her for a refill. She shook her head.

"I'm not plying you with liquor either."

He slanted her a glance. "I suppose you won't be dragging me off to bed, either. Will you?"

Liv's mouth curved into a smile. "Well," she dropped her voice suggestively and saw his hands clench on the counter.

"Stop it," he said sharply. Suddenly he was all concentration, totally absorbed in meal preparation, blocking her out completely. Chastened and, on a moment's reflection, knowing that she had been playing with fire, Liv followed suit, fixing her attention on the salad dressing. By the time the dressing and hash browns were done, Joe bent to open the broiler and speared the steaks. He flung them onto the waiting platter and strode across the room to set it on the table. "Let's eat," he said briskly.

Liv followed his example silently, sitting down across from him and beginning to eat. *It was a good thing he didn't let me have that wine,* she thought, *or who knows how idiotically I might have acted!* Had she really been baiting him? She looked up guiltily, but Joe was intent on cutting his steak. Obviously he was immune to her. She thought she was relieved, but she wasn't sure.

"It's good," she offered tentatively.

He nodded, mouth full. "Thanks. So's your dressing."

The tension abated a bit, and he began telling her about his two weeks' journey all over the country, giving speeches. She was impressed again by the seriousness of his commitment. There was no money in it for him, no great publicity. Some people even disliked him for speaking out. She thought again of the magazine's comment about people not knowing the real Joe Harrington at all and was glad that she'd been given a glimpse.

"I'll do the dishes," she offered afterward, but he shook his head.

"My mommy taught me to do dishes, too. If we do them together we'll have more time for other things later on."

Liv didn't ask what the other things were. She thought she would find out soon enough, so she ferreted out the dish-washing liquid and squirted some into the sinkful of water, washing up while Joe got a dish towel and dried. It ought to have been that simple, Liv thought. She must have washed dishes several thousand times in her adult life, but she had never felt so aware of the man helping her. She found herself watching as his strong hands smoothed the towel around the curve of a wineglass or whisked droplets of water off a plate. And she couldn't think of a thing to say to save her life. She was submerged in an awareness growing between them so powerfully that it was almost tangible. And yet it was odd, too—they were doing dishes together, just like people who had been married for years and years.

"Just like an old married couple," Joe's voice broke into her thoughts and she looked up at him, astonished. How had he read her mind? Her look of astonishment must have unnerved him, she thought, or maybe he didn't really realize what he had said, for suddenly an uncharacteristic tide of red crossed his neck and face and he said, "Tell me about your work."

And Liv did, gladly, allowing him to lead their conversation into an avenue where they would both feel safer.

"Let's go for a walk," Joe suggested when the last dish was put away.

That sounded safe, Liv thought. Safer than staying inside, anyway. When you walked, you had your feet on the ground at least. And the way she felt the sexual tension building between them, on the ground was just the place her feet needed to be. It was a lucky thing, she reflected, that her wine had gone down the drain. Tonight was turning out to be a heady enough experience even when she was sober.

"Want a sweater?" he asked, leading her out the door.

It wasn't really that cool, but she was tempted, just to feel Joe's sweater around her shoulders. Resist it, she told herself. "I'm fine," she said.

Joe shrugged but pulled a nylon, fleece-lined Windbreaker off the hook by the door and tied the sleeves around his neck. "Just in case," he said. "We can share it."

She should have accepted the sweater. It would have been less dangerous after all. Ah, well. She giggled a little; the thought of sharing his jacket wasn't bad either. *Control yourself, Olivia,* she admonished herself sternly. But just then his warm hand closed over hers and all resolution failed. A giddy warmth filled her as she curved her fingers willingly around his.

Had they stayed to eat at her house they would have been able to walk down the street past other equally unimaginative houses until they reached the neighborhood convenience store. And if they had gone a block further they could have passed the chain-link-fenced playground of the kids' elementary school. But here they had an enchanted woodsy park, a moon peeking through pine trees, the smell of pine resin and damp leaves and the sound of the lake lapping on the shore.

"I love to go to sleep hearing the sound of water," Liv said as they skirted the edge of the lake.

"Me, too."

"You'll sleep well tonight, then." She sat down on a rock outcropping and Joe settled himself next to her, pulling her between his legs so that her back rested against his hard chest.

"Not likely," he growled in her ear.

"But—"

"How in hell do you expect that I'll sleep well, knowing that you're a mile and a half away with five little kids?" His arms came around her, and she turned her head so that his lips, warm and demanding, brushed her cheek, before he shifted and found her mouth in a long, shattering kiss. She shuddered under the impact of it.

"Cold?" he murmured, arms tightening, his cheek scraping hers.

"N-no." She was burning. A heat like molten lava coursed through her veins and, unthinking, she shifted onto her knees facing him, putting her arms around his neck, winding her fingers through his thick, dark hair.

"Let's go in," Joe whispered, his mouth moving against her cheek. His eyes were closed and she could hear his heart thudding as loudly as her own. Wordlessly she allowed him to draw her to her feet and slip the jacket around both of them before they walked as one person back along the lakeshore to the house.

"Our architect was a romantic, too," Joe said softly as he moved ahead of her into the living room and lighted the bank of candles on the mantel. The room took on a golden glow, looking as seductive and unreal as Liv was feeling. She stood just inside the doorway and watched Joe as he padded across the room in his jogging shoes, his hair mussed, the planes and angles of his features softened by the shadows of the candlelight.

"Come here." His voice was husky, slightly unsteady, and he moved toward the sofa and sat down, patting the space beside him.

Liv went, drawn like a moth to a flame. "I must be crazy," she mumbled in a voice as unsteady as his. But she curled up beside him, snuggling against his hard chest, feeling in spite of all her common sense that what was happening was right, that this was where she belonged.

"Liv," Joe groaned, his hands slipping under her halter, caressing, seeking, finding. "You don't know what it's been like these past two weeks."

"Mmm? Don't I?" She knew what they'd been like for her. Two years. His fingers sought the curve of her breast. There was no bra to stop him and Liv didn't pull away. On the contrary she felt as though something had finally happened to thaw her out. The block of ice that she had been since Tom's defection had protected her from other men, had been her shield against all intrusions into her life. Nobody had come close to penetrating it until now. But Joe was like a forest fire, relentless, uncontrollable, melting her in his arms. And she knew that, at the moment anyway, she had no desire to control him. Her hands were as restless as his. Chains of restraint loosened; she tugged his shirt out of his jeans and slid her hands up across the smooth muscles of his back, kneading his shoulders, stroking his neck, skipping down his spine.

"Yes," he muttered, "Oh, yes." And he slid sideways, pulling her down on top of him and removing her halter top in one easy movement. Very clever, she thought. Years of practice. But suddenly it didn't matter. Nothing mattered but Joe, the feel of him, the taste of him. She nibbled an earlobe and felt a tremor rock through him. The candlelight flickered, making his expression almost unreadable. But Liv could see enough in the heavy-lidded eyes to know how much he wanted her. As much as she wanted him. She tried to pull back a bit to see better this man who was making her forget every resolution she'd made in the past two years, but his hands drew her back down to him, his mouth seeking her breast, suckling gently and causing her the same torment she knew she caused him. Her hand moved down his chest and sides, stroking, learning the shape of him, the bony ribs, the haired chest, the flat, hard stomach. Her hand trailed lightly across the skin above the waistband of his jeans. He sucked in his breath sharply, his mouth drawing, tugging on her, reaching the center of her being. Then he nuzzled against her, murmuring, "Go on, Liv. Please." His own hands were fumbling with the snap on her jeans.

"I hear a car," Liv said, staying his hand in its quest, though she ached for him to go on.

"Naw. It's probably just the creek where it goes over the rocks to the lake." His hand continued. The snap was undone, the zipper partway down. He was probably right, she thought fuzzily. No one else lived nearby; no one would be coming to see them. Anyway, her hands were not moved by reason tonight; they only wanted to know him, to touch him. His jeans unsnapped even more easily than hers. She traced a narrow line of hair down below his navel even further.

"The car's still here, so she must be," a childish voice announced on the porch, breaking the sounds of quickened breathing and the dull rush of water over rocks.

"That's Ben!" Liv hissed, sitting bolt upright on Joe's thighs. "Oh, my God!" She scrambled off him, frantically searching for her top, finding it behind the sofa and pulling it on—wrong. "Cripes," she muttered and tugged it off and on again.

Joe cursed and sat up slowly, staring dumbly, as if he'd been asleep and had only just come around. His were not, she reflected with the barest hint of humor, the reactions of a man used to making love in a house full of children.

The knock on the door made her jump. She ran a hand through her hair helplessly, knowing that it was only too obvious what she'd been doing. But none of that mattered. Something was wrong at home. Otherwise Ben wouldn't be here. What was wrong? How had he got here? Who brought him? A neighbor? Frances?

"Would you answer the door?" she said to Joe, who was still dazedly fumbling around. She wanted to shout, *or at least zip up your jeans before I open the door,* but she didn't. He looked very uncomfortable and she supposed he was. Ben's voice had had the effect of a cold shower on her, and she didn't imagine it was any more pleasant for Joe. He ran a pocket comb through his hair to no effect whatsoever and, shrugging wryly at the sight they presented, opened the door.

"I don't think we've met," said a cold, formal voice that sent Liv's stomach plummeting to even greater depths. "But I've come to deliver an urgent phone message for you, Mr. Harrington."

It was Tom.

Chapter Five

What could he have said?

The question had been plaguing Joe for hours. The whole scene had been compressed into a kaleidoscope of nightmarish impressions—Tom, overbearing and judgmental; Ben, dazed and disoriented; himself, aching and fumbling, stammering responses; and Liv. Yes, Liv! He would see her white, strained expression forever. Guilt. Anger. More guilt. All there on her face. Liv, who had held and caressed him moments before, wouldn't even look at him. Except, he recalled angrily, when Tom had said the message that was so urgent came from Linda Lucas. *Then* she had looked at him! The hurt and loathing in her expression had twisted his stomach.

He shifted uncomfortably in the narrow seat of the L.A. bound plane, but he couldn't escape the image of her face. He had wanted to shout, no! Nothing Linda Lucas had to say mattered to him at all! But he knew it wouldn't do any good. She had only had to hear Linda Lucas's name, to believe, however erroneously, that Linda had some claim on him, and the evening was over. They would never be able to recapture the moments they had shared before she'd heard Ben's voice on the porch. And not even the great Joe Harrington could convince a self-righteous ex-husband to leave so that he could continue making love to his former wife.

No, he had lost the opportunity forever. And, he reflected grimly, he had probably lost Liv too.

There had been no point in arguing that the message wasn't important. She would never believe it. Why should she? There was his wonderful reputation, for one thing. And he hadn't denied that Linda meant anything to him when Liv had mentioned the pictures she had seen. Maybe if he had. . . . Damn! His fist slammed down on the armrest, and the old man sitting next to him sat up with a jerk.

"Sorry," Joe muttered, and the old man subsided into gentle snores.

Sorry. Was he ever! He had tried to say it to Liv on the way to the airport, but the word wasn't adequate. Words that covered things like inadvertently waking strangers on airplanes couldn't begin to cover what he felt about the disaster they had just been through.

Anyway, he acknowledged, she wasn't having any of it. She had, once the immediate shock of Tom and Ben had been absorbed, become brisk and matter-of-fact, practically pushing Joe out the door. She was again the Olivia who emerged whenever she had to cope with something distasteful and nearly beyond her depth. The Olivia he had first met at the Sheraton.

"I'll take you to the airport," she had said, thrusting his jacket at him and blowing out the bank of candles as effectively as the north wind. "You drive Ben home," she told Tom, "and I'll be right there."

"Can't," Tom said with a falsely apologetic smile. "I'm expected elsewhere. You'll have to take Ben with you."

It was very neat, Joe thought. You couldn't find a better chaperon than a ten-year-old boy, especially one who never blinked. So Liv had driven Joe to the airport, ignoring him all the way with her tight lips and angry eyes, only bothering to answer Ben's mundane questions and to laugh once when he told her something Jennifer had said at dinner. She never once looked at Joe or spoke to him directly again until she drove up into the glare of lights outside the air terminal.

"Thank you for the dinner," she said in her best well-brought-up tone, staring straight ahead. The engine was idling and he knew she wasn't going to park and come in with him.

"Can't we see him take off?" Ben implored, hanging out the window to peer at the jet just landing.

"We don't know when the next flight will be," Liv said, and Joe knew she couldn't wait to be rid of him.

"I might not even get a seat on it," Joe said with an attempt at lightness he didn't feel.

"You will," Liv said bitterly. "I imagine they'd bounce the pope to give Joe Harrington a seat."

"Damn!" he muttered. Why did it have to end like this? She was the one woman he'd ever really liked as a person. He flung open the door and dragged his suitcase out after him. "I'm sorry," he grated. "I know you don't believe it, and heaven knows why you should, but I am. Linda Lucas doesn't—"

"If you say, 'Linda Lucas doesn't mean a thing to me' I'll scream," Liv said tightly and revved the engine. Joe bent down, staring at her hard for a long minute, willing her to turn her head. She didn't.

"Thank you for the ride," he said finally with icy politeness and, slamming the door, he walked into the brightly lit terminal and didn't look back.

In his mind he couldn't stop looking back. Playing it over. Rehashing it. *Too bad you couldn't have a second take in life instead of having to muddle through with the mess you made of the first one.* He leaned his head against the coolness of the window, feeling the throb of engines through the painful pounding in his temple.

"Something to drink, Mr. Harrington?" the flight attendant asked, smiling at him as though it wasn't just a drink she was offering. Another night he might have smiled back, chatted with her and waited for her after the plane got in. It had happened before.

"No, thanks." His voice was colorless. He put his hand over his eyes. The only smile he wanted tonight was Liv's—one of her wide, happy grins, or the smile she had given him when he was chopping the potatoes, or the tiny, wistful smiles he sometimes caught on her face when she thought he wasn't looking. If he couldn't have that, he didn't want anything. He only wanted to be left alone. Completely alone.

"LEAVE ME ALONE!" Liv could hear the high edge of hysteria in her own voice. Sly remarks and innuendo from Tom were generally unwelcome, but never more so than this morning. She hadn't slept at all last night. She had chivied the kids outside after a quick breakfast so she could nurse her headache—and heartache—without interruption. And she didn't need a phone call from Tom now—or ever.

"You should have more sense," he went on, undeterred. "All he wanted was to get you in the sack."

"What does it matter to you?" she nearly screamed at him. Of course he was right—she was nothing more than an interlude, a small tidbit to tide him over until he could go back to Linda Lucas—but she didn't need Tom to tell her that!

"I'm concerned about your welfare, that's why it matters," Tom said with pompous self-assurance that made her want to strangle him.

"Garbage," she raged, the sunlight blurring in her tears. "If you were so concerned about my welfare, why did you go off with Trudy? Or any of those other women?"

"I, well, I...."

"So don't preach at me, Tom James. Goodbye!" There would have been more satisfaction in slamming the receiver in his ear if she hadn't been crying so hard. Damn him anyway! And damn Joe Harrington! *And damn me for letting them matter!* She rubbed a fist across her eyes and blew her nose on a paper towel.

"How about an aspirin, Mom?" Noel appeared in the doorway, a concerned expression on his face.

Liv managed a wan smile. "No, thanks, dear. I'll be all right."

"You don't look all right." Noel ambled into the room and perched on the edge of the kitchen table. "Did Dad make you cry? Or was it Joe?"

"Both of them. Or maybe it's just me. I don't know." She couldn't have said even that much to anyone else, but Noel had seen enough to understand.

"I'll tell Dad to lay off."

"You don't have to do that, Noel. I already did."

"Well, Joe, then."

"I don't think he'll be back." She forced herself to say the words.

"But Theo said he rented a place nearby."

"I think that was a spur-of-the-moment thing. I doubt if he'll be around again." She was virtually certain he wouldn't be. Why would he willingly come back and face her? As far as she could see, she would be nothing more than a source of annoyance and embarrassment to him—not to mention what he would be to her.

Noel looked unhappy. "That's too bad," he intoned. "I thought he seemed like a pretty nice guy. But if he hurt you—"

"He didn't hurt me." *Not the way you mean, anyway,* Liv thought. Her hurting was from wanting too badly what she had no business wanting. Was it possible to tell yourself, I told you so?

"You're sure?" Noel still looked as though he'd willingly punch someone in the nose.

"I'm sure. But thanks. I'll survive." She reached over and ruffled his hair, feeling uncommonly good that he cared. She could make it, she thought, with just the boys and Jennifer. She didn't need Tom. She didn't need Joe. Without him life would be quite nice enough.

"NICE," LIV REFLECTED for perhaps the thousandth time several days later, being the operative word. Not "exciting" or "sparkling" or "vibrant," in fact, none of the things she had experienced when Joe Harrington had so briefly been a part of her existence. But safe, she thought, and relatively comfortable.

The trauma of the night at his house had receded in her mind to where she could get through several hours, if not a whole day, without dwelling on it. At first all she could do was remember how agonizing it had been finally to let her wall of reserve down slightly, to trust a man at all, and then to have another "other woman" thrown in her face. Then she felt a fool, as blind and stupid as could be. And finally she became angry, furiously angry at herself and Joe. But at last she had become numb to the pain of it all, and was even able to face Tom again without stammering and looking away when she talked to him.

Oddly enough, she began to realize with a certain amount of amusement, that Joe Harrington had, if nothing else, rekindled Tom's interest in her as a woman. It was as though she had suddenly acquired the *Good Housekeeping* Seal of Approval or, perhaps, she thought wryly, more likely the *Playboy* Guarantee of Quality. At any rate she was not a little surprised the first night that he called and suggested that they get together for a drink.

"Why?" it was the last thing on earth she wanted to do that night.

"Well...." It was Tom's turn to sound uncomfortable. "I thought we could discuss how to divide up the kids for the summer. Who takes whom when, you know?"

"Fine," Liv said, her mind more on the story she was trying to write than on dealing with Tom. "Drop by tonight after supper. The kids will all be here then and we can discuss it."

"But I thought just the two of us could—"

"It's the kids' summer, Tom," Liv said flatly. "I won't make these decisions without them. And I don't want to have a drink with you." She was not going to have Tom complicating her life right now, not for the kids' sake or any other reason. He was part of her past, not her present, and she had no intention of getting involved with him again.

Everyone at the office commented about how involved she was becoming with her work. And that was fine with her—just the way she wanted it, in fact. When she was busy, she wasn't thinking about Joe Harrington.

I am getting over him, she congratulated herself as the days went by and she coped very well. It was an aberration, nothing more—like a reaction to a vaccination. It was just that she had been so long without a man who made her feel like a woman that she had overreacted, read too much into his attentions and had acted like a fool. Well, it wouldn't happen again. She was sure of that. Anyway, he was gone for good, no question about it. So she was shocked on Thursday when George Slade popped into the office to pick up Frances for lunch.

"I'm glad your friend, Mr. Gates, was satisfied with the Traynor house."

Liv's eyes widened as if she had been jolted by electricity. She had told George that her friend Tim Gates wanted the house, since Joe didn't want it in his name. "It's not a retreat if everybody knows you're there," he had said. But she had imagined that Tim had called George and said he had changed his mind. "Was he?" she asked, trying to sound only vaguely interested. "Satisfied, I mean?"

"Sent me six months rent the other day," George said happily, a Cheshire cat smile on his round, ruddy face. "Have to give you a cut if you keep on bringing me clients."

"N-never mind that," Liv stammered, her stomach churning. He couldn't really be considering coming back, could he? If he did, what would it mean? What does it matter, she asked herself crossly. *You're not going to get involved!* She stabbed the pencil lead so fiercely into the paper in front of her that the point snapped off and skidded across her desk to the floor.

BEING ALONE WASN'T the answer, Joe discovered very quickly. Brooding was what he did best, and, as usual, it didn't solve a thing. He went directly to his house in the hills above Malibu. It was odd, he thought, how much more at home he felt in the architect's house in Madison, where he had spent one day, than he did in his own home. A decorator's idea of how a successful Hollywood actor's house ought to be furnished, it did nothing for Joe. It was a place to hang his clothes, to take a swim, to entertain women, and to catch some sleep in between movies. It had never been a home like his parents' or like Liv's. But he hadn't cared. In fact until he walked in the door now, he hadn't even noticed. The earth tones of the conversation pit ought to have been pleasing, but they simply looked empty, stark, rather like a desert. He sighed and rubbed a hand around the back of his neck. He wasn't usually given to thinking of this house in poetic images. What on earth was happening to him? Shaking his head he wandered through the rooms, trying to get a feel for his home. But the only feelings he had were lonely and unfulfilling. *It's because you're frustrated, idiot,* he told himself sharply. And it was, of course, the truth, but not all the truth. He just couldn't stop comparing the house to where he had been with Liv. And that brought back thoughts of the ending of the evening. Groaning he kicked off his clothes and threw himself down in the middle of his king-size water bed, praying for the oblivion that sheer exhaustion promised. Unfortunately, he didn't sleep.

Instead he spent the rest of the night—what little there was of it—lying there awake thinking of all the things he should have said, should have done, bumping into his own thoughts over and over again. In the morning he drove to

Linda Lucas's apartment, figuring that by now he was probably weak enough from lack of sleep that he wouldn't have the strength to kill her, even though he wanted to.

"What did you think you were doing, calling me in Madison?" he demanded, shouldering past her wide-eyed rumpled self when she finally opened the door to his furious pounding.

"I, well, I...oh, Joey, I missed you so!" she gurgled and flung herself onto him, her bare legs tangling with his so that he stumbled over onto the sofa.

"Linda, stop it!" He took her hand out from inside his shirt and wriggled away from her, trying in vain to sit up and put some space between them.

"But, Joey, Luther Nelson said he thought you should come to his party last night. He has a great new script for a Steve Scott movie, and he said I might get a role and—"

"For that you called me in Madison? For a lousy, stinking— How in hell did you get the number anyway?"

"Tim?" she offered a smaller voice now, sensing perhaps that his anger was real and not easily quenched. Still, though, she kept up a steady stroking of his thigh until he clamped his hand over hers and forcibly removed it.

"Tim?" he was aghast. Tim had strict orders not to give out such numbers to anyone except in emergencies. "What did you say to him?"

"I told him it was an emergency," Linda said uneasily, one hand tangling in her long golden hair nervously. She giggled. "Me getting a part *is* a bit of an emergency, wouldn't you say?"

Another time Joe might have thought it was funny. Now he was just furious. "It might be," he said with ominous coldness. "You might never work in Hollywood again."

"Joe!" She stared at him, shocked, the wheedling, kitten-softness gone, replaced by spitting indignation. "You wouldn't!"

"I could," he said, extricating himself from her grasp and going to stand across the room from her, staring out at the palm tree before his eyes. For once she didn't follow him and hang on him like Spanish moss.

"I'm sorry," she pouted, the indignation vanishing as quickly as it had come. She looked at him with pleading blue eyes.

"So am I," he said roughly. Sorrier than he could have imagined. Just seeing Linda again had made what had happened with Liv all the more distressing. Linda couldn't hold a candle to her. Liv was substance, depth, understanding. Linda was cotton candy, a dandelion puff, as insubstantial as smoke. Suddenly he couldn't be bothered anymore. He had said what he had come to say; now he only wanted to be gone. "Good-bye, Linda," he said, meaning it, and strode to the door.

"But, Joe. . . ." She ran after him, one hand barely keeping the front of her pink negligee together.

"Don't push it, Linda," he warned, amazed that he could contemplate her curvaceous body practically nude and not feel a thing. "And tell Luther I am not interested in a new Steve Scott."

"Are you . . . are you going back to, um, Manchester?" Linda asked, gripping his wrist.

"I don't know," Joe said, letting the Manchester bit pass uncorrected.

"But what are you going to do?" Linda demanded.

"I don't know," he said again, prying her hand off his arm. "What would Steve Scott do?" he mocked, and dropping her hand, he shut the door firmly between them.

Who cared what Steve Scott would do, he thought. Except the millions of people who thought he was, somehow, a real person—a person who always had the answer, who always knew how to solve the problem, how to win the war, how to get the girl. He sighed and rested his head on the steering wheel of his maroon Jaguar. Steve Scott had it easy. Steve Scott had scriptwriters. What did Joe Harrington have?

Ellie, he thought. *I have Ellie.*

"LOOK WHAT'S ON the porch," Mike McPherson yelled to his wife an hour later. "What did you do?" he queried as Joe brushed through the door past him, suitcase in hand. "Run away from home?"

"Home?" Not that elegant monstrosity tucked away in the Malibu hills, certainly. "What's that?" he asked, heading directly into the den at the rear of the house and opening the double doors of the Spanish-style armoire that served as a liquor cabinet and pouring himself a straight Scotch. He gulped it down, feeling it burn all the way to his toes.

"You look ghastly," Ellie said easily, studying him from the table where she stood folding clothes. She eyed him with such intensity that he instinctively ducked his head, staring at the bottom of the glass in his hand. "Leave the unshaven look to Harrison Ford. It doesn't suit you."

"Thanks very much," Joe muttered. He should have known better than to come here—Ellie never pulled her punches. Other people might be polite and say that he looked tired or exhausted. Ellie always came right to the point.

"Too many speeches or too many women?" she asked.

Joe winced. One woman too many, that was for sure. How relatively uncomplicated his life had been before Olivia James had got under his skin. He poured himself another Scotch, and Ellie swooped across the room and confiscated the bottle, capping it and thrusting it back into the liquor cabinet, banging the door.

"It's only one in the afternoon," she chastised him, and he wished again that he had never come. It was a bad idea all around. Steve Scott had doubtless been an only child. No nosy, bossy older sisters for him. "What's this I hear about your doing another Steve Scott flick for Luther Nelson?" she asked as she took an undershirt from the laundry pile and deftly folded it.

"What?" It was a yelp of indignation.

"I saw him on Wednesday," Mike said, "when we were doing budget projections for his next picture. Your name came up, of course." He grinned. "Big box office draw and all that. Luther said he had been talking to your Linda and—"

"She's not *my* Linda!"

"Tell her that," Mike suggested, grinning from his post by the door. As a CPA he had only to deal with Luther's money flow, not the women.

"I did. Just before I came here." Joe wished he still smoked. A cigarette sounded heavenly just now.

Ellie stopped folding clothes and regarded him curiously. "Someone new, is there?"

Joe lurched out of the chair where he had been sitting and crossed the room to stand with his back to the fireplace. "There's always someone new, isn't there?" he asked more lightly than he felt.

"Apparently," Ellie replied grimly. "I wish you'd stop riding off into the sunset and get the girl for once."

So do I, Joe thought suddenly, and choked on the last of his Scotch. Was that really what he did want? His eyes swept over the homey comfort of Mike and Ellie's home—scattered newspapers, stacks of laundry amid thick rust-colored carpet and heavy Spanish oak furniture. More comfortable than elegant, more cozy than luxurious, warmth without suffocation. It had none of the starchiness of the home he had grown up in, none of the front-parlor mentality he had been running away from for years. His mind could easily see Liv moving through these rooms. He tried to picture her in his lonely but elegant palace on the hill. It didn't work. That was a Linda Lucas sort of place, not a home but a showplace. Chrome and glass, stark and polished. Lots of flashy surfaces, not much depth. He shook his head, his mind reeling.

"How about it, huh, Joe?" Ellie prodded him.

"Huh? What?" He tried to focus again on what she was saying.

"Panicked you, didn't I?" she teased, misunderstanding. "All I've got to do is mention settling down and you blank me out."

"Not really. I—" he began, but she cut him off, shaking her finger at him imperiously and saying, "I think you're a case of arrested development, Joseph Harrington. You're wonderful when it comes to commitments to films, to causes you believe in, to getting inside a character and acting him out. But when it comes to your relationships with people...." She flung her hands up in the air in disgust.

"What's wrong with my relationships with people?" Joe demanded, cut to the quick. He turned and glared at her.

Ellie pursed her lip. "Deep down where they count, they're shallow," she said.

That stung. Damn her anyway. She had no right to condemn his choice of life-style. Would she rather have seen him shackled to Patsy Everett for the rest of his life? He strode across the room and picked up his suitcase with a jerk; then Mike laid a hand on his arm.

"Lay off, Ellie," Mike said easily. "He looks as though he could use a few hours of sleep, not a tongue-lashing."

Ellie dropped her hands, sighing. "You're right." She gave Joe a sheepish smile. "I'm sorry, love. I just get carried away sometimes."

"It's your evangelical fervor coming out," Joe said, forgiving her. It had always been this way between them. She had saved his sanity when they were younger and he was growing up under the thumb of his all-too-knowing father and never living up to the old man's expectations. Ellie stuck up for him then, but no sooner had she done so than she would turn around and upbraid him herself. Only from her he could take it. Usually. "Mike's right," he said now. "I am bushed. Can I sack out here?"

"Of course. Tony's on some white-water canoe expedition. Take his room," she said, waving him away, all disagreements forgotten.

This time sleep came more easily. As he settled into the down comforter, Joe's visions of Liv were less the grim-faced, censorious ones, and more the laughing, gentle ones. And when he woke up, he knew that he couldn't just walk away and forget her. She had touched something in him that no one else had. What it was he didn't know yet. But if no one else had ever reached it before, maybe no one ever would again, and that, he knew, he was not prepared to risk. He would risk her wrath and go back to Madison instead.

"You're right, you know," he said to Ellie when he came downstairs after his five-hour nap in his nephew's bed and perched on the edge of the kitchen counter. He had shaved and showered and looked every bit as attractive as his playboy reputation warranted. He wondered if Liv would think so. Or did he even want her to think along those lines? She didn't seem to find his sex symbol identity a plus any more than he did. Still, he'd never get back into her good graces looking like something the cat dragged in.

"Right about what?" Ellie asked. She was chopping onions and looked up at him with tear-streaked cheeks.

"My relationships. Riding off into the sunset and all that. So I just thought you'd like to know, I'm renting a house in Madison."

"Madison? As in Wisconsin?" Ellie looked stunned; tears streamed into her gaping mouth and she wiped at them ineffectually, as if getting rid of them would improve not only her vision but her hearing. "Did you say you rented a house in Madison, Wisconsin?"

"Yes." Telling someone made it official, he decided. He would be more likely to go through with it then.

A grin split through the tears. "Joe, that's the first step on the road to respectability!"

Joe grimaced. She would say something like that. He hopped off the counter and fetched a beer from the refrigerator, glowering at her as he snapped off the top.

"It's not a bad word, Joe," she teased. "Really. Some of my best friends are respectable."

"Yeah," he said sourly, "and your relatives, too. With their split-level ranch in Sioux City, their nicely behaved 2.5 children and their cocker spaniel puppy and—"

"Joe," Ellie said quietly. "Some of them aren't a bit like Dad."

He took a long draught of beer. "Yeah, I know," he muttered grudgingly. "It's just if you were to distill people and come up with something called 'essence of respectability,' Arthur Harrington is what you'd get. I get the shudders just thinking about it."

"Don't think about it, then. Your career, your life—they're your choice. Just be sure that they're what you want, not just what he *doesn't* want. Besides," she went on with a grin, "your career wasn't the only career he didn't approve of. You should have stuck around long enough to hear some of the things he said about playwrights."

"Yeah, but you redeemed yourself by marrying a CPA," Joe said glumly.

"You could, too," Ellie offered. "There's one in Mike's office. Carla, I think her name is."

"Very funny." It amazed him how often marriage seemed to crop up these days. Cripes, he'd gone years during which it was scarcely mentioned—except by his parents over long distance—and now he thought about it all the time. It was a word that seemed to come with Liv. And it petrified him. Marriage meant commitment, and commitment meant responsibility, and together they meant sameness and ruts and all the things that he'd been avoiding for years. He'd never even got as far as living with someone. Even that was more than he wanted till now. And now? Now he didn't know what he wanted. He only knew he had to find out.

"What's in Madison?" Ellie asked. "Or should I say, 'Who?'"

"No, you shouldn't," Joe snapped, completely unprepared to talk about Liv to anyone. Acknowledging that his past relationships left a lot to be desired in no way meant that he was willing to subject the disastrous beginning—or ending—of this one to Ellie's probing mind. "It's just a nice university town," he said. "Some culture, some variety, some pace, but also some peace and quiet. And right now I want that."

Ellie gave him a quizzical look but refrained from commenting.

"I've been thinking that I want to write a screenplay," he told her. "I'm fed up with Steve Scott and the adventure boys and all that rot. That's why I'm saying no to Luther. I'm sick of the notoriety and all the hoopla that goes with this sex symbol crap. I'm a person too—not just some stud. And as long as I keep on acting and doing a little directing, nobody's going to believe it. But if I write something. . . ." He felt himself warming to the idea even as he expressed it. It seemed right somehow. He could almost see bits of the story in his head, like film clips, as he talked. He had to do it, had to try, anyway. He needed more in his life than being just a jumped-up actor who rescued fair maidens and shot the bad guys while flexing his muscles and looking tough.

"So you're going to Madison to write a screenplay?" Ellie's expression went from quizzical to incredulous. "I don't believe this."

"Believe it," said Joe. He grinned at her, feeling the enthusiasm growing inside him, flowering. He had visions inside his head—visions of himself bent over a typewriter, clattering away, pouring out his thoughts onto paper while happy children's voices floated through the open windows and Liv hummed to herself in the other room. He dipped his head, avoiding Ellie's penetrating gaze.

"There is more to this than meets the eye," Ellie said, her tongue tracing a circle on the inside of her cheek.

"Umm," Joe mumbled. A part of him wanted to tell her about Liv, to ask her advice. But he couldn't—not yet. Not until he knew better himself what he felt. Chances were he would get Liv out of his system as quickly as he had got all the others out. And he would wish that he'd never mentioned her to Ellie then. But maybe she was different. He'd been thinking about her constantly, ever since he'd left her that first time in Madison. He saw hundreds of lovely women every day, day in and day out, but all he had yearned for was to see Liv, to talk to her, to touch her. The phone conversations, far for appeasing his hunger, had whetted it more. He'd had obsessions before—infatuations—but nothing like this. It was weird. He found himself wondering what she'd been like as a child, if she had had Stephen's gamin grin or Theo's freckles. He grinned as he remembered her combative feistiness, her willingness to toe the line against the zoning commissioner or—heaven help him—himself. He remembered those moments at his house before Tom had shown up—her passion, the fires burning just beneath the surface, the promise of things to come. And he ached. He ached with such wanting as he had never known. And he ached with shame because he had not known how to handle what had happened next. Joe Harrington, the Mr. Cool of the Romance League, had acted like a gauche kid caught making out with the minister's daughter. Ten thousand times since then he had told himself that he should have stayed, should have told Liv's ex-husband where to put his hypocrisy, should have told her until she believed him that Linda Lucas meant nothing, absolutely nothing, in his life. God knew it was true! But somehow he had been speechless—caught flatfooted by Tom's righteous indignation, Liv's total embarrassment and his own confused emotions. All he could think was that if he left it would be better for everyone. But he had been wrong. He felt Ellie's hand on his shoulder.

"Hang in there," she said, giving him a quick hug. "It'll be fine."

Joe wished he was as sure as she was. A pity she couldn't write him a happy ending as she could for one of her books. And what would it be, he asked himself mockingly, draining the last of his beer. He didn't know. He only knew the next step—he had to get back to Madison as soon as possible.

"Can I use your phone?" he asked Ellie. "I want to tell Tim to take a six-month lease on the Traynor place starting Monday."

LIV WAS REACHING FOR the last white undershirt to pin it to the clothesline when she saw Stephen and Theo hurtling down the hill on their bikes. The stiff breeze carried their first words away from her and she called, "Be careful when you cross that street!" But the boys were oblivious, grinning like fools, and at last she heard "Joe's back!" and the wind slapped the undershirt across her face.

Chapter Six

It wasn't exactly a surprise. Liv had been anticipating the moment since George Slade told her that Tim Gates had sent him the money for six months' rent two days earlier. It was almost a relief to know—like discovering what disease you had, so you could at last go about finding a cure for it.

"Really?" She finished pinning the shirt and carried the wicker laundry basket over to the patio. "How nice." Her tone was carefully neutral, even if her emotions weren't. She didn't want the kids thinking that he had hurt her badly—a conclusion that Noel had already jumped to earlier, and not without grounds, she had to admit. But she didn't want to sound eager to see him either. For one thing she wasn't—really. For another, even if she were eager, she would be a fool to encourage Joe Harrington. Relationships like ones he was used to were exactly what she didn't need.

But she needn't have worried. They had no intention of dragging him home. "Me an' Stephen are going to the hardware store," Theo announced breathlessly as he skidded in the gravel and dropped his dirt bike with a thud. "For Joe," he added importantly.

"The hardware store? What for?" Liv asked. Heavy-duty springs for his bed?

"For nails," Stephen explained, a broad grin on his face.

"Nails?" That sounded permanent.

"We're buildin' a tree house." Theo said. "Joe an' Ben are gettin' the wood."

"You shouldn't bother Joe," Liv began, but Stephen interrupted.

"He's not bothered. He suggested it."

"I bet he wouldn't have if you hadn't been standing there," Liv said firmly. The boys had trekked the mile and a half to Joe's unoccupied house almost daily since he had left. Liv hadn't said much about it, thinking that his absence would be the best discouragement. Now she was beginning to wish she'd forbidden them to go.

Theo shrugged. "Who cares?"

I do, Liv thought. It meant they would be at his house at all hours, and chances were that he'd come home with them. She would have to see him, talk to him—resist him. That was the crux of the matter.

Once she had got over feeling angry and humiliated and indignant with herself and Joe and Tom, she had had to face how she really felt about what had happened that night. And nothing betrayed her feelings more clearly, she discovered with dismay, than hearing that Joe had, in fact, rented the Traynor house for six months. Completely unbidden a tiny stab of elation pricked her. He's coming back, she thought. And then what, she had immediately demanded, cross with her own perverse happiness at the thought.

There was no way she was going to let such a man get close enough to hurt her again. She wanted a steady man, a reliable man—if, indeed, she wanted a man at all. What she definitely did not want was a man like Joe Harrington who had the reputation of being a hundred times the Don Juan that Tom James was. No, if Joe was coming back she would have to squelch that renegade bit of happiness, snuff it out before it could flicker to life again.

"Wanta help us build it?" Stephen asked her, swinging back onto his bike.

Liv shook her head. "No, thanks." She wasn't going to go near Joe's place. She didn't want the boys to go, either.

But she couldn't think of a convincing reason to stop them, so she managed a weak smile and waved them off, praying that Joe Harrington would have as little desire to see her as she had to see him.

God and Joe, however, seemed to have other ideas. When five o'clock rolled around and she was just about to put Jennifer in the car and drive over to Joe's place to fetch the boys home—a move that she desperately did not want to make—she heard talking and laughing on the patio; the kitchen door burst open, and Theo, Stephen and Ben all trooped in, carrying a large bucket of fried chicken and coleslaw, a six-pack of soda pop, another of beer, followed by Joe Harrington armed with a sheepish grin and a fistful of daisies. He held them out to Liv with a quizzical, hopeful look on his face.

Her heart was crashing around in her chest like waves crashing on a beach in a storm, and she wiped her hands on the dish towel, gripping it to stop them trembling. "Hello," she said coolly, and she knew from the look on his face that he'd sensed the drop in room temperature, even if the boys hadn't.

"We brought you dinner," he said, thrusting the daisies into her hand and nodding at the flurry of activity going on around them as the boys slapped plates on the table and clanked down the silverware.

"You needn't have," she said. The daisies were burning her hand, and she turned to grab a glass out of the cupboard, stuffing the flowers into it and running water to the brim. Anything not to have to look directly at him.

"I know," he said, and the grin flashed again, a bit more hopeful this time. "But I didn't figure you'd invite me to stay, otherwise." He cocked an eyebrow and she thought, damn his boyish vulnerability anyway. But she shrugged, knowing that the battle was already lost. The troops were all on his side. She could hear Stephen chattering away about two-by-fours and Ben's calculations of how many steps they would have to make up the side of the tree, and she knew there was no use in fighting him now.

"I suppose you're right," she said ungraciously and turned to get her tossed salad out of the refrigerator. Fortunately she wasn't required to make scintillating conversation. The kids were saying enough for everyone. Their enthusiasm was enormous, and in spite of her own misgivings she was pleased that they were getting to make this tree house.

It wasn't something that Tom had ever bothered about. Tom would come and watch their ball games occasionally, or take Noel out to play golf with him. But he'd never bothered to go swimming with the kids or to build things with them, and Liv thought now, listening to them, how odd it was that Joe Harrington should be acting more like their father than her ex-husband ever did.

"Use your napkin, not your sleeve, Theo," Joe said, and she thought, Lord, he even sounds like a father. He had certainly come a long way since the first time he had sat at this table and fussed about having to eat peas. She lifted her eyes from her plate just long enough to glance at him.

He was grinning at her and her eyes dropped immediately. The look he gave her was far too sensuous, far too provoking, far too reminiscent of Albert Finney playing Tom Jones, gnawing on a chicken leg while he seduced Mrs. Waters with his gaze. They should do a remake, she thought. Joe Harrington would be a natural Tom Jones.

"Can we go back and work on the tree house some more now?" Ben asked Joe when they had finished eating.

"Ask your mother," Joe said. "It's all right with me."

All eyes turned to Liv, whose first reaction was to say no, shove Joe out the door and bolt it from within. But that was a selfish reaction, albeit a safe one, and after hearing an hour's worth of enthusiasm about the tree house, she couldn't do it. Besides, just because the kids played at his house it didn't mean she she had to have anything to do with him. "All right," she said with what she hoped Joe would hear as indifference.

The whoops and hollers quickly changed to groans when Joe said, "Dishes first, though," and mobilized the kids as though he were a drill sergeant, not an actor.

"There," he said when the kitchen was spotless. "Come on." The kids raced on ahead out of the kitchen, and Liv stood behind one of the kitchen chairs regarding Joe warily, as if the chair's flimsy wooden frame would protect her from his formidable presence and charm.

"Not me," she said, shaking her head. "I'm not coming." Because she knew that was what he was waiting for.

Joe didn't say anything for a moment. His eyes traveled slowly from Liv to the daisies on the windowsill and back again. The warm evening light bathed his features in a kind of golden glow, and Liv felt an ache deep within her. He sighed and scratched his ear. "Liv," he said carefully, "we have to talk."

"No, we don't." There was nothing he could say that she wanted to hear. Whatever he said, she knew, would undermine her resolve against him.

"Something special was happening between us that Saturday night," he persisted.

Liv grimaced. "I bet you say that to all the girls," she retorted sarcastically, her knuckles white as she gripped the chair back. What did he know about "special?"

Joe shook his head, a red flush staining his cheeks. "You're *not* all the girls!" he grated angrily.

"You can say that again!" Liv snapped. "But I was handy, wasn't I? Not too bright and not too beautiful, but better than nothing, huh?"

"Stop it! It wasn't like that and you know it!"

"How do I know it?"

Joe's shoulders slumped, and a look of helplessness overtook his features. He shook his head defeatedly and stared unseeing past the blue gingham curtains into the yard beyond. "I don't know," he said in a low voice. "I don't know."

Liv's anger faded somewhat as she stared at his baffled face. She had expected an angry response, not confusion. "What do you mean, you don't know?" she demanded, thrown off balance.

"Well, I mean, how can I prove it?" He shrugged helplessly, like a man condemned. "I can't point to my sterling reputation and ask you to believe me, now, can I?"

Liv shook her head. "Never mind," she told him. "Forget I asked."

The screen door flew open and Ben poked his head in. "Hey, c'mon Joe, we're ready?"

"Yeah, just a sec. Listen," he beseeched her, "I'm not leaving Madison. I meant what I said, Liv. I don't want to lose what we had that night...."

"We didn't have anything," she protested. "Lust, that's all."

"No," he argued. "I think I know lust a damn sight better than you do. That wasn't lust."

Liv knew her face was crimson. Why couldn't he just drop it? "I want them home at eight," she told him, wringing the dish towel in her hands.

"You have to talk to me sometime, Liv."

"Eight," she reiterated, her spine so rigid that she thought it would crack. She turned away from him and began rearranging the spices in her cupboard. Anything, just so he would leave her alone.

"All right," he said finally, moving to the door, his eyes still boring into her. She ducked her head to avoid the penetrating gaze that made her feel as though he were trying to touch her soul. Alphabetical, she thought. First allspice, then basil. Cinnamon. Her hands moved mechanically.

"Thank you for the nice dinner," she mumbled as the door banged after him; but she didn't budge from the cupboard till she heard his car drive away. Then she went into the living room and sank into the sofa, wondering at the weak, spineless creature she had become. Where was her willpower that she could feel her knees buckle at the sight of his handsome face? But, a more perverse side of her argued, it wasn't just his handsome face doing it, though heaven knew it was attractive enough—it was the way he acted with the kids, firm but enthusiastic, the thoughtfulness of the fried chicken and the daisies, the teasing friendliness of their early phone conversations. There were so many things that made Joe Harrington difficult to resist.

But he must really think I'm dumb, she thought, *if he figures he can just come in here and feed me some line about "something between us" and have me drop into his arms like some roast duck.* He might be hard to resist but he wasn't impossible. It would be easier from here on out, she told herself. Now that she had seen him, she could steel herself against him, avoid him, ignore him. Sooner or later he would go away.

SOONER OR LATER she would crack, Joe told himself. She couldn't keep on being Miss Stainless Steel forever. But for two weeks she hadn't been doing too bad a job of it, he admitted, ripping another sheet out of his typewriter and crumpling it up.

The floor was littered with paper—his screenplay—but his mind was littered with thoughts of Liv—Liv saying, "No thank you," when he invited her to dinner; Liv saying, "I'm busy," when he suggested going for a swim; Liv saying, "I can't, but I'm sure the kids would love to," when he offered to drive them to Milwaukee to the zoo or a ball game. Nothing he came up with made the slightest dent in her refusal to have anything more to do with him. And nothing he could do succeeded in banishing her from his mind.

How he'd tried! After he figured out that she was going to do her iceberg imitation every time he came near, he thought that if she could do it, he could too. That was when he discovered how limited an actor he actually was. He couldn't stop himself watching her every move, couldn't pretend indifference to her curtness, couldn't feign coldness if she ignored him whenever he came around. It wasn't his nature. Instead he tried harder, agonized more, and ached to the very core of his being.

His salvation—if he had one—was the kids. Their cheerfulness made her coldness bearable. They arrived enthusiastically almost every morning, stayed all day, mucking about in the kitchen and yard as though it were their own home, hurrying to tell him their latest accomplishments or bemoan their setbacks. They invited him to all their games and swim meets, some of which Liv attended, too, when her work permitted, and to impromptu picnic suppers, swearing that "Mom said it was okay." Oddly enough they gave him a comfort and an anonymity that he hadn't had in years.

A man surrounded by five bouncing, babbling children—even though he might be a dead ringer for famous actor Joe Harrington—scarcely got a second glance. Everybody knew that the lady on Joe Harrington's arm would never be a five-year-old with straw-colored pigtails!

He could hear Jennifer giggling now, her shrill laughter ringing out above the boys' as they hammered and sawed, and he got up out of his chair in the den and went to the window to watch them. Usually Jennifer didn't come—she stayed most days with her regular baby-sitter, Margie, and, nominally, he supposed the younger boys did, too. But though Margie might be their official baby-sitter, Ben, Stephen and Theo spent nearly all their time with him. And before he had left for scout camp the day before, Noel, too, had become a fixture here.

Liv, as far as Joe could tell, tolerated the situation. She seemed to realize that if she forbade them to come it would be worse—rather like forbidding one's children to see undesirable friends, he thought ruefully, wondering how his straight-laced parents would feel about that. They had done it to him often enough. Probably, he decided, they would agree with Liv. In any case, Liv hadn't actually objected, though she did spend an inordinate amount of time when he was around her cautioning them not to bother him and to remember their manners, in such a way that he felt her disapproval even if they didn't.

"Hey, Ma! Hi, Ma. C'mere!" He heard Theo shout, and Joe craned his neck to see Liv coming around the side of the house, looking very proper in a navy knit shirtdress, her hair piled in a severe knot on her head, and her gray eyes hidden behind owlish sunglasses.

Liv? Here? That was a first. His stomach roiled and he rubbed suddenly-damp palms on the sides of his faded denim cutoffs. Taking a deep breath he went to the door and opened it. She was standing on the porch, seemingly undecided whether to knock or to cross the yard to where the kids were in the tree, waving at her.

"Well, look who's here," he said with a false heartiness that he knew didn't mask his nervousness at all. Why had she come? Had she finally decided to give him a chance? His mouth felt dry and he licked his lips hurriedly.

She seemed to be looking at him from behind the dark lenses, but then almost as quickly, her head turned back so that she was looking toward the children in the tree, and she said expressionlessly, "I've come for an interview."

"What?"

She shrugged. "You didn't expect it to be a secret that you were in town, did you? Frances saw you in the grocery store." She grimaced behind the glasses as though plagued by a distasteful memory. "Even got your autograph, I hear. So Marv wants a follow-up story on the one I did earlier."

Joe dragged a chaise longue over into the sun and motioned her into it, fetching himself a chair. "And you decided to do it?" he asked, unable to disguise the hopefulness in his voice. He was ready to take advantage of any opportunity at this point.

"I didn't have much choice," Liv told him flatly. "If I hadn't come, he'd have sent Frances. And I didn't know *what* you'd tell her."

He wished she'd take the glasses off so that he could see her face. How else was he supposed to know what she was thinking in that suspicious little mind of hers. "I don't kiss and tell, if that's what you're implying," he said coolly.

"No, you just kiss a lot."

Well, she hadn't softened her stance toward him, that was certain. He leaned forward in the chair, his forearms resting on his knees, hands loosely clasped. "I haven't kissed anyone since you, Liv."

"I want an interview, not a confession story," Liv said coldly, and sat up on the very edge of the chaise longue, perching precariously like a very stiff crane about to take flight.

Joe sighed. He wanted to reach out and stroke her, take her hair down and run his hands through it, soothe the stiffness out of her, ease the tension he saw in her shoulders. And all he could do was talk. One move would be disaster. One touch and she would flee. "All right," he said heavily. "Shoot."

Liv looked at him uneasily, as though she hadn't expected him to cooperate willingly, if at all. "Very well," she said finally, and reached into her purse for a notepad and a small cassette recorder. "Do you object?" she asked, indicating the recorder.

"No. I only object to one thing."

"What?" she asked warily, as if she would rather not know.

"The glasses. I don't like talking to people I can't see." He needed access to her face. If he couldn't touch her, at least he had to have that. He lifted one brow in silent entreaty. "Please?"

Slowly Liv's hand went to her temple and she lifted the glasses off, like a knight removing his armor, and just as reluctantly. Her eyes mirrored just the turbulent storm he had expected, and his mouth lifted slightly at one corner. She wasn't as indifferent to him as she pretended. Good.

He dipped his dark head, concentrating on the toes of his bare feet, leaving the next move up to her. That she was here was enough. He wasn't about to say anything to spook her now. Let her take the lead.

"I—I suppose that Marv wants to know why you're back in Madison," she began awkwardly. He could hear her shift uncomfortably in the chaise longue, but he didn't look up. The sun baked his back, drying up his nervous perspiration.

"I'm working on a screenplay," he said slowly. "In Hollywood everyone is on my back about Steve Scott. Scripts pop out of the woodwork, directors and producers call at all hours. There isn't a moment's peace." He spread his hands helplessly.

"Poor you," Liv mocked unsympathetically and wrote something on her pad. The cassette whirred on.

"Your understanding is overwhelming," Joe muttered. Damn her, couldn't she give an inch?

"I'm not being paid to understand you," Liv replied, "only to interview you."

Joe sighed and shifted uncomfortably in the creaky deck chair. "I used to think you understood me," he said quietly.

Something flickered in Liv's eyes. "What do you mean?"

"When we talked on the phone all those times, when we cooked dinner, when we—"

"Never mind about that," Liv said abruptly, cutting him off. "How long will you be here?"

"I'm not going to tell you."

"What?"

"Unless you listen to me about what I want to talk about, I won't give you the interview."

Liv glared at him, her fingers clenching, snapping her pencil. "Damn!" she muttered.

"Come on, Liv," he pleaded. "All I want to do is talk."

"That's not all you want to do!" Liv snapped, her jaw tense, the sensitive cords of her neck standing out.

"It's all I want to do now!" Joe retorted. "What do you think I'm going to do? Ravish you right here on the lawn in front of four of your children?"

"You nearly did in front of one of them!" Liv said angrily, her hand going up to brush her already severe hairstyle into even greater order.

"Well, you sure weren't fighting me off!"

"The more fool I! I should have had my head examined, going out with you, eating with you...." Her voice rose and then trailed off as if she couldn't bring herself to finish what she was going to say.

"Making love with me," Joe finished for her, and Liv exploded.

"No! You don't know what love is!"

"And you're the world's greatest expert, I suppose?" he said scornfully, and immediately wished he hadn't. She looked stricken, as though he had hit her in the most vulnerable spot there was.

"Hardly," she said bitterly in a voice that made him ache. A speedboat roared by towing a water-skier, and Joe watched the wake of the boat, unable to look at Liv and see the hurt he knew was in her face.

Finally he rubbed an anxious hand across the back of his neck, lifting the sweat-dampened locks of hair that clung there. "I'm sorry, Liv," he muttered. "I shouldn't have said that."

"No, no." Her voice was shaky; her hands twisted the broken pencil in her lap. "You're right. And I can't blame you for what happened that night. As much as I might like to. I was as willing as you were. But it was a mistake."

Joe shook his head violently. "No. It wasn't."

Liv jumped to her feet and crossed the porch, her back to him. He got up and followed her, stopping a few feet behind her, held back by an invisible shield that wouldn't let him get any closer. "Yes, it was. I don't want that sort of relationship. I want love, commitment, marriage, all those things I thought I had with Tom—" Her voice broke and her head bent. Then she shook it angrily and spun around to face him. "I won't be one of your women, Joe. I let my passions take over that one night. I won't do it again!"

The stormy, tornado-cloud-gray of her eyes held his green ones in silent battle, and he swallowed hard, his mouth dry. She reminded him of a doe, frightened and defenseless, facing a hunter with a loaded gun. If only she knew he was just as scared of her as she was of him, he thought. But then he realized that it wasn't just him that she was seeing. "Tom really hurt you, didn't he?" he ventured.

Liv frowned, a tiny line appearing between her brows, accentuating her vulnerability. He wanted to take her in his arms, comfort her, but he knew if he even heaved a sigh or took a step she might vanish. So he held completely still, not even breathing. Her gaze slid past him to concentrate on the grove of trees near the lakeshore. "Yes," she said woodenly. "I guess you could say that. I was devastated at the time."

"Wha..." Joe began, and then knew he couldn't ask. If she were willing to tell him, that would be fine. But he couldn't force her confidence in him.

But Liv, obviously guessing what he wanted to know, shrugged and gave him an ironic look. "What happened? Nothing extraordinary, I assure you. He was the classic roving husband. I was the classic unsuspecting wife, convinced that it could never happen to us. I actually thought he was working late, going to out-of-town seminars, studying latest techniques. He was—only the subject wasn't dentistry!"

"When, I mean, how...." Joe stumbled, embarrassed by her frankness and afraid of making her dredge up a past that was painful, but still unable to contain his questions.

Liv crossed the porch to lean against a planter filled with geraniums. "It took me a while to wake up, actually," she said. "It had been going on for a couple of years before I wised up. I guess maybe Tom thought I never would, so he stopped being quite so discreet. People we both knew saw him and mentioned it to me. They didn't know he was lying to me about where he was and who he was with. It wasn't intended maliciously, but it was enlightening just the same. Anyway, once I had accepted the fact that it was a possibility, a lot of other things fell into place. I confronted him finally when he came home from a 'weekend seminar' and I discovered, to my surprise, that it was all my fault." She snorted derisively, but her hands trembled and she clasped them behind her back.

"Your fault?" Joe echoed, his forehead furrowing.

"Oh yes, definitely. You see, I was always too busy with the raising of the kids to go places with him. This one was sick or that one had a game or we couldn't get a sitter. So, if he couldn't go with me he found someone to go with. First Janice, then Patty, and Di and several others. Now it's Trudy. Anyway, all of them were women who were, according to Tom, better able to help him fulfill himself than I was."

Liv couldn't hide the bitterness and hurt, didn't even try to, and Joe wondered if love was even worth it if this was what it got you. For a moment he thought that maybe life with a succession of Linda Lucases was a better idea after all. But he was finally beginning to learn that even that solution had its drawbacks. He wondered if Tom would figure them out. The man was a jerk to leave a woman like Liv for a succession of empty-headed, full-busted broads, and Joe didn't mind saying so.

"Well, thank you," Liv said wryly, "but it wasn't quite like that. They were none of them dewy-eyed, dumb blondes like Linda Lucas." Instantly she turned beet red and clapped her hand over her mouth. "I'm sorry," she mumbled, obviously mortified.

Joe's mouth twisted. "Don't be. Your honesty is one of your most appealing qualities." His tone was dry.

Liv made a face. "I suppose my other is that I look you right in the eye. Other women are appealing because of their smiles, their eyes—"

"Dewy," Joe supplied, grinning. "No, your other most appealing quality is your sense of humor."

"The kiss of death! No wonder Tom divorced me," she said with a smile that didn't quite eliminate her hurt. "He used to tell me how well I coped with adversity. 'You always come up with a smile,' he used to say. I sometimes wondered if he didn't want to see if he couldn't come up with something that I couldn't bounce back from." She sighed and plucked the leaf off a geranium. "He did a pretty good job."

"He ought to be shot," Joe said wanting to kill the man for hurting her, yet at the same time, a part of him was perversely glad Tom had, so that she was free, so that Tom had no more claims on her.

"Probably," Liv agreed. "There was a time I would have done it myself. I sat home night after night, wondering what all those years of struggling through grad school and opening his practice and coping with teething and bumps and bruises and croup were for. I guess I'm one of those people who believes in delayed gratification. I don't mind the sacrifices. I figured we'd have a lifetime together to even things out." She snorted inelegantly. "Well, I was wrong."

"Maybe I should have neglected the kids, I don't know," she went on. "Anyway, it's too late to worry about it now. That's over and done with. What I can do is make sure it never happens again." She was looking at him squarely now. "I don't fancy being one in a string of women. Not Tom's. Not yours. So, if you'll just excuse this digression and give me the interview, I won't bother you anymore."

Joe dragged a hand through his already mussed hair. Where did he begin, for heaven's sake? How could he tell her that she wasn't just another of the women in his life, a successor to Linda Lucas? Because as surely as he knew that he didn't want her to be that, he didn't know what he really did want, either. "What if I said, 'Let's just be friends?' " he asked.

"Friends?" Liv looked at him as though he'd lost his mind.

"Why not?" He plunged ahead. Improvise, the drama coach had yelled at him time and time again. "I mean, you and I hit it off pretty well, once you decided that I wasn't going to rape you that first night, didn't we?"

"Yes, but—"

"And when we talked on the phone, we were friends, weren't we?" he pressed her.

"Well, yes."

"And leaving off the ending of our Saturday, we got along tolerably well, wouldn't you say?" He was pacing back and forth on the porch, the sun beating on his neck and back, feeling like a klieg light boring down while he played Clarence Darrow in a courtroom drama.

"Leaving off the ending," Liv agreed.

"So, why can't we just be friends? Look—" he stopped pacing and turned to face her, fighting for his life, wishing he knew why it mattered so much "—I've had enough of strings of women like Linda Lucas, too. They're one of the perks of my job, really." He grimaced ironically. "Or one of the pains. In any case, I want something other than that. I'd like it if we could be friends." He was holding his breath, watching her, waiting.

"Friends?" Liv seemed bemused by the idea, examining the word in her mind, like a scientist probing a foreign object.

Joe waited. His chest hurt, his throat was tight. The hammering from the tree house had nothing on the wild beating of his heart. Somewhere on the lake a speedboat cut loose.

"All right. I suppose we can give it a try," Liv said cautiously and offered him her hand as though expecting an electric shock, not a truce.

He took it, feeling her hand warm and slightly damp in his. He wanted to rub his thumb against the sensitive skin of her wrist and stroke her palm. His breathing quickened.

Friends? He groaned inwardly. *God help me, what have I done now?* But he schooled his features into what he hoped looked like cheerful friendliness and made his handshake a firm one. "Good," he said, and hoped she didn't hear the tiny break in his voice that he heard.

"Now, about that interview," Liv said, removing her hand from his and going to sit on the edge of the chaise longue. She was more like the Liv he remembered from before the Saturday night disaster, and Joe sat down opposite from her and began to talk. He found himself opening up to her, telling her about his proposed screenplay, about his disgust with the continual pressures of being a Hollywood star, of sharing his life with Steve Scott, and he was amazed when she finally shifted on the lounge and said, "I really have to get back. It's past three. If I'm going to write this up...."

"Write it up?" he yelped, stung. It wasn't an interview! He had forgotten entirely about that. He was just talking to her, sharing, one friend to another. He opened up his mouth to protest, but Liv shook her head.

"Don't worry," she told him. "I've read enough interviews with Joe Harrington to know that nine-tenths of this was off the record. Trust me?" It was a question, and Joe removed his own glasses and rubbed the bridge of his nose. It was a fair request, he realized. If they were really friends, then he would trust her not to do him in, not to spread his plans, hopes, fears and insecurities all over her newspaper. She was trusting him, after all, not to make her into just another Linda Lucas in his life. But just as it hadn't been easy for her, letting her have free rein with this material wasn't easy for him. He was tempted to tell her to forget the whole thing, that the whole interview was off the record, that he'd send her a press release tomorrow instead.

And then where would they be?

Back to square one, he acknowledged. And she would believe that his offer of friendship was just as insincere as she might have feared it was.

"I trust you," he said, and wiped damp palms on his bare knees.

Liv smiled, a little tentatively, a little warily, but at least she smiled. "Tell the kids to be home by five, please. And tell them that I really will stop and see the tree house soon. But I do have to get back to work now." She turned and walked down the path around the side of the house, and Joe followed her, hands stuffed in his pockets. She didn't wait for him to catch up, but when she got to the car she stopped, and gave him another smile. "I'll send a copy of the article over with the boys in the morning," she promised. "If you don't like it, we won't print it."

Joe shook his head, refusing the out she gave him. "No, that's okay. I trust you. Really."

Her smile grew. "I guess we are friends," she said softly, and she got into the car and drove away. Joe stood, hands in his pockets, staring after her long after the car had disappeared over the hill.

His trust wasn't misplaced, either. The article, which appeared in the Sunday "People" section of the paper, was flattering without being gushy, discreet but not vague. Liv gave him credit for concern with peace and human rights, for a sincere effort to improve his craft of acting, for his desire to go beyond the acting and directing he had done so far to write his own screenplay. Of his heretofore widely touted amorous exploits, she reported nothing. The only reference to his marital status was a lead-in to one paragraph that said he was a thirty-six-year-old bachelor who divided his time between his career and many worthy causes. It didn't claim that one of them was bed-hopping. It said nothing about his rantings and ravings about the Steve Scott identity crisis he was having, or about his complaints that his fame kept him from leading a normal life. It did say that he liked Madison because it offered him some of the everyday experiences and anonymity denied him in California, and that he appreciated the willingness of many local fans to simply ignore him.

She quoted him as saying that it was hard to walk the line between being grateful to people for his success and wanting to be a private person whom no one recognized. "I am working on it," said the quote in the paper, "with a little help from my friends."

Joe grinned as he read it. One friend in particular, he thought, going to the telephone to call her and tell her what a good article it was. How nice to have a friend who could put words in his mouth—the right words—words that said that she knew almost more about him than he knew himself.

Chapter Seven

Friends? Liv wondered as the days passed and July faded into the even hotter days of August.

Friends with Joe Harrington? It wasn't as impossible as it sounded. She soon discovered that when he wasn't leering at her anymore, she could relax and enjoy his company. She put the lid on her own desire for more than friendship with him. It wasn't realistic. It wasn't even sensible. So she took what she could get and was grateful for it.

It was lovely to have an adult around again—someone who didn't think that batting averages were the height of sophisticated conversation, someone who didn't consider a meal containing eggplant an abomination, someone who read more of the newspaper than the sports section and the comics. And if Frances thought there was more to it than that, she was wrong.

"I think he's smitten," Frances said, knitting needles clicking away faster than the computer terminal on her desk.

Liv shook her head. "He likes my honesty and my sense of humor," she quoted, not even bothering to ask whom Frances was talking about. Frances never talked about anyone else.

"But he calls you all the time," Frances protested.

"Maybe he just wants me to make him laugh," Liv said. "For heaven's sake, of course he calls me up all the time, Frances. My kids are always over at his house, bugging him.

He wants to know things like can he give them an ice-cream cone half an hour before dinner, or how to get the grass stains out of Theo's beige jeans. It's not at all what you think!"

But no one told Frances what to think. She had her own ideas, and nothing Liv said would change that. But Liv tried. She had told Joe not to call her at work, but he didn't mind very well. "I forgot," he'd say, unabashed, or "It'll just take a minute," and he would then proceed to tell her something that made her laugh or ask her an inane question that she knew he must have worked hard to think up. But she didn't try too hard to stop him because she liked the calls. She liked Joe. He was a bright spot in an otherwise pleasant but not too exciting, hard-working life, and she needed that.

The phone rang. "It's for you," Frances said with her customary Joe Harrington giggle, and handed Liv the receiver.

"Now what?" Liv said automatically, her eyes skimming down the columns of print she was scanning.

"Stephen's sick" Joe said without preamble.

"Sick?"

"Not dying or anything. I was going to give him some aspirin and keep him here, but I thought I should check with you."

Liv glanced at her watch. It was barely two. She couldn't skip the meeting Marv had set up for three-thirty, but she had no right to stick Joe with a sick child either. And Margie wouldn't want him if he was ill; she had three of her own to think about. "I'll call Tom," she told Joe. "He can come and get him."

"I don't mind having him," Joe said hastily.

"No." Liv was decisive. "Tom's his father. He can take time off and come and get him."

"Whatever you want," Joe said finally, his voice flat and impersonal. "Goodbye." He hung up abruptly and Liv was left staring at the receiver.

"Stephen's sick," she told Frances.

"With what?"

"I don't know," Liv said helplessly. Darn Joe anyway. He had hung up without telling her anything. No symptoms, no temperature, nothing. "I've got to call Tom to go get him." She dialed Tom's office number, trying to think what she would say to him when he asked about Stephen's symptoms and how she would explain why he was at Joe Harrington's. "This is Olivia," she said to his receptionist. "I'd like to talk to Tom."

"I'm sorry, Mrs. James. He's in Phoenix."

"Phoenix?" What on earth?

"He'll be back Monday," the receptionist went on relentlessly.

Monday? Liv hung up. Phoenix! And he hadn't even bothered to call and let her know that he was going out of town. What about his promise to take the boys boating on Sunday? Damn him.

Hastily she called Joe back. "I'm sorry," she said as soon as he answered. "Tom's out of town. Will you keep him until I can get there?"

"Of course."

"I'll hurry from the meeting."

"Take your time. We'll be fine," he assured her.

But when she got to Joe's house shortly before five, she wasn't sure. Joe looked worried, harassed, harried. Parental, she thought, and she couldn't help smiling.

"How is he?" she asked, her own worries surfacing again.

"Hot. He's got a headache," Joe said, leading her through the living room and up the stairs to a bedroom where Stephen lay, flushed and still, under a summer-weight quilt. "I looked for a thermometer, but our architect didn't seem to have one," he said to her as she felt Stephen's forehead. "It's probably nothing serious. Kids get bugs all the time."

"I know." But it was never very nice when they did. And if it lasted, who would stay with him? Noel was at camp.

Tom was gone. Baby-sitters, even competent ones like Margie, didn't like diseases. Liv's thoughts were winging all over the place.

"Let him sleep a while," Joe urged. "Come on downstairs and sit down. You look beat." He took her arm and she let him lead her, unprotesting, down to the living room. He pushed her into an easy chair.

"Relax," he told her.

"I can't. I have to go home and get dinner on the table. Then Theo has a ball game tonight and—"

"I'll go buy a couple of pizzas."

"No. I have to take them home."

"Why?"

"Um, well, because...well, you shouldn't have to be bothered with us, with Stephen, with the rest of them. You don't want that kind of hassle." She wished he wouldn't look at her with that compassionate expression in his eyes. It was all too tempting to just lay all her burdens on him.

Joe's features softened further, his mouth quirking into a grin that quickened her heart. "Why don't you just let me decide what I want, huh, friend?"

"But...." Her shoulders sagged. How could she say no to a grin like that?

"Pepperoni?" Joe asked with a smile that said he knew he'd won.

"Whatever you want." Liv waved her arm wearily. "I don't know how to thank you."

The green in Joe's eyes seemed to flame for a moment, but he shook his head as though banishing his thoughts. "Don't worry about it. What are friends for? Come on, gang," he said to Ben, Theo and Jennifer. "Let's go buy some pizzas and give your mother a rest."

Then they were gone. Liv's eyes flickered shut. She wouldn't sleep, she told herself, but it wouldn't hurt to rest for a minute. If Stephen were really ill, it would be a long time before she would get much rest again. That was one of the realities of single parenthood that she had discovered early on. Hell, she thought tiredly, what was she going to do?

"LEAVE HIM HERE TOMORROW," Joe said flatly when he got back and plopped a plateful of pizza onto her lap.

"But—"

"He's usually here, anyway," Joe went on. "And then Ben and Theo can keep working on the house without him feeling left out. He can supervise from inside. Anyway, he might be fine tomorrow."

"Well. . . ." It was tempting. All her problems would be solved if Joe kept Stephen. Well, maybe not *all* her problems, but all the ones she was allowing herself to think about. She wouldn't even consider the ones that might arise as a result of agreeing to Joe's proposal.

"Please, Mom?" Ben and Theo pleaded on Stephen's behalf.

She gave up. "All right," she said, "but I won't feel right about it. I pay Margie Cunningham for baby-sitting Jennifer."

Joe ground his teeth. "So pay me. Whatever will ease your incredible conscience."

"At least I have one," she flared, and immediately regretted it. She hadn't baited him about his woman-filled past since they'd agreed to be friends, and now she was wondering if she had spoiled everything. "I'm sorry," she said, dropping her head.

"I forgive you," he said gruffly. "Anyway, as far as consciences go, you might be surprised. I'll expect you to drop them off at eight." He got out of his chair and carried his plate into the kitchen. "I'm going out to take a walk," he said, one hand already opening the screen door. "Don't lock up when you leave, please."

He really knew how to make an exit, Liv thought. She wondered if he had taken classes in it. But she had deserved it. He had been trying to help her out, to be nice, and all she could do was make sarcastic remarks. Damn her sharp tongue anyway.

"Come on, kids, finish up," she said. "Then you can clean up the dishes and I'll fetch Stephen and we can go home. I think Joe's had enough of us for one day."

IN THE MORNING, though, Joe was waiting on the steps when she brought the kids at eight and dropped them off. He hustled them inside with the efficiency of a day-care-center professional and gave her a perfunctory wave that implied, "Don't call me, I'll call you." So she waited until he did.

She wanted to call and ask how it was going, if Stephen was all right, but she didn't want to sound as if she didn't trust him. Oddly enough, she did. He had shown his concern for the kids continually over the past few weeks. Sometimes she thought that Tom could have taken lessons from him, Tom, who was in Phoenix doing who knew what—playing golf and other games no doubts—while Joe Harrington, of all people, cared for his sons. She ground her teeth and went back to roughing out an article on the upcoming concert series being held at the university, one ear listening for the phone.

It didn't ring all day—at least Joe didn't call—and she was nearly a nervous wreck when she got out of the car that night. He called her five times a day when nothing was wrong. Why didn't he have the decency to call once now?

"How is he?" she demanded as she burst in the door. Joe was sitting at the typewriter in the den, hands poised over the keyboard. Theo and Jennifer were watching the "Electric Company" on TV, and Ben was up in the tree house, hammering away.

"Not bad," Joe said, getting up. "He's in bed reading. He's still got the fever. Theo does, too. And now Stephen's got these blisters on his face."

"Blisters?" That didn't sound like flu. Liv flew up the stairs into Stephen's room, with Joe padding after her as though she were the doctor and he the concerned parent.

"Let me see your face, Stephen," she said to her son, who had his nose buried in a book.

Stephen looked up and blinked. Half a dozen or so clear blisters dotted his cheeks. She brushed back the hair on his forehead and found three more. "Pull up your shirt," she told him.

"Cripes, more," Joe said. "What kind of flu is that?"

Liv managed a sour smile. "Try chicken pox."

"Chicken pox?"

"I'm afraid so. And probably Theo has it, too. And Jennifer will be next," she moaned, thinking of the implications. "What am I going to do?"

"Just what we did today, obviously," Joe said. He was leaning casually against the door frame, barefoot, in cut-off jeans and a yellow short sleeve shirt with the tails flapping against his thighs. It was funny how Tom, wearing virtually the same outfit, could contrive to look unkempt, while Joe looked only sexy. It's all in the mind of the beholder, she told herself firmly. Just remember he's your friend. But how could she keep thinking that if she saw him virtually all the time when she wasn't at work for the next week or so?

"No. It's impossible," she said, needing to reject his suggestion.

"Why?"

"You can't know what you're letting yourself in for. I mean, this is a communicable disease. The city health department even gets into the act."

"To do what?" Joe looked fascinated.

"Oh, fill out forms, keep the kids out of school for thus and such many days—if you're in school, that is. That sort of thing. We did it when Noel and Ben had them."

"Sounds like fun," Joe said, maddeningly calm.

"You don't want sick kids for a week!"

"Got any better ideas?"

She opened her mouth, but nothing came out.

"You don't, see?" He reached out and gently closed her mouth. "So why don't you just drive home and get whatever you and the kids will need for a week or however long this takes, and come back. We'll eat in about an hour."

"You mean *move in here?*"

"Well, I could move to your place, but it'd be less crowded if you came here. And we'd get a bit less notoriety, I imagine."

"There won't be any if I don't move in," she protested, fumbling for excuses that seemed just out of reach.

"But you won't have a baby-sitter, either," he pointed out.

"I'll hire one."

"Who?"

"I'd rather have Joe, Mom," Stephen interrupted, looking up from his book to add his unfortunate opinion.

I wouldn't, Liv thought, feeling trapped. But she didn't see any other way out of it. Margie wouldn't take them. She couldn't find anyone else on short notice. She stalled, studying the wallpaper, the pine needles scratching on the window screen, the assorted blues in the hand-braided rug underfoot. "All right," she said reluctantly. "I don't know what else to do." Probably, she thought, Joe would get sick of his magnanimous gesture within two or three days, anyway. Surely he couldn't keep up this concerned-father role for more than a week. And then maybe she could just take a few days off work. Marv wouldn't mind a week, but stretch it into two and he would flip.

"I knew you'd see sense," Joe said, chucking her under the chin. "Now, off with you. The chef gets mad when he has to eat cold pork chops."

Liv went, her mind reeling. She had visions of running into Frances on her way home. "What are you up to?" Frances would ask. "Moving in with Joe Harrington," Liv would reply. It was good that Frances didn't have a heart condition.

By the time Liv returned, she had the whole week mapped out in her head. "The only way it will work," she told Joe with the brisk efficiency of a first-grade teacher, "is if we have ground rules."

Joe looked at her from over the top of his newspaper, a grin twitching at the corner of his mouth. "Oh, yes?" he inquired politely.

"Yes. Now the way I see it, we can put Theo and Stephen in the blue bedroom because they're both sick. Jennifer and I can use the bedroom at the back, and Ben can sleep on the couch. He's already had the chicken pox, anyway. We'll use the blue bathroom and leave the gold one off the master bedroom for you. I'll cook breakfast and dinner and I can make the kids sandwiches and leave them for lunch. I went to the store and got plenty of food—Ben's putting it away now. Then, as soon as I come back at night, I'll be sure they stay out of your way. We'll go into the den or the bedrooms and play games or something and—"

"You missed your calling."

Liv stopped midsentence and stared at him. "What?"

"I said, 'You missed your calling.' You'd have made a terrific traffic controller—or prison warden." Joe eased himself out of the chair and crossed the room to where she was standing by the window. Liv backed instinctively toward the kitchen until she ran into a bookcase and was trapped. "Calm down," he said softly.

"But...." She was trembling at his nearness.

"Calm down." His hypnotic green eyes measured her from head to toe. "You are as uptight as a stretched-out rubber band. One more ground rule and you're going to snap." His hand reached up and snaked behind her neck, closing on her nape and massaging gently. "That's better," he murmured as though he felt her muscles relaxing—as indeed they were relaxing, against her better judgment. He led her, unprotesting, to the sofa and pushed her down gently but firmly. She felt a momentary frisson of panic as she recalled the first time they were on this couch together.

"Cut that out," Joe said firmly. "I'm not going to attack you. I haven't attacked you yet, have I?"

"No," she allowed shakily. *But it doesn't mean you won't,* she thought, *or that I might not attack you.*

"Was that a note of disappointment I heard?" His voice was teasing, but she thought she detected a note of hope in it.

"No!"

"Rats." He sat down next to her, the couch sinking under his weight, and turned her shoulders away from him, continuing to massage them with his large, strong hands, working the tensions out of her. "Now," he said lazily, his voice a rough whisper almost caressing her ear, "listen to my version of the ground rules. Your sleeping arrangements are fine—I'm not expecting you to share my bed. You can cook breakfast if you want, because I'll probably never get up early enough to eat it anyway. Lunch, however, is my job, and so is dinner. Hush," he commanded as she started to protest. "I make terrific peanut-butter-and-jelly sandwiches."

"I heard," she murmured wondering how he could talk about peanut butter at a time like this. His breath was warm on her shoulder. She could feel it through the thin shirt she wore as it raised goose bumps on the back of her neck.

"Right. And I want to cook dinner. When I'm doing a movie I never have time. Now I do, and I have people to do it for. So the job is mine."

"If you insist." His hands were reducing her to putty. She should get up and move away, but it felt so good and she'd had a long, hard day.

"I insist. I also insist that you stop worrying that you and the kids are an unwelcome burden and stop trying to hide away in a closet somewhere. That's ridiculous. If you persist I will have to take measures to see that you behave." His thumbs were massaging the sensitive cord at the back of her neck, and she felt as though she would melt against him in another second.

"Whatever you say," she mumbled, trying and only just succeeding to remain upright.

Joe chuckled, his thumbs working their way down the column of her spine, teasing each ridge as they went. "I've never seen you so malleable and amenable."

"You're hypnotizing me," Liv complained. If he could reduce her to jelly with no more than a back rub, what could he do if his hands had her whole body as a playground? The thought hit her like a bolt of lightning and she jumped up.

"What's wrong?" Joe was staring at her, astonished, as she scurried across the room and took refuge behind an overstuffed chair.

"We need a rule about that, too," she said, her voice so breathless that she was humiliated. She cleared her throat.

"About what?"

"About...about your touching me," she mumbled, avoiding his eyes, feeling like a first-rate fool.

"What?" His face was all innocence, but for the twinkle in his eyes. "No back rubs?" He lifted an eyebrow in amusement.

"Something like that." She groped about for an explanation that wouldn't sound too inane. "When I was in high school, our drama teacher had a rule he used to call the one-foot rule."

Joe's mouth quirked. "Which was?" he prompted.

"Well, it was dark backstage, and people kept, um, bumping into one another and, um, well, you know...." She knew her face was the color of Theo's toy fire engine. "So he had this rule that said that everybody had to stay a foot apart."

Joe's grin was all over his face. "Are you making this up?"

"Of course not! I wouldn't be capable of making it up, it was too stupid."

"And yet you're suggesting the same thing now," he reminded her softly, still grinning.

"Well...." Liv shoved a nervous hand through her blond hair, wishing she had pinned it up again when she'd changed into more casual clothes. It made her feel more businesslike that way, more remote, more able to resist the likes of Joe Harrington. "I still think we need something," she maintained.

"A treaty? With boundaries?" Joe asked, cocking his head so one dark strand of hair fell across his forehead.

"Yes."

"To keep me in my place?" His eyes bored into hers.

"Yes," she said, and then, because she wanted to be honest with him, she added, "And to keep me in mine."

Joe's eyes widened momentarily. "You can touch me all you want," he said magnanimously. "I don't mind if we have an affair."

"No. But I do," Liv replied, her fingers clenching in the nubby tweed fabric of the chair. "I couldn't handle it."

Joe didn't say anything for a moment. He chewed on his thumbnail, considering, and then scratched his nose. Liv watched him warily, thinking how unutterably stupid she had been to come here in the first place. How could she ever think that she could live in a platonic relationship with Joe Harrington in the same house for more than a week? How could she have imagined that he would even go along with that?

"All right," he said slowly now, nodding his head.

"All right what?" she asked, wanting to get it straight, not willing to believe that he was agreeing.

"All right, I won't seduce you. I won't touch you. I won't *do* anything," he said roughly, jamming his hands in his pockets and dipping his head so that he looked for all the world, Liv thought, like a boy whose mother had just slapped his hands away from the cookie jar.

"Thank you," she said, wondering if she was losing her mind. She was certainly losing her sense of propriety—and, she thought ruefully, her sense of danger. Otherwise she'd be backing out the door this minute, saying, thanks but no thanks, no matter what he promised. "I'm sure we can work it out," she said, more to convince herself. "After all, we are adults."

"That," Joe told her scathingly, "is the whole problem." And he turned and walked out of the room without looking back. It was Liv who rescued the pork chops burning in the kitchen.

IT MIGHT BE A PROBLEM, Liv thought, but it definitely had its compensations. For one thing, it was glorious to have another adult in the house full time. Life was so much smoother when there was someone else besides herself to say "Time to brush your teeth" or "Pick up your tennis shoes before you go upstairs." She smiled thoughtfully as she curled into the corner of the couch and remembered hearing Joe herd the kids upstairs to bed. He had read Jennifer a story while Liv finished doing the dishes, and had poked his head into the boys' room while she was saying goodnight to tell her, "I'm going to take a shower now."

It was as though they were a family, she mused, and then corrected herself. They were living together, for convenience's sake, for a week. He was a famous Hollywood star, she was a divorcée with five kids. He was doing her an enormous favor and she was giving him nothing in return. Absolutely nothing, she thought, remembering his reluctant agreement to what he had referred to all evening as The Chicken Pox Treaty.

Well, at least he had been a good sport. Given the press coverage of his libido she would hardly have suspected it. She sighed and opened the book she had taken from a shelf of the late-architect's library. It was a novel written about two years ago that, like almost everything else written since she had become a full-time single parent, she had never read. But it was immediately absorbing, and she sat bathed in the pool of light from the table lamp, reading and listening to some lilting, haunting music by Debussy until she heard Joe's footsteps on the stairs, and she looked up to see him come into the room.

He was wearing clean jeans and a pale blue open-necked sport shirt, buttoned only halfway up his chest. Her heartbeat quickened, and she swung her feet off the couch planting them firmly on the floor. "How was your shower?" she asked, hoping for a noncontroversial topic.

"Cold."

He gave her an ironic grin that accelerated the thuds inside her chest even further, and she buried her nose in her book, intent on ignoring him. Joe must have had similar intentions, for he didn't comment further, just padded silently on bare feet over to the bookcases built into the wall next to the fireplace and poked through them, eventually extricating a book, which he took to the chair farthest from her and sat down.

Liv's eyes flickered once or twice to glance at him in the warm, golden lamplight, but he was motionless in his chair, scowling at the book in his lap. Gradually, then, she relaxed, burrowing deeper into the corner of the couch, tucking her feet back under her and laying her head against her arm as it rested along the back of the sofa. The haunting softness of Debussy's music wove a spell around her, and she closed her eyes, reaching over to shut off the reading lamp beside her. Gentle breezes blew through the open windows, and cicadas hummed in the trees by the lake. Her body drifted on the sounds, mellowed by the music, the steady hum of the insects, and cushioned by the plush softness of the corduroy couch beneath her.

The sound of bare feet hitting the polished wooden floor with a thwack jolted her. She opened her eyes to see Joe striding across the room to the stereo, pausing only to flick on the bright overhead light before he jerked the needle off and yanked the Debussy record off the spindle. Liv stared openmouthed as he bent down and riffled through the records in the cabinet below, pulling out another album and slapping it on the turntable. Moments later the sounds of John Philip Sousa reverberated throughout the room.

"What the...."

Joe spun around, hands on his hips, legs spread slightly, enough to tauten the material across his thighs. "Do you want this treaty to work or don't you?" he growled.

"Of course!" Liv was astonished, looking into the full brunt of his glare.

"Then don't sit around in half-lit rooms, playing soft music and wearing that skimpy top without a bra!"

"It's hot!" Liv retorted, bounding to her feet and flinging the book down on the couch. "And I've been wearing this skimpy top all evening and you haven't said a word till now!"

"What was I supposed to say in front of all those big-eared children, 'Put a bra on, sweetie; seeing you falling out of that shirt is driving me wild'?"

Liv made a strangled sound, wrapping her arms across her breasts. "The only thing you think about is sex!"

"I'm human," he said. "Put a normal human male in the same room with a woman he's attracted to, dim the lights and play seductive music and dress her in tight jeans and a flimsy shirt that—"

"At least it's buttoned," Liv shouted, her eyes raking his chest which was still visible beyond the open front of his shirt.

"Turned you on, did I?" he mocked, his hands going to his shirt front, doing up the buttons with a seductive slowness that was calculated to drive her mad. Only Joe Harrington, she thought, could make getting dressed seem sexy.

"No," she lied. "After all these years I'm quite familiar with the male body. I shouldn't think yours is substantially different from Tom's." Which was, she realized, almost as absurd as saying that a Maserati wasn't much different from a middle-of-the-line Ford.

"It's not the body, it's the performance," Joe replied and stuck his tongue in his cheek, a grin twitching the corners of his mouth. "But in the interests of preserving your blasted treaty, I'll forbear—for the moment—to demonstrate mine."

Thank heaven, Liv thought, trembling all the way to her toes. If he knew how strongly he affected her their treaty would be in shreds in seconds. She'd never been one for believing in a strong defense, but with Joe Harrington she could definitely see merits to that argument for the first time. "I would appreciate it," she said coolly, having paused long enough to get a good grip on her emotional response to him. "In any case, since your tolerance for seeing my body appears to be severely limited, I'll just remove it. Good night."

She was halfway up the stairs when she heard him snort, "Good?" and that one word echoed in her mind all the while she was brushing her teeth and getting into her thin cotton nightgown that she was desperately glad Joe wouldn't see.

Even after she had checked on the children and had got into bed, her cheeks still burned and her heart pounded as she remembered the look on his face as he stood glaring at her. The march music ended abruptly downstairs and she heard his footsteps pass her room on the way to his. Moments later the shower was running again. Cold, no doubt, she thought. She wished she were taking one herself—anything to soothe the heat that coursed through her body as she remembered his gaze. It was going to be a long week.

IN FACT IT WAS nowhere near as trying an experience as she had imagined it might be. Joe's march music the first night set the tone for the entire interlude. The days were upbeat, peppy, cheerful—at least as much so as a household full of children whose entire vocabulary ran to "I itch," and "Mommy, I'm burning," and "Mommy, can I have some Kool-Aid?" could be. She marveled that Joe stood it as well as he did; he saw them for far more of the day than she did.

But he was unfailingly easygoing and seemed to cope far better than the average father might have.

It's because they aren't his, she reminded herself. He knows he can tell them when to leave. If they bug him enough we're the ones who will be out on our ears, not he. But she suspected that she was selling him short. She had to, however. If she didn't it was far too easy to simply let her fantasies run away with her. What would it be like to come home to him every night, she found herself wondering more than once.

"Don't be stupid," she said aloud now as she shut off the light in her room, having determined that Jennifer, whom she was sharing the bed with, was fast asleep. "He's not going to turn himself into a house-husband just for your convenience," she told herself and pulled the door shut, padding down the hall to the room Stephen and Theo were sharing. The thought of Joe as a house-husband was almost laughable. A pity it was also so tempting.

"Can't we stay up?" Theo asked plaintively when she went to switch out their light. "There's an old movie of Joe's on tonight."

"You're too young for any of Joe's old movies," she said, smiling as she kissed his scabby nose. "Besides, the real thing is right downstairs."

"Yeah, but he isn't half as exciting," Stephen grumbled, shutting his book.

"Tell me about it," Liv said lightly. He was quite exciting enough, thank you, she thought as she kissed Stephen and put out the light. "Good night," she told them both. "Maybe you won't itch so much tomorrow."

"Don't talk about itching," Stephen growled. "It just makes it worse. It's terrible being reminded."

"I know what you mean," Liv replied. "I'm sorry." She gave him a short wave of her hand before pulling the door closed. A living reminder of her own personal "itch" was right downstairs. It wasn't just a physical itch, either. That she could have rationalized away. *That* was the sort of thing she could have joked about with Frances. What she was beginning to feel about Joe was far more than that. Of course she was aware of him as a man. Who wouldn't be, she almost snorted as she went down the stairs. His smoldering glances were even more effective in person than in widescreen technicolor. But then, so was everything else about him—his caring, his gentleness, his patience with the kids, his tolerance of her treaties and her one-foot rules. He might be a famous actor, a talented director, and a struggling screenwriter, but he was also just about the most marvelous man she had ever met. She stopped at the foot of the stairs to stand and simply look at him.

Joe was hunched over his typewriter, where he had been since helping her with the dinner dishes. She had hustled the kids out of his way, determined to give him some time for himself, and occasionally she had heard the tap-tap of the machine while she was bathing them and reading them stories, but now he sat unmoving, his head resting on the top of the machine, hands limp in his lap, looking like a sacrifice to twentieth-century technology. Liv felt an almost overpowering urge of longing for him, wanting to go up behind him and rub the tension out of his slumped shoulders and run her fingers through his thick disheveled hair. But that, she knew, would be extreme foolishness, especially when it was because of her wishes that they had a treaty at all. So she crossed quietly to the sofa and sank down, observing as she did so, "You look exhausted."

Her voice caused Joe to raise his head, but he didn't turn around, staring instead at the sheet of paper half-typed in front of him. "I am," he confessed, the weariness evident simply in his ragged tone of voice.

"The kids are too much for you," Liv said quickly, smote by another pang of guilt for all she was taking from him while giving nothing in return.

"No," he disagreed. "It's not the kids at all. It's this play." He waved a hand at the paper in the typewriter and the crumpled ones in the wastebasket beside the table.

"What's wrong with it?"

"Everything. The characters are flat." He sighed and stretched his arms over his head. "The scenes don't move. You name it, it's wrong."

"May I read it?" She didn't know how she dared ask it, except that somehow she had the notion that perhaps it would help him to share some of the frustration he obviously felt.

Joe looked at her skeptically.

"I do know something about writing," she went on hurriedly. "It is my job and all."

He seemed to consider this, then a half smile tugged at his mouth and he shrugged. "Sure, why not? But it isn't very good," he added self-consciously. He handed her the thin manuscript and watched as she settled back against the cushions and began to read. Then he got up and paced to the sliding doors overlooking the patio and came back again. Once she had the manuscript in her hands, she didn't notice him again, starting instead to read. When she finally looked up, having finished as much as he had given her, she found him leaning against the fireplace, arms folded across his chest, his hooded green eyes watching her carefully.

"I'm not much of a writer, I'm afraid," he said apologetically before she could speak. "I'm just beginning to find that out."

Liv shook her head emphatically. "On the contrary, I think you have the core of a really intriguing story here. A love story set against a revolution like the Spanish Civil War has a lot of potential."

"More than I have," Joe said with a humility that she found strangely touching. "But the period has always interested me and, well. . . ." He shrugged, embarrassed.

"I think you have a really good start," Liv said, tucking her knees under her and snuggling more comfortably into the corner of the couch. "But I think you have to give Elena more of a chance to prove herself. She's flatter than Pío as a character, less of a mover, more of a pawn. But even now and then she shows flashes of spirit that make me like her a lot." She tapped the manuscript with her fingernail. "You've got to let her go."

Joe frowned, but not angrily, merely as if she weren't making herself completely clear. "What do you mean?" he asked, coming across the room and sitting down beside her.

"Here." Liv pointed to the scene she had just finished reading. "She is furious with Pío, and rightly so, I would think. But just when she's ready to tell him off, she inexplicably calms down. Why?"

Joe grinned. "I guess I was empathizing with Pío."

"Well, I empathize with Elena," Liv retorted, then grinned self-consciously because she had, in fact, felt a real rapport with Joe's fledgling character. "How about just letting her follow through with her anger? What would happen?"

Joe rested his elbows on his knees, closing his eyes, considering her question. Then he nodded slowly. "Yeah. I see what you're saying. If she really spoke up, then...." He opened his eyes, a glimmer of excitement shining in them. "You're right, I think. Let me try it." He bounded off the couch and sat down at the typewriter and began banging away. "Will you read it again when I've got this?"

"Of course." Meanwhile she simply relaxed, enjoying the luxury of just studying him. He typed for almost an hour, and she was nearly dozing when he handed her several pages. She read them, immediately caught up again in the lives of his two protagonists.

"Well?" Joe demanded, hands on his hips, regarding her almost belligerently.

"I like it." She smiled.

So did he. Then reaching for the pages, he said, "Let me add some more while it's still fresh in my mind. Okay?" He gave her a boyish grin of sheer enthusiasm and Liv grinned back.

"Go to it."

He was still at it two hours later when the Seth Thomas clock on the mantelpiece chimed twelve and Liv uncurled from her catnap on the couch and stared at his fingers moving quickly over the typewriter keys. For a man who was weary hours ago, he seemed to have got a second wind. His hawklike concentration was evident in his profile; he scowled intently at the keys, pondering, then typed some more. Liv smiled and stretched. Joe typed. She yawned and got slowly to her feet, trying to loosen the crimps in her back and neck she had got by falling asleep on the couch. Her loose peasant blouse stuck to her, a remnant of the sultry summer night, and she shook it, trying to get a breath of cool air. Joe had left the screens open to the patio and she heard the buzz of cicadas over the hum of the air conditioner she had turned on in the boys' room earlier that night. She remembered nights like this when she was married to Tom, when she had fallen asleep while he sat up watching a late film. "Just like an old married couple," she remembered Joe saying the first night they had washed dishes together in this house. Yes, she thought, it was. She looked at his dark head bent over the typewriter and longed to go over and tousle his hair, to give him a kiss and promise to meet him upstairs. If they were married, she would.

If they were married! How many times had she thought that lately? It was a hazard of agreeing to share his house. But at times it seemed as if they were married—they were sharing a closeness, a partnership. And tonight they had even shared his work. For a change she had given something, even though it was only some simple ideas, and Joe had taken them. In that, at least, they were closer than she and Tom had ever been. What would Joe do, she wondered, if she did bend over and kiss his cheek before going up the stairs? She hovered, considering. But she didn't consider long. The evening had been beautiful. They had relaxed together, shared something together, something important. She didn't dare spoil it even if, deep inside, she knew she was tempted to ask for more. For years to come all she would have of Joe Harrington would be her memories and she wanted them to be good ones—ones she would look back on with joy and fondness, not ones that would cause her heartache and tears.

"Good night," she whispered beneath the clatter of the typewriter, and she blew him a kiss. Then she went upstairs to dream.

IT WAS ALMOST two in the morning when Joe ripped the sheet of paper that ended the scene out of the typewriter and sagged across the keys. What would happen if he let Elena have her say? Wow! Fireworks, that was what! People talked about characters coming alive. Well, Elena had tonight. And so had Pío. Only, as he wrote, Joe had trouble keeping them black-haired and brown-eyed Spaniards. Elena kept turning into a blonde, slender and dynamic, with fiery depths to her cool gray eyes. And Pío? Ah, yes, Pío. Pío wasn't sure what he wanted. Was it the revolution? Was it Elena? Could he make up his mind? Joe snorted. It hadn't been hard to identify with Pío at all. He was a man in turmoil. A man who longed to get close to a woman for the first time in his life and who hadn't the faintest idea how to do it. Everything he did worried him. Should he marry her? Shouldn't he? Should he go away and fight or not? Did she care or didn't she? Joe stood up wearily and flexed his shoulders, trying to shift the weight of his newly created world off his back. He had certainly written himself a pile of questions tonight. He wondered what Liv would think when she read it. He turned back to the couch, expecting to see her still sitting there, scowling when she was not.

"Liv?" He frowned and rubbed his eyes, knocking off his glasses. When he retrieved them he saw the clock. No wonder she had gone to bed! Inside him there was an urge to go and wake her, to share with her what he had written. It wasn't great, but it was better than anything else he had done so far. He was sure of that. Shutting out the lights and locking up, he weighed the manuscript in his hand. Then, on impulse, he carried it up with him. Maybe, just maybe, she was still awake.

There was no sound from her room, though, as he walked past it down the hall. He stopped and went back. The door was slightly ajar and he peeked in. He smiled. She was curled up, facing away from him, her slim body lightly covered with a sheet. Next to her he saw Jennifer in a relaxed sprawl. For a moment he closed his eyes and ached. Not, he was surprised to discover, the purely physical ache of desire unfulfilled, though there was of course that. Rather, he felt a yearning to share with her on all levels, mental and emotional as well as physical—a yearning to crawl into bed beside her and hold her, to wake her and share with her this marvelous thing he had just written, to share with her the only way he knew how, what she was coming to mean in his life.

Ah, Jennifer, you lucky kid, he thought and smiled wryly. How far he had fallen if he was in a position to envy a five-year-old girl with chicken pox!

Chapter Eight

The sound of cupboards banging woke him. Joe was amazed that he had been asleep at all. Visions of Liv and his yearning to be with her had kept him awake until he heard the first birds of morning begin their song. To have finally fallen asleep to dream of her, only to be jerked awake again seemed cruel until he realized that the banging was very likely to be done by Liv herself. What on earth was she up to? He scrambled out of bed and stumbled out into the hallway. The light in the kitchen was on, so he made his way cautiously downstairs.

Liv was hunting through the cabinets, and he paused in the doorway, croaking, "What's up?" His voice breaking as she turned to face him and he saw the outline of her lissome figure through the sheer pale blue gown she wore. Just what he didn't need on top of his dreams!

"Sorry," she apologized, her eyes raking him with the same intensity with which he looked at her. "I didn't mean to wake you. I was, if you can believe it—" she gave a small laugh "looking for a packet of Kool-Aid. It seems to be the one thing that would make Stephen happy." Her eyes were wandering away from Joe's face to his chest to his navel and below. Damn it, why hadn't he thought to grab his jeans? All she had to do was look at him and all his dreams promised to come true. He raked a hand through his hair, trying to control feelings that threatened to overcome him. Remember the treaty, he told himself.

"I know where some is," he managed, his voice jerky. "Hang on a sec'." He bolted out of the room and back upstairs, pulling on his jeans as quickly as he could. Stop it, he told himself firmly. *You might want it, but she doesn't.* He took deep, cleansing breaths trying to convince himself that it was true. But even as he thought it, he knew it wasn't.

She did want him—probably on all the levels that he wanted her—that was the whole trouble. Liv was no more indifferent to him than he was to her. He had thought so even before this week, but since she had come to stay, he felt more certain every day. The way she looked at him, the way she knew what he was thinking almost before he'd even thought it, all pointed to a sense of sharing, of oneness. It pointed, he thought grimly, to making love, didn't it? Then why were they fighting it? He snapped his jeans, and his hands stilled at his waistband as he considered the question.

"Because she isn't ready," he said softly, the words echoing in the quiet of his room. *And are you?* he asked himself. "Of course I am," he said into the stillness. But as he went back downstairs he wasn't sure.

He met Liv again in the kitchen where she was now dressed in a robe that looked respectable enough for his own mother. She gave him a shy grin, sheepish almost, that made his heart pound like an awkward teenager's. He shook his head wryly, wondering at the feelings this woman evoked in him, and bent to fish through the cupboard for Kool-Aid. "And the treaty lives another hour," he muttered, shoved his hand behind the soup cans and came up with the requisite packet.

"Thank you," Liv said primly. "You can go back to bed now. I'll make it."

"No. I can. You have to go to work in the morning."

"He's my son," she argued, tilting her chin and facing him. She looked weary and rumpled, even though he could see she had tried to comb her hair, and he wanted nothing more than to fold her into his arms and soothe away all her cares. He felt a warm protectiveness that caused him to reach out a hand and brush a stray tendril of hair back from her cheek, his fingers stroking the softness of her skin. For once she didn't jerk away. He closed his eyes against the temptation, his teeth clenching so that he felt a muscle in his jaw twitch. Liv didn't move; she stood rooted, her eyes dark and luminous, drinking him in, so that when he opened his eyes he was stunned by the look he saw on her face. Then, abruptly, she seemed to recollect where she was, like a sleepwalker come awake, and turned to pour a glass of grape Kool-Aid with only slightly trembling hands. Nothing like his own, which were shaking violently.

"I can manage now," she told him, speaking to the window over the sink, where the darkness reflected their closeness. She sipped the Kool-Aid in her hand.

Joe's hands went to her shoulders, and he stood directly behind her, his breath caressing the nape of her neck. His lips ached to touch it. "Liv, I, we...."

"Stephen's waiting," she mumbled, stiffening under his touch.

Joe sighed. "All right, we'll take it up together."

He put the pitcher in the refrigerator and turned off the light, following her up the stairs, not wanting to let her go, though he knew that if he had any sense he ought to. She was getting skittish again, ready to bolt, their closeness of the evening before evaporating, replaced by a tension as taut as an electric wire. Let her be, he told himself. But he couldn't. Following her around in the dark of night, seeing her with sleepy eyes and tousled silvery hair was such a refined, exquisite form of torture that he was insane to do it, and helpless not to.

"Thanks for coming, too," she said when they came out of Stephen's room. "I know he was glad you came." She looked as though the idea worried her, as though Stephen's pleasure were not her own, but she was too polite to say so.

"You're welcome," he muttered, wishing for a little pleasure from her, too. The silence lengthened between them, neither of them moving in the dimly lit hallway. Then Liv began to turn away and his control broke. His arms went around her like a drowning man reaching for a life belt, and his mouth came down on hers hungrily, seeking, tasting. She was so warm, so sweet, and he needed her so badly. In their mingling he tasted the grape Kool-Aid and felt his rough cheek move against the petal softness of her own.

"God, Liv, you don't know what you do to me!" he rasped, willing her to respond, to yield, to hold him as he held her. Finally, with aching slowness, her arms did creep upwards, did encircle him, did press him more closely into the softness of her worn chenille robe.

"I do know, Joe," she whispered, her hands stroking his back, sending shivers through him as they moved up and down his spine. Her voice trembled with an aching he didn't understand. "I do. But it won't work."

"Why?"

Liv's hands stopped and she stepped back to put a tiny distance between them. Joe inched forward to close it again, wanting—no, *needing*—her softness against him. But she put her arms between them, pressing them against his chest, holding him off.

"Look at me, Joe," she commanded. "I mean it. Really look at me." She stepped back even farther so that he could not help but stare down at her whole body, taking in the slender figure barely camouflaged in the nubby robe, the pale face with its generous mouth, regal nose, and wide, sad eyes, the shoulder-length hair almost silver in the moonlight.

"I'm looking," he said hoarsely.

"Then ask yourself if this is the woman you want to follow in the footsteps of Linda Lucas, Shallie Holmes, Trisha Kingdom and whoever else." She named several actresses with whom he had been linked in the news as she stared into his eyes, daring him to answer.

He felt as though she had hit him. Even to think of her in the same terms as those women appalled him. But when he shook his head mutely, unable even to articulate how ghastly the comparison was, she nodded slowly and said, "See?" and turned to walk away.

"Liv! No, you don't understand," he gasped. "You're not like them at all. But that's good, don't you see? That's good!" He grabbed her arm and turned her back to face him, but the look on her face was not encouraging.

A small, almost wistful smile touched her mouth. "Good?" Her words echoed his with a hint of mournfulness he didn't quite comprehend. "Yes, I guess it is," she said with something like regret in her voice. "But just where does that leave us, Joe? What about you and me?"

The very question he had left hanging between Pío and Elena just hours before. Joe swallowed. The question had ceased to be an academic one. And just as Pío was left dangling, so was he. Olivia James was nothing like Linda Lucas or any of the other lovelies he had hustled and seduced for so long. So what did he want of her? And what would he do if he ever got her? Love her and leave her? Have a fling and forget her? Marry her?

Marry her? He broke out in a cold sweat that owed nothing to the hot August night. "I don't know, Liv," he said softly, his voice low and confused. He ducked his head, not wanting to look at her, not wanting to see the censure he expected to find in her eyes. And after a moment he heard her footsteps receding down the hall. There was a faint click as she shut the door to her room behind her.

"I don't know," he muttered to the silent hallway. "God in heaven, I really don't know."

HE DID KNOW that he couldn't get a damn thing written on the screenplay the next day because whenever he tried to write dialogue for Elena, he saw the moonlit blond Liv in his mind and heard her voice asking, "What about us?" He began to wonder if he would even be able to finish the play until he had answered the same questions it asked in his own life. He hoped so, or he was likely to be in for a very long haul.

Shaking his head wearily he crumpled up another paper and tossed it at the wastebasket. He missed. Ben and Theo booed from where they sat on the floor playing Chinese checkers.

"Stuff it," Joe growled, but couldn't help grinning when Stephen picked up the paper and faked a dribble around the den before hooking it over his head into the metal wastebasket. "Show-off," Joe grumbled. "Go lie down. You're supposed to be sick."

"Naw, all I've got are scabs now," Stephen contradicted. "I just itch." He made apelike scratching motions and beamed at Joe out of his scabby face. "Hey, there's the doorbell. Shall I answer it?"

"No. You'd probably scare whoever it is to death," Joe said, getting up to answer it himself. A moment later he wished he had let Stephen do the honors.

"What in heaven's name are you doing here?" he demanded as Ellie swept past him into the living room and dropped her suitcase in the middle of the carpet.

"And I'm delighted to see you, too," Ellie replied with her hands on her hips, grinning like a fool as she surveyed her surroundings.

"Do come in," he said belatedly, knowing his sarcasm wouldn't touch her. He shut the door and glared at her, part of him annoyed, but part of him enjoying the expressions that flitted across her face as she surveyed his kingdom—the boys sprawled on the floor of the den, the towheaded girl with the remains of a peanut-butter-and-jelly sandwich on her face, playing with some blocks in the corner, his typewriter and the scattered sheets of paper on the desk and floor.

"I haven't come to the wrong house, have I?" Ellie asked, her eyes taking in the rooms once more before they settled on him in wide-eyed amazement. "You *are* my brother? You *do* live here?"

"Mmm hmm."

"Then, pray tell...." she waved an all-encompassing hand.

"It's a long story," he said, not wanting to discuss it.

"I'll be here a while."

"They've all got chicken pox," he said discouragingly.

"I've had it."

"What do you want?"

"A number of things. Offer me a cup of coffee and I'll tell you."

It was obvious she wasn't going to be got rid of easily, so Joe motioned her to a chair and escaped into the kitchen in search of coffee. When he returned, she was in the den playing Snap with Stephen, and Ben and Theo had abandoned their checkers game to watch. Even Jennifer, who had been in a fit of sullen itchiness for two days, seemed to have forgotten her own misery enough to leave her blocks and crouch on the floor beside Ellie, giggling at Ellie's groans and moans as Stephen won time after time.

"That's all," Ellie said when Joe handed her the mug of steaming coffee. "I quit. You're too good for me," she told Stephen who beamed from ear to ear.

"Did you let him win?" Ben asked suspiciously.

"Me?" Ellie feigned horror. "Never! I always play to win. Ask Joe."

"She plays to win," Joe told him with the voice of years of experience. "She never let me beat her once. She picked on me constantly. Still does."

"Absolutely," Ellie agreed complacently. She stirred milk into her coffee and settled on the corduroy-covered sofa, regarding Joe silently over the rim of her cup. Then she smiled and said, "And I'm going to start again now. Picking on you." She took a sip of the coffee and grimaced, waving a hand in front of her mouth to cool it. "My word, that's hot. Are you trying to burn me alive?"

"We'll see," Joe said equably, taking the chair across from her. "I won't decide till I know why you're here."

"Well, Luther sent me to—"

"Luther! I told him no Steve Scott!" Joe sat bolt upright in fury, slopping his own coffee onto his pants.

"Luther sent me to see what you were up to. He couldn't believe that you were just really writing a screenplay."

"I *am* just really writing a screenplay," Joe said firmly, mopping up the coffee and then reaching for Jennifer who stood by his chair, lifting her onto his lap. She cuddled against his chest, her fair hair nestled beneath his chin, smelling of Liv's shampoo. His hand came up to stroke her hair absently and he wished Liv were here.

"Ummmm," Ellie said, her gaze flickering over the kids to the typewriter and its accompanying sea of paper. "So I see," she said. "But that's not all, is it?" she probed, her eyes darting back to the children.

"They're friends," Joe said flatly.

"Obviously good ones."

"So why else are you here?" he demanded, wanting her back on a subject of his choosing.

Ellie shrugged. "Curiosity," she admitted. "Mike said to leave you alone, but when I didn't hear anything for ages and ages after you left, I began to wonder again what the real attraction to Madison was." She grinned. "I must admit, I'm more curious than ever, now that I'm here."

Joe scowled, but she went on blithely.

"The third reason is that I need a place to hole up for a while, so I can work on the plot of my next play. You know I can never do the plotting well at home with Mike and Julie around and all my interruptions and—"

"No," Joe said. He knew exactly where this conversation was headed now.

"But this place is simply perfect," Ellie decreed looking around proprietarily.

"No."

"But you're not even going to be here!"

"What?" That was news.

"That's the fourth reason I'm here. You've got an invitation to speak on world peace at the symposium at the UNO in Vienna a week from Saturday!"

"Huh?" Surely he hadn't heard her right. Vienna? As in Austria?

"I'm serious. Tim Gates called me when he knew I was coming here. He said you have received an invitation to speak to the general assembly of delegates from all the nations attending the conference."

Joe stared, unable to believe what he was hearing.

"That's a coup, little brother," Ellie said proudly, smiling at him. "You can't turn that down."

He couldn't, and he knew it. It was exactly the sort of high visibility speech he had been angling for, the sort of thing that would lend credence to all his talks around the country and that might even have some effect internationally. It meant that people were really taking him seriously. But what about Liv, he wondered. He couldn't leave her. Not now. There would be no getting his foot back in her door if he left her now. "I'll think about it," he told Ellie.

"What's to think?" Ellie was looking at him as though he'd gone right around the bend. "If ever there was a footloose lad, it's you, my boy. You can pick up and go at a moment's notice. At least that's what you've always told me, at any rate."

"Yeah, but...."

"But?" Ellie's eyebrows arched speculatively.

But there was no need even to articulate it because at that moment the door opened and Liv came in. She slung her tote bag onto the bench just inside the patio door. "I'm home," she announced.

"I see," Ellie said, her words overflowing with meaning.

"No, you don't see!" Joe snapped, leaping to his feet, depositing an openmouthed Jennifer on the floor. He moved quickly to Liv's side and slipped an arm protectively around her, feeling her stiffen as he did so. His arm tightened. "This is my sister, Ellie McPherson," he told her. "Ellie, this is Olivia James. You've met her kids."

"All of them?" Ellie asked, her gaze swiveling over the four assembled in front of her.

"No," Liv said easily, relaxing a bit against him. "There're really five. The oldest is at camp."

Ellie looked as if she'd been hit by a beer bottle. "Five?" She turned to Joe. "And where do you fit in? Is this the secret family you've been keeping from Dad all these years, just to spite him?"

He grinned, a part of him wishing, momentarily at least, that it was true. "No, actually I'm just the lowly baby-sitter. Chicken pox tends to limit the options of the working mother."

"Well, I'm glad you're making yourself useful," Ellie laughed, but she was looking at him with a strange light in her eyes, and Joe found himself avoiding her gaze. "Where do you work, then?" she asked Liv, who was looking suddenly very self-conscious and trying to move away from Joe.

"For the *Madison Times,*" she said. "That's how I met Joe, actually. I interviewed him."

"Joe doesn't give interviews."

Liv grinned suddenly, and Joe saw her glance up at him, a mischievous glint in her eyes that he hadn't seen recently. "I didn't think so, either," she agreed, digging her elbow into his ribs. "But for some reason he wanted to give me one."

"I wonder why," Ellie said dryly.

"So did I," Liv said demurely. "Especially after he met the kids."

"Hey," Joe jerked his head up, suddenly aware that, if he allowed it, these two were capable of ganging up on him. The way they were grinning at each other made him decidedly edgy. "I'm just a nice guy, that's all. A soft touch."

"I'm glad to hear it," Ellie said, picking up her suitcase from the floor. "In that case you won't mind showing me to my room."

Joe's eyes narrowed and he opened his mouth to protest again, then reconsidered. Maybe having Ellie there wouldn't be a bad idea. She could certainly help defuse a potentially combustible situation between Liv and himself. After last night he had doubts about his control lasting where she was concerned; at the same time he was more convinced than ever that, until they had a better idea of what they wanted from a relationship, her treaty was a good idea. "The couch is all yours, my dear," he drawled, gesturing at the one she had tossed her sweater on in the living room when she passed.

"What about me?" Ben demanded. It had been his bed.

"We can go back to our house," Liv offered.

"No," Joe cut in. No way was she going to leave now—not with all these questions she had stirred up in his mind. "You have two choices," he told Ben. "You can sleep with me or on the floor."

Ben looked disgusted.

Well, I don't want to sleep with you much, either, fella, Joe thought glumly, *but I don't reckon your Mom would have me at the moment.* One look at Liv told him she knew what he was thinking and that he was right. "Put your suitcase in the hall closet," he told Ellie. "Since you won't be staying long...."

"A month or so, I thought," Ellie replied, still looking from him to Liv and back, as if weighing the possibilities. He could almost see her mind ticking over, putting things together and coming up with—Joe grimaced—coming up with God knew what!

"A month," he groaned. "Hardly."

"But I have a whole play to plot."

"Rent a cottage."

"Too expensive."

"You could buy and sell me," he protested. "You're one of the richest playwrights in America."

Liv's jaw dropped. "You're *that* Eleanor McPherson?"

Joe's nose wrinkled in distaste. "You didn't know I had such a famous sister?"

"I never would have guessed," Liv admitted. She was looking stunned, and he hoped it wasn't yet another strike against him. Then she smiled and he felt relieved, although he wished she'd smile at him. "I love your plays," she told his sister.

"Thanks. Joe doesn't brag about me, that's for sure," Ellie said as she deposited her suitcase in the closet. "It doesn't go with his image. I keep trying to marry him off in them."

"Life doesn't always imitate art," Joe said gruffly, wishing she'd shut up.

"More's the pity. But—" and here Ellie gave him an arch look that spoke volumes "—I never give up hoping."

"More's the pity," Joe countered in turn and left the room.

LIV DIDN'T KNOW how Joe felt about his sister's arrival, but she was delighted that Ellie had come. Another day or, worse, another unchaperoned night in the same house with him—and four children sleeping were *not* chaperones—and she wouldn't be able to answer for what she would do. The temptation to let go of her scruples, her sanity, her judgment, was almost overwhelming. Why not have a fling, she asked herself almost hourly. Lots of people had them—Tom, for heaven's sake, had had dozens of them—and everyone she knew had lived to tell about it. Most people even appeared to emerge from such affairs relatively unscathed. Why not Olivia James?

He was driving her insane. He had only to look at her and she burned with wanting him. Never again would she smirk over all those starry-eyed girls who drooled over the men they saw in magazines. They, at least, had the excuse of youth and naiveté. She had no excuse at all. All she had was willpower and The Chicken Pox Treaty, and the first was fading fast and the second would end in four days.

So, thank goodness for Eleanor McPherson, Liv thought as she set the table for dinner the following night. There must indeed be a God, and Ellie had been sent as his instrument for her salvation from Joe Harrington! Or so she believed until she sat down to dinner.

"I've just come up with a marvelous plot for my next play after this," Ellie announced with an enthusiastic grin. She swallowed her mouthful of mashed potatoes and continued, "I've been watching you two cope with this three-ring circus for three days, and I've decided that—"

"No!" Joe cut in, his fork arrested halfway to his mouth. He glared at Ellie with fire in his green eyes. Liv was glad she wasn't on the receiving end of that look.

Ellie just giggled, fairly bouncing with enthusiasm, and Liv wondered how Joe could bear to squelch that until she heard the next words. "Movie star falls for lovely divorcée with five kids! I'll make it six in the play. Will he win her? Will he succeed in breaking down her reserve? How juicy!"

"Damn it!" Joe spat.

"You wouldn't!" Liv's fork clattered to her plate, and she stared at Ellie in crimson-faced horror.

Ellie was overcome with amusement. "Touchy, aren't we?" she teased.

"I'll sue you for invasion of privacy," Joe snapped, and looking at him, Liv thought he very well might.

"Well," Liv shrugged with good-natured indifference, "it's not even necessarily true, is it? I mean, unless you've really fallen for Liv...." she baited, letting her voice trail off into nothing.

Liv's eyes dropped to the piece of gristle left from the roast on her plate, not caring to look at Joe or the kids. She couldn't imagine what his face looked like. The kids, she knew, would have eyes like one-hundred-watt bulbs. The silence went on for eons.

"Pass the peas," Joe said to Stephen, and practically snatched them from him, shoveling a huge amount onto his plate.

"I thought you hated them," Jennifer piped up.

"Don't be impertinent," Joe warned through a mouthful. He stared across the table at his sister who was watching him in openmouthed wonder. "Have some peas," he commanded. "And if you behave yourself, after dinner I'll let you plot a love affair between Pío and Elena for *my* screenplay. Maybe it will help you stick to fiction."

Liv hoped so. Things between Joe and herself were strained enough without Ellie threatening to make them characters in one of her plays. It was sufficient that she saw herself in Elena without that. She didn't say anything, though, trusting from Joe's quick intervention that Ellie would back off. Too much protest might give his sister the idea that more existed between them than really, in fact, did. So she quietly helped Ben with the dishes, then sent him out to frolic with Joe while she read the paper in the den. But the paper was hard to concentrate on. Her mind drifted to Joe and to the shouts and splashes just beyond the yard. Giving up on the news, she got up and went outside, sitting down on the grass.

She was watching the sun go down, admiring the lake in all its golden, sun-streaked beauty and trying to forget the dinner-table conversation when Ellie came and sat down beside her.

"I always tease Joe about being the hero in my plays," Ellie said, settling herself on a beach towel. "Ordinarily he just ignores me. Obviously he has more at stake here. I didn't mean to embarrass you."

Liv wrapped her arms around her knees and wondered what she could say to that. "You didn't," would hardly be honest because she had rarely been more embarrassed in her life. But, somehow, admitting it to Ellie made her dreams seems possible, made it seem as though something might really be happening between herself and Joe, made it seem that all her crazy, unbelievable fantasies weren't so crazy and unbelievable after all. It was rather like being in junior high school and hearing that the boy you had a crush on also had a crush on you.

"Umm," she mumbled, unable to come up with a sensible response. Her eyes were fixed on Joe and Ben cavorting in the water. They followed Joe's lithe, muscular form wherever he went, wanting him, needing him.

"You're exactly what he needs," Ellie went on in her no-nonsense fashion.

Liv felt the color rise in her cheeks. "Hardly," she snorted. "I'm not quite his type—except as a momentary diversion." She had to keep telling herself that or she would be heartbroken when he was gone.

"No." Ellie tucked her knees under her chin and rested her elbows on them. "Joe's quite good at finding momentary diversions all over the place. That's what his life has been for the last eighteen years—one momentary diversion after another. You're something else."

"I certainly am," Liv agreed dryly. It was folly even to let herself think that what Ellie was so broadly hinting might actually be true. "I'm a middle-aged damsel in distress," she went on. "And I think he sees me as his goodwill project of the month. His cause. Like world peace."

Ellie clicked her tongue against her teeth, shaking her head in dismay. "And you looked like such a bright girl," she chided.

Liv laughed. "Not really. Just sensible. Joe's a good friend," she said sincerely. And sexual attraction or not, she reminded herself, that was very likely all he would ever be. She gave Ellie a small smile and the other woman cocked her head as though considering what Liv had said. Then she turned and watched her brother give Ben a piggyback ride through waist-deep water.

"You know," Ellie said finally, "I don't think I've ever heard a woman tell me yet that Joe was a good friend and mean it." Liv looked at her curiously, but Ellie was staring out over the water, talking softly, the breeze ruffling her brown hair. "I mean, she might have said, 'Oh, he's just a good friend,' to cover up an affair she was having with him or something, but never because she meant she really liked him, thought of him as a valuable person to have around, to be with, to share with." She sighed. "He's been used, one way or another, by nearly everyone in the industry. He has acquaintances by the score, and he's on everybody's party list. For a while, of course, that's fine. He even wanted it like that."

"What do you mean?" Liv couldn't contain her curiosity any longer. She couldn't imagine that sort of existence appealing to anyone, much less to a sensitive man like Joe.

"I mean that momentary diversions were all he wanted for years. You have to understand that my father is a bit of a steamroller."

"Like someone else I could mention," Liv said.

"Very much," Ellie agreed. "But what my father wanted out of life for Joe and what Joe wanted for himself were two very different things. They clashed from day one—over classes in school, activities, careers, places to live, universities, the girl Joe was supposed to marry."

"He was engaged?" Liv knew she was staring but she couldn't help it.

"No, but not because our father didn't try. He had the girl all picked out. Daughter of a lawyer he knew. In the days of arranged marriages my father would have known no equal. But he met his match in Joe." She shook her head in wry amusement, her eyes remembering. "'If I want a prison sentence, I'll commit a crime,' Joe told him when Dad announced that Joe ought to marry Patsy. There was no compromise, no middle ground. Neither gave an inch. And after he left home to be an actor—something else Dad didn't like—Joe never came back."

"Never?"

"Three times in eighteen years. And then he stayed at a motel. He took my parents out, showed them he was a material success—which was his way of telling Dad he'd made it on his own—and that was that." Ellie shrugged. "Joe is a stubborn man. Too stubborn for his own good." She smiled slightly, and Liv's heart quickened when she saw the resemblance to Joe in that smile. "Or he was," Ellie amended, "until he met you."

"Don't start that again," Liv protested, but Ellie just smiled like a fairy godmother about to grant wishes that Liv wouldn't even admit to because they were so hopeless and absurd.

"We'll see," Ellie said archly. "We'll see." She got to her feet and picked up the towel, folding it under her arm. "The muse beckons," she said. "I think I'll go type for a while, see if Joe's right about my sticking to fiction!"

Probably he was, Liv mused as she sat in the lengthening shadows and mulled over what Ellie had said. It was insane to get her hopes up, to believe it when Ellie told her that Joe's relationship with her seemed different than the ones he'd had with other women. But it had the effect at least of making her see him in a different light. Now, knowing about his father, she could impute another motive to his having a harem than pure undiluted hedonism. Now she could see it as a rebellious reaction to a father who had tried to control his life. She sat watching him as he dried off briskly, his body silhouetted against the flaming orange of the sky, and she was overwhelmed by the surge of affection that washed over her.

All week the tension between them had been tautening. Emotionally as well as physically the bonds linking them grew stronger. Now even their gazes, their accidental touches, their stilted conversations were like currents of electricity. Her awareness of him, especially since the night he had kissed her in the hall, had become a physical, almost tangible thing. Shivers in her knees, goose bumps on her arms, tiny hairs that stood at attention on the nape of her neck, all presaged Joe's entrance into a room. His gaze made her hot, his voice made her cold, and his complete domination of her mind had made her drive past the Elvehjem Art Museum four times before she remembered that that was where the recital was that she was supposed to be covering for the paper.

She saw him sling the towel around his neck and begin walking toward her, his arm around Ben's shoulder as they came. Like father and son, she thought, and knew in a moment of stark truthfulness that she wished it were so. She wished that Joe Harrington were the father of her children, that she could have *his* children, that he would be her husband and she would be his wife.

Oh how I love him, she thought as he loomed ever closer, and her knuckles whitened as her fingers clasped her knees.

"Your mother's a foolish woman," Joe was saying conversationally to Ben, his grin teasing her as he approached. "She never swims with us!"

"I'm afraid I'll drown," Liv managed, her voice shaky, stunned by the realization of her love for him.

"I'll save you," he promised. He pulled her to her feet and slipped his arm around her, drawing her to his side.

"Will you?" she asked in a little more than a whisper. A nighthawk circled and dived above their heads.

"Mmm hmmm." He was cool and damp, his hard hip pressed firmly against her own as they walked as one toward the lighted house beyond.

And Liv thought, *I hope so, because like it or not, I'm going down for the third time.*

Chapter Nine

Joe did all his research, made all his plans, advised all his troops, anticipated all Liv's arguments and allowed for all contingencies before he asked.

"Will you come with me to Vienna?" he said. They were sitting in her VW bus overlooking Lake Mendota because, having gone out for supper and been mobbed by autograph seekers, having gone to the movies and been mobbed, and having stayed away from home where, if there wasn't a mob there was the nearest thing to one, Joe had given up on trying to find the appropriate moment and had finally just driven to the end of a dead-end street, snapped off the ignition and popped the question.

Just as he was about to open his mouth with the first of his well-reasoned and thoroughly rehearsed arguments, he heard her say, "Yes."

"What?" He couldn't have heard her right.

"I said yes." She was looking at him steadily, without her sunglasses on for once, with just clear, gray eyes, and saying it again. "Yes."

"You will?" He couldn't believe it.

"Well, why did you ask if you didn't want me to say yes?" she demanded, exasperation showing.

"I do," he said quickly. *"I do want you to!"* Did he ever! It was the stuff of which fantasies were made!

"Well, then...."

"I... I'm just surprised, that's all." That hardly covered it. Amazed, stunned, baffled, thrilled, delighted, ecstatic, rapturous, astonished. This list could go on and on. He felt as though he must be grinning all over his face.

"I'll have to arrange with Marv for some vacation, though," she said to him, her eyes thoughtful. "And ask Tom to take the kids."

"I already did," Joe said. That was part of his preparation before he'd even dared to ask her.

"What?" Now it was Liv's turn to be incredulous. "You asked Tom to watch the kids while I went with you to Vienna?" She started to laugh.

"No, I asked Ellie. She agreed," Joe said quickly. "And I asked Marv to give you the time off. He will, but he wants one travel feature on Vienna and a follow-up on my speech at the UNO to tie in with the one you did earlier on my speech here."

Liv stopped laughing abruptly. "You talked to Marv?" She looked horrified. "My God, what will he think?"

Joe shifted uncomfortably in the seat of the VW, banging his knee on the steering wheel. "Nothing he wasn't thinking already," he said gruffly. The twinkle in the older man's eye, which fell just short of a leer, was fresh in her mind. "Your friend Frances what's-her-name assured him that I would take good care of you."

"Frances?" Liv was looking more horror-struck by the minute.

Joe shrugged, wishing he'd kept his mouth shut. Everything he said seemed to be undermining his position rather than strengthening it. "She thinks I'm just what you need," he offered hopefully as a last resort.

Liv rolled her eyes. "She would. Frances is a born romantic. She firmly believes that innocence can reform the worst of rakes."

"And you don't?" Joe saw a faint flicker of something he wanted to believe was hope in her eyes, but it was gone almost instantly and her face was closed again.

"Not anymore," Liv said, matter-of-factly. "In my experience innocence implies gullibility. I found that out with Tom. I intend to learn from my mistakes." She was looking at him with an intensity that unnerved him, and he felt as though he was missing something that ought to be as plain as day.

"Oh," he said, filled with a faint but growing uneasiness. He ought to be rejoicing, oughtn't he? He'd just pulled off the coup of the century—he'd talked Liv into going to Vienna with him, hadn't he? Had he?

It's just that you didn't really have to work hard at it, he comforted himself. *You put in all those hours thinking up reasons, and you didn't even need them.* Why not, he wondered as he stared blindly out over the wind-whipped orange-streaked lake. Why had she suddenly stopped fighting him off?

The answer was simple. Liv had even told him it, spelled it out—she learned from her mistakes. And the biggest thing she had learned from the failure of her marriage to Tom was that she needed to take an active part in any future relationships she wanted. It wasn't enough to expect that things would work out if you were just nice, pleasant, helpful, faithful and a good mother. That sort of thing was fine for cocker spaniels, Liv decided, but it wasn't much good for wives.

She felt oddly exhilarated as she sat in the wind-rocked VW watching Joe contemplate the water, knowing that he was trying to fathom her complete reversal. It was like being dealt a good hand in bridge, like getting the inside lane at the track meet—a tiny edge, a taste of power, and for the first time in their relationship, she felt as though she wasn't the one running away.

On the contrary, she was advancing. Once she realized that she loved him, there was no running away from involvement with him. She had to act. And acting, in this case, she knew meant going to Vienna with him. Her mouth quirked up at the thought of it. *Way to go, Liv,* she reflected. *If you're going to pursue a guy, what better place to do it than a fabulously romantic city like Vienna.*

"When do we leave?" she asked him.

"Thursday. Do you have a passport?"

"No."

"We'll get you one."

"I thought it took weeks," Liv protested.

But with Joe Harrington, passports, like everything else, appeared like magic. A drive to Chicago, a Joe Harrington smile, a shuffling of papers, and a few hours later Liv had a passport, a ticket and a new piece of lightweight luggage—a gift from Frances, who'd said, "You can't travel with Joe Harrington carrying that eighty-pound monstrosity that Aunt Martha took west with her on the Oregon Trail."

The suitcase wasn't the only lightweight thing about her, Liv thought as the next three days passed by in a blur of activity. There was her mind as well. She must have been insane to agree to this, she thought again and again, mostly when the pace slackened and she had a half a moment to reflect on what she was doing. But then she would catch a glimpse of Joe, or hear his voice, or just have a second's vivid memory of him—his grin, his after-shave, the taste of his skin—and her doubts would be overcome by love. She might be crazy—everyone but Frances, given knowledge of what she was about to do, thought so—but she had to try to make this relationship work. She loved him, for better or for worse, and if he wasn't the loving kind, wasn't the marrying kind, it would be because he chose not to be, not because she gave up without ever trying to let him know how she had grown to feel about him.

But the doubts lingered, even though the kids were properly envious of their globe-trotting mother, and Frances spent half of Liv's last workday gushing lots of advice and innuendo. It all washed over Liv in a wave of babble and enthusiasm. She only saw clearly Ellie's thoughtful frown when she was telling them goodbye, Tom's incredulous expression when she'd told him that, yes, she definitely did know what she was doing going off to Vienna with "God's-gift-to-women-Joe-Harrington," and lastly, Joe's rather nervous, "You haven't changed your mind, have you?" on their way in to Chicago that morning, which made her wonder if he wished that she had.

But the qualms all disappeared as quickly as O'Hare Airport did when the plane took off that afternoon. It was impossible to dwell on the negative, not to be excited. To a woman who had never been farther from home than Detroit in one direction and Fargo, North Dakota in the other, she could as well have been going to the moon as to Vienna. She glanced quickly at the man sitting next to her, the man who was responsible for her being here and wondered again if he regretted asking her.

But Joe didn't look like a man with regrets. He was smiling at her indulgently, rather like a father enjoying his child's first view of a Christmas tree, and she felt the color rise in her cheeks as she smiled back at him.

"Glad you came?" he asked, his voice soft in her ear and seeming the tiniest bit uncertain.

"Oh, yes." But the real reason, she knew, wasn't their destination—Detroit or Fargo would have done as nicely—it was the person she was going with. Wanting to share that with him she reached out and laid her hand on his knee, then leaned across the armrest to brush her lips across his. "Yes, I am."

Joe blinked as if this new, more aggressive Liv would take some time getting used to. His eyes followed the length of her arm down to where it rested on his knee. "Liv," he growled sternly, sounding more like her father than the man she had come to love.

"Sorry." She lifted her hand and settled it demurely in her own lap, trying to rein in feelings which had been growing stronger every day. "I'm just amazed that I'm here, that's all," she tried to explain. "I seem to be acting out of character lately."

Joe's brows lifted above the dark frames of his glasses. "Yes," he agreed seriously, "you do." He looked as if he still couldn't believe that she was coming with him. But then, the plane hadn't quite left the ground yet, so maybe he thought she might still back out. Liv could have told him she wasn't about to do that. From here on out there was no turning back.

"I wonder what the movie is," he said, shifting uncomfortably in his seat, as if her warm smile was making him nervous.

Liv took out the in-flight magazine and searched through it, trying to appear thoughtful while she was still bursting with enough psychic energy to propel the plane all by herself. Unfortunately, when she found out what the movie was, all her thoughtful discretion dissolved in laughter. "Guess what!" she chortled.

"What?" He regarded her warily.

"Steve Scott."

"*What?*" Joe snatched the magazine away from her and stared down at the page she indicated. There it was in black and white: Joe Harrington as Steve Scott in *Hills of Thunder.* "Hell," he moaned and sank back into his seat.

Liv grinned. "Your alter ego lives."

Joe groaned. "You don't want to see it, do you?"

Liv had no trouble detecting a strong note of hope in his voice, but, in fact, she did want to see it. She hadn't seen a single movie of Joe's since she had known him. It didn't matter which one she saw, but she knew she wanted to bring her knowledge of the man to his films and see what, if anything, she learned.

"Why not?" she challenged him. "It was good."

Joe looked skeptical, rather like Steve Scott when confronted by a particularly unpleasant new plot twist, Liv thought.

"Please," she implored.

Joe shrugged, his expression grim but resigned. "If you want, go ahead," he said gruffly as the plane hurtled down the runway. "But don't expect me to. I brought a book on the Spanish Civil War to read."

He didn't read it, however. Instead he watched Liv watching Steve Scott and grew increasingly morose. She seemed enchanted, enthralled, intrigued. Was it Steve Scott she really wanted? A master of all situations? A clever, charming, intelligent, superb lover? A superman in jeans and polo shirts? Joe closed his eyes and stifled a groan. There was no way he could be all that, even if he tried! But then why had she come to Vienna with him? The question of the century, he thought as he studied her profile, watching her smile as Steve Scott saved the day once more. Good old Steve, he had all the answers. Joe wished he had the answer to this one.

"You were really wonderful," Liv told him when the lights came back on again, and the flight attendants moved back down the aisles offering another round of refreshments.

"Um," Joe grunted. He wished he could muster up some enthusiasm himself. She sounded positively thrilled by what she had seen and that depressed him further. "How about something to drink?" he asked, hoping to divert her.

"Not now," Liv said, eyeing him curiously. "What's the matter?"

"Nothing." He plucked irritably at the armrest, then muttered. "I hate Steve Scott." He couldn't help himself.

Liv didn't hate Steve Scott. But she wouldn't have gone to Vienna with him, either. He was too perfect, too macho, too predictable—he was the prototype from which movie star idols were made, and undoubtedly there were bits of him in Joe. But Joe had a humanity, a vulnerability, that was lacking in Steve Scott. And it was more than part of him that Liv loved than the movie star hero. In fact she thought that Joe must find him difficult to live up to. It must be terrible to have to pattern your life on a cardboard character who only had virtues. Heaven knew her own failure to be a magazine version of Superwife and Supermom had been hard enough to take, and she was the only one expecting that of herself. Not like Joe, who had an image that legions of sex-starved women expected of him.

"I can see where he'd be a bit of a cross," she said, and Joe looked over at her, wary and assessing, as though he didn't believe she had really said that, so she went on, "Hard to live up to, I mean. After all, how often does one have the opportunity to rescue fair maidens from headhunters or deadly plagues, or to defuse bombs?"

"Not often," Joe agreed, a faint grin twisting the corner of his mouth.

"Still," Liv said, taking a sip of the orange juice the flight attendant had handed her, "I think you're better at real life."

"Oh?" It didn't come out as noncommittal as he'd obviously intended it. Liv heard a sharp note of interest in his voice.

"You rescued us from chicken pox," she said, "which, while it may not be deadly, was certainly heroic of you in my book."

"Anybody would have—"

"And if not bombs," she continued, starting to laugh at the memory of it, "you certainly managed to defuse Tom."

"That bastard!" Joe straightened in his seat, his face a mixture of irritation and amusement. "That self-righteous prig! How dare he come banging on the door at two in the morning, drunk as a skunk, demanding to know my intentions toward his ex-wife?"

"Well, I think you convinced him that it wasn't any of his business," Liv giggled. "Although turning the garden hose on him seems a rather crude method of dampening his anger!"

"It was the quietest way I could think of. Did you want the kids to hear him?"

"No." She shook her head adamantly. "He is their father. Even if he no longer has any rights in my life." She met his eyes steadily, trying to tell him without words the commitment she was making by coming with him.

For longer than she would have liked, Joe didn't respond. Then, slowly, his eyes changed, becoming the same warm inviting green that the sea was on a summer day. "Good," he said, and Liv thought she heard satisfaction in the word and, she hoped, a wealth of promise.

I am drowning, she thought again, remembering with startling clarity the night by the lake when she had realized she loved Joe Harrington. There was no other man to compare with him. Tom didn't matter anymore; only Joe. And she smiled at him with a certainty that, for the first time since they had boarded the plane, he seemed unreservedly to return. She felt his hand touch hers, wrapping her fingers snugly in the warmth of his palm and she sighed and leaned her head against his shoulder, confident that things would work out. It wasn't long until she slept.

Their flight, by way of Amsterdam, arrived in Vienna in midmorning. Swept through customs, yawning and stretching, they were met by another one of what Liv had determined must be Joe's fast-lane friends. Uli Carvalho, an Austrian-Portuguese charmer who, Joe said laughingly, "had feet almost as quick as his hands," was, she discovered, a professional soccer player. He hustled them through the airport with the facility he might have shown moving the ball downfield, and the next thing she knew, Liv was seated in the back of his black BMW with Frances's suitcase for company. She listened intently while Uli caught Joe up on the amorous events in his life and hoped, ears burning, that he would be discreet about theirs.

Not that they had any, she thought as they sped down the main road through Schwechat toward Vienna. But what was Uli supposed to think when a woman—obviously no young virgin—accompanied a man with a reputation like Joe Harrington's halfway across the earth? Exactly what he did think when she heard him say, "I have moved my things to my mother's flat. You and Olivia can have mine."

Liv sucked in her breath like a tightrope walker about to take her first fatal step, when she heard Joe reply, "No. Liv can stay with your mother."

Uli's expression was comical, mirroring, Liv imagined, her own. Where was the playboy of the western world now? She stared at Joe's dark head in front of her, but there was no way she could tell what he was thinking. But whatever it was, apparently it wasn't a foregone conclusion—at least to him—that they would share an apartment. She didn't know whether to be hurt or relieved.

"Whatever you want, then," Uli said carefully. Liv could almost see him rearranging his thinking. The gaze he shot her in the mirror was both curious and speculative. "Anyway, you will have both flats to yourselves after tonight. I go to Stuttgart tomorrow for a game. From there we go to Amsterdam. And my mother goes to Stuttgart tomorrow also, to spend two weeks with her sister."

"Really?" Joe said, but it was impossible to discern anything from that. Liv scowled and wished she didn't always feel at sea with him. It was more than a little difficult loving a man she couldn't figure out. She tried, but he distracted her almost immediately by pointing out Karlskirche as it came into view, and before she knew it, they were nearly there. Uli was concentrating on probing his way through the busy traffic on Vienna's narrow streets. Five- and six-story buildings rose on either side, huge brown and gray stucco monoliths, some plain, some decorated with bas relief sculpture and gargoyles. In front of one Uli double-parked and ushered them in. "Go on up," he told Joe, once he had led them into a dark, cavernous hallway that led to a curving cement stairwell. "Three floors up, yes? My mother is waiting."

Uli's mother was every bit the stereotypical rosy-cheeked, blue-eyed Austrian that her son was not. She also spoke not a word of English. But even that, combined with Liv's inability to speak more than ten words of German, didn't deter Mrs. Carvalho from making them feel very welcome.

Deluged with cherry kuchen, cream cakes and strong Viennese coffee liberally laced with milk, Liv enjoyed Mrs. Carvalho's maternal cluckings and hoverings, which reminded her of her own mother's. She barely roused herself from the armchair where she sat when Joe left. Then, yawning, she accompanied him to the door when he left for Uli's flat to have a quick nap.

"Wish you were coming with me?" he asked, laughter lurking in the sea-green depths of his eyes.

Liv wiped a speck of cherry kuchen from his upper lip, pleased at this teasing, more lighthearted Joe. He seemed to have made up his mind about something on the plane. At least he wasn't staring at her quite so intently anymore. Maybe he sensed that she knew what she was doing. She hoped so. "No," she told him, teasing him back. "I've always rather fancied those Latin types with the dark, soulful eyes."

"Oh you have, have you?" Joe growled, his arm sweeping around her to draw her against his hard, virile length. "We'll have to see about that."

"When?" Liv asked, playing with the buttons of his shirt, wanting to slip her hands inside and feel the warmth of his body.

Joe made a face. "Later."

"Promises, promises."

He bent his head, nipping her earlobe, sending a shiver of anticipation clear through her. "Watch it, sweetheart," he cautioned. "When Uli and Mama are in Stuttgart and the speech is in the minds of all peace-loving peoples everywhere, who will save you then?"

"Why you, of course," Liv said, her fingers continuing to trace erotic patterns on his chest, then slipping down toward the flat plane of his stomach. "You promised always to save me, remember?" she said. "That night at the lake?" *The night I realized I loved you,* she added silently.

Joe gave her a wicked grin. "I lied," he whispered, and after kissing her hard on the lips, he turned and vanished out the door.

THE ANTICIPATION made it bearable, Liv thought, coupled with the fact that Vienna was such a lovely city to explore. The following morning while Joe went over his speech notes for the last time, she went for a walk in the immediate neighborhood, savoring the feel of living in history in a way that she had never felt in Madison. The abundance of sculpture amazed her. Everywhere she went, stone was carved, sculpted, swirled, bringing vigor and life to the drabbest of corners. She wandered through one of the parks along the famous Ring and shopped in some lovely stores she found along Kärtnerstrasse as she ventured further from Uli's flat. When the speech was over, they would come back together, Joe had promised. "I'm not lying about *that,*" he had assured her. "We'll work it in somehow." And she smiled as she thought about what he intended to work it in between. And she hoped that they would because she saw so many things that she wanted to go back and share with Joe.

"Where did you eat?" he asked when she got back to Mrs. Carvalho's apartment, footsore and content, brimming with thoughts to share of places she'd been and things she'd seen. He was sitting at Uli's mother's dining-room table, surrounded by piles of notes scribbled in spiky handwriting, and a plate of cherry pits.

"Demels," she told him, licking her lips in remembrance of the plate of green peppers and tomatoes with vinaigrette dressing and the scrumptious strawberry tart she had enjoyed. "Like any other self-respecting tourist on her first day in Vienna."

"Damn," he muttered good-naturedly. "You're not saving anything for me to show you."

"You can show me the local bars and coffeehouses," Liv consoled him. "Uli says that's your strong point anyway. What did you have for lunch?"

"Wurst, cheese, cherry kuchen. I didn't starve. Mrs. Carvalho made sure of that before she left." He shoved back his chair and tipped it back on two legs, balancing it precariously as he leaned his dark head against the wall. "I'll be glad when this speech is over."

"Three more hours," Liv said, consulting her watch. "Do I get to come and watch?"

"Of course. Give moral support, hold my hand and all that."

Liv blanched. "Not really?"

Joe shrugged. "Why not? It's not exactly like going in, delivering my lines, saving the girl and riding off into the sunset. This is serious business." He chewed his lip thoughtfully. "Maybe I bit off too much."

"No." Liv went over to him and tipped his chair forward again. Standing behind him she began to knead his shoulders, her thumbs pressing against the cords of his neck and back, working out his tension.

"Mmmmm, fabulous," Joe breathed. His head tipped back and his eyes closed. "Don't stop. It helps my head."

"Have you got a headache?"

"A bit. Nerves probably." He smiled. "Even we movie idols have them, in case you wondered." She saw the corner of his mouth lift and she wanted to reach over and touch it, but then his head dropped back even farther, so that his dark hair brushed against her breasts, and an even better opportunity presented itself. She bent over him and touched her lips to his.

"You kiss fantastically," he murmured against her mouth. "Even upside down. Such talent."

Liv nibbled his nose. "You should see what else I can do."

Joe groaned. "Don't tempt me. What would they say if I didn't show up?"

"That you were in bed with a beautiful woman, no doubt," Liv said dryly. "What else?"

"What else indeed?" Joe grinned. "Sounds great. Let's do it." Liv shoved his chair back on all four legs and lifted his head away from its resting place. "No way. There's a time and place for everything."

"And this isn't it?"

She shook her head, smiling at the consternation battling with laughter in his face. "This isn't it," she agreed.

"I suppose not," Joe said reluctantly. "But it won't be long."

I hope not, Liv thought, and marveled that she would admit thinking it. Loving Joe was a dangerous business. For a woman who, after her divorce, had decided that she wanted a life in a safe harbor, a relationship with Joe Harrington promised to be a sail on very unpredictable seas. She could drown, she kept telling herself. She very well might. He had made no promises. He had never said, "I love you," to her. He went through women like her boys went through socks, and there was every possibility that he would fly off to Majorca or Malibu tomorrow or next month and never give her or the kids another thought. She looked down on his dark ruffled hair and an ache pierced her so sharply that her fingers dug into his shoulders for support.

"What's wrong?" Joe asked, looking up concerned over his shoulder.

"Nothing." *Everything. I love you,* she thought. *I want you. I need you. Now. Tonight. Tomorrow. Forever.* But she couldn't say it. Not yet. Ever since she had talked to Ellie, she had been wondering if Joe would ever commit himself to any woman. He had been running from marriage for a long time. She had no right to expect that she would be the woman to change him. And just as she couldn't change him, she realized that she couldn't change herself. She couldn't stop herself from loving him even if in the end she lost him. At least, she consoled herself, she would have memories.

"I know it hasn't been much of a great vacation so far," Joe said. "But the fun is just beginning." He leered at her and got lithely to his feet, wrapping his arms around her and hugging the breath out of her.

The warmth of him enveloped her and her throat closed with emotion. Stop it, dummy, she commanded herself. You haven't lost him yet, for heaven's sake. He's right here. Time enough later for regretting that her time with him was over. Time now to get on with living. "I'll go take a bath before we go," Liv told him. "Are you going to shower up at Uli's?"

"I'll share with you," he offered.

"I'll take a rain check, we might not get there otherwise," she told him, grinning, feeling the desire in him. She pulled away, stopping to press a light kiss on his warm cheek. "I'll be ready in an hour."

Joe was ready even before she was. He looked formidable and distant in a dark blue, severely cut, superbly tailored suit, his hair neatly combed, his cheeks smooth. There were lines of fatigue or worry around his eyes—more visible since he wasn't wearing his glasses that she had become used to but that weren't a part of his public image—and a paleness around his mouth that made Liv realize that he hadn't been kidding about his nervousness. She gave him a bright smile and squeezed his hand encouragingly. He returned the smile with a ghost of one of his own, and his damp palm encircled her hand firmly and didn't let go.

He hung on to her hand all through their long taxi ride through Vienna and across the Danube to the UNO complex, kept her fingers locked with his throughout the introductions to various dignitaries, with whom he spoke in both English and reasonably passable German, and when he dragged her along to the general assembly room where he was to speak, Liv wondered if she would be standing beside him at the podium, her fingers still intertwined with his, while he gave his talk.

She wasn't. A voluble, portly Austrian spirited her away just moments before Joe mounted the platform to give his speech and found her a seat off to the side where she could listen and where Joe, at his insistence, could still see her.

And where he could find her again just moments after the speech was over. His forehead was beaded with perspiration and his hands were shaking as he reached for her. "You were fantastic," Liv said, hugging him, sensing that he needed physical reassurance at that moment. He looked so ill.

"Think so?" He smiled, but his eyes looked glazed, and she could feel his heart hammering against her chest.

"Definitely. What now?" She felt his arm around her shoulders and she curved easily and naturally into his side, her arm around his waist, feeling as though she belonged there.

"Press conference. A short one fortunately. Then we're free. Okay?"

"Fine." Liv followed the Austrian who was in charge down one of the halls to a room where reporters from all over the world were waiting to bombard Joe with questions. She felt him stiffen against her a moment before he plunged into the room, leaving her out of the glare of the lights against the back wall. She hung back, happy not to have to share the spotlight with him, proud of him for doing it so well. He answered the questions intelligently, honestly, capably, and she glowed as she watched him. She remembered the first time she had seen him speak, that night in Madison when Marv had coerced her into interviewing him and attending his speech. Listening to him then, her view of him had undergone a radical change. And it had kept right on changing, she thought, growing from grudging respect tinged with sexual attraction, to genuine liking, to loving with all her heart. Something close to a sob strangled her as she watched him dredge up an extra ounce of energy from somewhere to do a good job here, too. How she loved him. Did he realize? Did he know? He would soon, she vowed, if he didn't already. She would tell him, show him. The moment they had both been waiting for would come. Soon. And what would happen then?

"Let's get out of here." Joe's voice was suddenly right by her ear, as he was pressed against her by a crush of reporters, all trying to ask him one last question.

"You're done?" She linked her arm in his, trying to muster smiles for the reporters, many of whom were staring at her in unabashed curiosity.

"Who's the lady, Joe?" one of the American reporters asked.

Joe gripped her arm just above the elbow and steered her in front of him through the press of the crowd around them, ignoring the question. But Liv could tell he was annoyed; his jaw jutted out defiantly and his brows were drawn down.

"Who is she, Joe?" another persisted, his voice as loud as his tie. And a third cried, "Who's the latest, Harrington?"

Liv felt suddenly cold.

Joe herded her out to the waiting taxi, the portly Austrian acting like an icebreaker in front of them, parting the crowd.

"Dreadfully sorry, my dear," the man said in his barely discernible German accent as he handed Liv into the taxi. "Don't let it upset you."

"No," Liv said shakily. Joe's latest? Oh, God. She didn't want to think about that. Not now.

Joe sat next to her looking like a cigar store Indian. The taxi poked its way back across the river and into the jumble of streets making up the ancient first district, the sounds of church bells and traffic and jackhammers wrapping Liv like a protective cocoon. Neither one of them spoke until the driver asked Joe something in German, and he roused himself from his wooden state long enough to consult with Liv before replying.

"Hungry? There's a good Greek restaurant in the sixth district. I know this isn't Athens, but...." His voice was brittle, jerky, and she managed a vague smile, nodding in agreement.

"That's fine." She wasn't hungry at all. She felt as hollow as a basketball, but it wasn't the sort of emptiness that food would fill. Damn those reporters anyway. Damn their dose of reality. And damn Joe for withdrawing like this. Why couldn't he deny it at least? Why couldn't he let her live a while longer with the fiction that he really cared? She followed him robotlike as he got out of the taxi and led her into a tiny restaurant, charming and obviously authentically Greek, and allowed him to order for them both because she was no more fluent in Greek than she was in German.

"I could kill them," he said finally, his voice harsh with anger no longer repressed. His eyes glinted in the candlelight, seeming more obsidian than jade in the dim golden glow. The ferocity of his voice shook her. "Damn them! Damn them!" His fingers clenched around the knife. "I'm sorry. If I had known they were going to get personal, I wouldn't have asked you to be there."

"It's all right," Liv said awkwardly after a moment, beginning to understand that his withdrawal had not been meant as a rejection of her. "It's—"

"It's not all right! It's my life! It's your life! What right do they have to stick their noses into it?"

"You earn a lot of money," Liv said slowly. "I guess they figure they own you."

"They don't." His voice was murderous. He was cradling the knife across both his hands now, elbows resting on the table as he contemplated it glittering silver and gold in the light. "You know," he said carefully, "that's the biggest temptation of Pío and Elena."

"What is?"

"Writing it. *Not* acting it. Being behind the scenes. Letting someone else be owned for a change." He sighed and set the knife down on the edge of the plate the waitress had just brought and set in front of him. "This wasn't exactly how I planned for the evening to go," he said ruefully. The anger in his voice was fading, replaced by a sort of wistfulness that assuaged Liv's hollowness better than the best moussaka in the world could have done.

"I know." She did, finally. She understood now that he had been as upset about their comments as she had been—and for much the same reason apparently. Suddenly she felt like singing. She smiled at him over the top of her wineglass. "Let's just forget them," she suggested, and was amazed that she knew she could. "They don't matter now."

Joe rubbed his eyes. "I'll try," he said. He drew his glasses out of their case and put them on. "I thought I'd be over this headache by the time I finished the speech. Seems like they're going to make sure I keep it a while longer." His mouth lifted in a faint grin.

"Perhaps you're just hungry," Liv said, but he didn't seem to relish his meal much either, good though it was. She ate heartily now, enjoying her moussaka to the fullest, but Joe picked at his shish kebob and shoved most of his rice from one side of his plate to the other. When Liv had finished and he was still rearranging his rice, she reached over and touched his hand. "Tired?" she asked.

"Sort of. Probably a combination of jet lag and stage fright."

"Well, if you're ready to go home, I am."

Joe struggled to sit up straighter. "I thought we'd go to the Twelve Apostles *Keller* later. You can't miss that."

"We can go another night. I'm tired, even if you're not." Liv stifled a yawn that she didn't even have to pretend. "Truly," she said when he looked skeptical.

"If you're sure." He didn't look as though he would take much convincing, and when she assured him again that she was, he signaled to the waitress for the check and escorted Liv to the door.

"God," he said when they finally got back to Uli's mother's flat and he opened the door to let her in, "This is the first night I've ever been alone with you, and all I want to do is sleep!" He looked positively disgusted.

"Listen to your body," Liv counseled, and Joe grinned.

"You never said that any other night!" he accused.

"No, but tonight I've only got to look at you to know where you belong. To bed, Mr. Harrington. Right now. I'll see you tomorrow when you're wide awake."

Joe looked forlornly up the stairwell. "You're really going to make me trudge up two more flights of stairs?"

"You were the stickler for chivalry," she reminded him. "Besides, how much rest would you get on Mrs. Carvalho's couch?"

"She has twin beds in the bedroom."

"And you'd stay in yours?"

"Well...."

Liv gave him an arch look.

He yawned. "All right. You win. When I take you to bed, I want to be awake enough to remember it." He ducked his head and gave her an almost brotherly peck on the cheek, which only served to emphasize just how very tired he was. She watched as he slowly mounted the curving stairway, wanting to follow him and love him, but knowing that tonight at least the time was not yet right. She heard him open the door of Uli's flat two floors above her. Then the door swung shut with a soft thud, and, chilled, she eased her own heavy door shut and extinguished the light.

BY ELEVEN the next morning Liv's second pot of coffee had grown stone cold. Tired Joe might have been, she thought, but this was ridiculous.

She had got to bed by ten and had awakened early, refreshed and ready to start the day. Knowing that Joe wouldn't likely be down at seven, she had busied herself writing postcards to Ellie, Frances and the kids. Then at nine she had made the first pot of coffee and had set out Mrs. Carvalho's rolls and jam, to be ready when Joe arrived. She finished off the first two-cup pot and made another. That one was half gone now and there was still no sign of Joe.

She poked through Mrs. Carvalho's cupboards and, finding a tray, set it with a plate of rolls, napkins, butter, jam and two mugs. Then, adding her freshly brewed third pot of coffee, she carefully mounted the stairs to Uli's flat.

She rang the bell three times before she heard him shuffling around. "Come on, sleepyhead," she called thinking that the smell of the coffee would surely wake him up.

The lock scraped back, the door opened and Joe stood before her, bleary-eyed and unshaven, wearing only a pair of faded denims. "Hi," he said dully, motioning her in, stepping back so that she could pass him. "I've got a headache."

She peered at him closely as she passed. "Oh Lord, Joe," she murmured, setting the tray down on the wooden countertop with a thump. "That's not all you've got."

"Huh?" He padded past her into the kitchen and perched on a bar stool, bending his toes around the bottom rung.

She reached out and touched a tiny clear blister on his cheek. "You've got chicken pox."

Chapter Ten

"That's not even funny." His head was pounding and he wanted to press his face against her breasts and feel her arms close around him. How could she joke when he felt so rotten?

"Oh, Joe." Her voice was wistful, gentle, and she smiled at him the way his mother used to smile whenever he had done something particularly stupid with the best intentions in the world. "I'm not kidding."

Her hand brushed softly against the roughness of his cheek, belying the harshness of her words, and he looked up at her stricken. His toes tightened convulsively around the metal rung of the stool. "No," he muttered. "No." It was as though someone were clubbing him senseless; his mind was blown, his hopes and plans for the rest of the week in ashes at his feet. He closed his eyes against the pain of it. The throbbing in his temples grew.

"Oh Joe," she murmured again, and stepped back to inspect his torso for more of the telltale blisters. Her fingers roved through the hair on his chest, and he felt a shudder course though him. "All those days with all those scabby kids. Why didn't you say that you hadn't had them?"

"I thought I had," he mumbled. "All kids have 'em."

She looked at him in dismay. "Apparently one didn't. I feel terrible."

"*You* do?" Oh, not her too!

"Not sick," she explained quickly. "Just terrible that my kids gave them to you. I feel so responsible. Oh, Joe, I'm sorry!" Then she did hug him, and hungrily he drew her between his legs as he hunched on the bar stool, luxuriating in the silkiness of her hair against his forehead and the cool hands that stroked his bare back. She rained gentle kisses onto his hair.

"I'm not sorry," he quipped hoarsely, managing the tiniest of grins. "Not if it gets me this." But he was, because it ruined everything. He'd had such plans—places to go, restaurants to try, favorite haunts to share with her, a day trip to Salzberg.

And now there was nothing. His throat tightened as he thought about it. He couldn't even look forward now to spending the week in bed with her. Who would sleep with a man covered with chicken pox?

"How about a roll and coffee," Liv interrupted his self-pitying thought.

"I'm not hungry."

"Too bad, you have to eat anyway," she said, and moved away from him to break a roll and butter it. He watched her glumly, remembering that she'd said the same thing to Theo in much the same situation.

"I'm not one of your kids," he bristled.

"Then don't act like one." She handed him the plate with the roll on it and then poured him a cup of coffee. "Here." She thrust it into his hand and then perched on the counter beside him, watching him like a mother eagle while he choked it down.

"Satisfied?" he asked finally, wiping his mouth on the napkin she gave him.

"For now. Back to bed with you, I think."

Joe groaned, but one glance at her implacable face and he slid off the bar stool and shuffled back into Uli's sitting room-bedroom and flung himself down on the crumpled eiderdown. "Care to join me?" he asked, wishing that she would. She was standing over him, looking all sympathetic, but he wanted more than that—much more—and he tried to grin. "I bet you've never been propositioned by a man with chicken pox before," he said, his voice cracking.

"Never," she agreed. "It's a first."

"Damn." He slammed his hand into the mattress.

"What's wrong?"

"Everything. Me. You. This." He managed a shaky laugh. It was better than crying, which was what he felt like doing. "I can't believe this. Chicken pox!" His fist slammed down again. "I didn't want it to be like this!"

She looked at him uncertainly. "It's all right. I mean, of course the chicken pox are rotten. But I think you'll be okay if that's what's worrying you."

"It's not. Anyway, what about you?" He couldn't contain his bitterness. "What'll you do all week?"

"Stay with you."

He snorted. "Some holiday that'll be."

"I don't mind."

"I do. You'd better fly home."

She looked at him horrified. "That's the stupidest thing I've ever heard. I'm not leaving you here alone and ill."

"I'll survive."

She looked exasperated. "Of course you will. But I'm not leaving you, either, so just drop that whole idea right now."

He rubbed a hand through his uncombed hair, blinking his eyes, hoping he masked the relief he felt. "If you want," he mumbled, ridiculously glad she wanted to stay. It shouldn't matter that much, he told himself gruffly. He'd got along fine on his own all these years. Surely he didn't need someone holding his hand now. But, almost without thinking, he reached for hers. Her cool, gentle hand slipped inside his hot one, and the other caressed his cheek softly.

"Sleep now," she advised. "I'll go back downstairs. Come down when you feel like it."

"Yeah." He felt her draw away, and bereft, he rolled over onto his stomach, burying his face in the pillow, moaning softly as he heard the door close behind her. So much for the romantic American hero who swept his lady off her feet in enchanting old Vienna. He bet Steve Scott never got the chicken pox!

"BORED YET?" Joe asked when she opened the door downstairs to let him in three hours later. He brushed past her into the living room and dropped disgustedly onto Mrs. Carvalho's chintz-covered sofa.

"Not a bit," Liv replied. She had spent the time writing the rough draft of her Vienna article for Marv and, finishing it, she opted for watching a soccer match on television. "How are you feeling now?" she asked him. He looked slightly better for all that he had three or four more pox visible on his face. He had dressed in a pair of gray corduroy jeans and a light blue polo shirt, open at the neck, and had made an effort to comb his hair, though he had not shaved. Liv found that she rather liked the effect of the stubble. It made him look even more roguish than usual.

He caught her glance and rubbed a rueful hand across his chin. "Like it? It's my new look. I can't shave until these things are gone."

"Oh!" The idea startled her. She'd never had to consider that with the little boys. "I hadn't thought about that!"

He grimaced. "Neither had I. Bad enough feeling lousy. Now I look it too."

Liv grinned. "A little movie star conceit?"

"No," he snapped, his voice harsh, and she was surprised by the vehemence of it because she had only meant to tease him.

"Actually I think you look quite dashing," she told him. He did—rather like a pirate, a glum, disgusted pirate who'd had a buried treasure snatched from beneath his very nose.

"Now you do," he grumbled. "Tell me that in a week."

"In a week you'll look more like a werewolf."

"Thanks very much." Joe looked even more glum at that and she decided that maybe teasing wasn't the answer. He was taking this all far too seriously.

"It won't matter," she assured him.

He snorted. "We'll see." But she could tell he thought he knew exactly what he would see—that she and everyone else would take one look at him and run for cover.

"Do you want something to eat?" she asked as he thumbed through one of the magazines she had been reading, then dropped it on the sofa and picked up another.

"No."

"Want to watch a soccer match?"

"No."

"Listen to a tape?" Uli's mother had a tape deck and some very tempting tapes, but Liv couldn't interest Joe.

"No."

Who said two-year-olds had a monopoly on negativism? "Go to bed with me?"

"N-what?" His head jerked up and the green eyes snapped open.

"Just wanted to see if you were paying attention," she said lightly.

"I am now." His eyes sparkled with amusement as well as with fever.

"Good. Give me your key and I'll bring your things down here."

"What for?"

"To move in. You can't be alone while you're sick."

Joe stared at her for a long moment before he fished in his pocket and handed her the key. "Would you have made the invitation if I were well?" he asked wryly.

Liv considered this, then met his eyes frankly. "I came to Vienna with you, didn't I?"

Joe let out a deep breath. "Yes," he muttered. "You did." He shut his eyes and looked suddenly so pained and ill that Liv was concerned.

"Are you all right?" she asked.

"Super." It was not convincing.

"Take it easy, I'll be right back." She began to feel faint pricklings of worry. He really did not look well at all. Was it worse, she wondered, if one had chicken pox as an adult? Were the complications more serious? At home she could have called a doctor friend and asked. In Vienna all she could do was bring down his suitcases and wait. "Maybe tomorrow you'll feel better," she said hopefully when she returned.

"I doubt it." He touched one of the blisters on his face gingerly. "Stephen didn't. Nor Theo, nor Jennifer." His hand dropped limply to his side. "Hell," he muttered. "Oh hell."

"IT ITCHES."

"Yes."

"Cripes, here's another one."

"Yes."

"Damn it, how could anybody get them between their toes?"

"Stop picking at them! And don't scratch!"

"Or I'll mar my handsome movie star face!"

"Yes, and everyone will say, 'Joe who?' this time next year."

"The werewolf of Vienna you mean?"

"Exactly."

Joe groaned. "It's not funny." He was sitting on the edge of the other twin bed in Mrs. Carvalho's bedroom, wearing only a short, lightweight blue robe of Uli's. "Tomorrow" he had not felt better, just as he had predicted, and as more and more pox popped out, broke and began to itch, he had shed more and more of his clothes, until finally only Uli's robe kept him within the bounds of decency. "Have you counted them?" He sounded incredulous. "I quit at four hundred and twelve, and those were only the ones I could see."

Joe was a dreadful patient. Sometimes, of course, he was stoical, uncomplaining and grateful. More often he was irritable, touchy and worse than Stephen, Theo and Jennifer combined. But when Liv finally said so, he replied fretfully.

"Yes, well, I've got it worse than the three of them combined, too."

As this was nothing but the truth, she shut up and brought him another glass of juice.

He had been sleeping on and off since she had brought his things down the previous afternoon. His head ached and his fever raged, and when she shut out the light and crawled into the twin bed across the room from his that first night, fully expecting at least one provocative comment, she got only a croaked "Good night, Liv" before she heard him shift onto his side and fall into the deep, even breathing of one obviously asleep. He awakened several times, parched and miserable, and Liv brought him juice or water, feeling oddly unselfconscious in her thin nightgown. Perhaps, she thought as she crawled back into bed for the fourth time, because he only saw the glass she held to his lips, never her.

By the morning much of his fever had subsided, but his irritability definitely had not. He seemed to take each new blister that appeared as an affront to his dignity or his masculinity or some ridiculous thing, and, in spite of her better judgment, Liv found it almost funny.

Joe did not. "Stop smirking," he ordered crossly. He glared at her as he sat hunched on the bed, his hands dangling between his knees. Irritably he leaned over and scratched one of the pox on his calf.

"Baking soda baths help stop the itching," she reminded him, hoping to find a useful distraction. She and Joe had run countless tubs of water for the children.

"If you want to look like a prune," he counted, wrinkling his nose.

"It's up to you. Would you rather be a prune or itch?"

"Some choice." But he hauled himself to his feet and walked gingerly across the oriental carpet to the bathroom. "God, they're even on the soles of my feet!"

"I'll get the baking soda," Liv volunteered. She made a dash for the kitchen and began poking through Mrs. Carvalho's cupboards, sniffing and rattling, trying to decipher the German as much by texture and smell as by the words on the box. At last she found something white and powdery and carried it back to the bathroom.

"I've got something called *Stärkemehl,*" Liv called over the noise of the running water. "Is that it?"

She heard Joe laugh for the first time since the afternoon he had given his speech. "Only if you want a bathtub full of gravy and an instant introduction to a Viennese plumber," he replied. "That means 'starch flour,' like cornstarch."

"Oh!" Liv scurried back to the kitchen, wishing she'd had more than two years of high school Spanish and a year of college French.

"Think bicarbonate," Joe called after her.

Liv did, but when she came back finally, she was bearing a green-and-white packet with a picture of a glass and a spoonful of white powder on it. It said *Speisesoda* and it both looked and sounded promising. She was going to say so. But when she opened the bathroom door all she could say was "Joe!"

He had shed Uli's robe and was stepping into the water in all his naked splendor—a splendor that his wickedly sexy grin and bedroom eyes had only hinted at. She felt as if she were dry kindling set to torch. "I...I should have knocked," she babbled, thrusting the box at him and backing rapidly toward the door, knowing that she should drop her eyes, avoid staring, and also knowing that she was incapable of doing so. Talk about masculine beauty and perfection!

"You're staring," Joe said petulantly as he shook the box over the water and chunks of baking soda fell into the water and foamed.

And how, Liv thought. "Um, sorry," she said hastily, about to turn and run.

"That bad, huh?" Joe glumly surveyed his pox-covered chest and legs.

Bad? Liv stopped, flustered, in the doorway and realized that they were seeing two different things. Where she saw only a lean, hard body, lithe and tanned, Joe saw chicken pox and nothing but.

He raked a hand through his spiky hair and looked away from her to inspect the grout between the tiles above the tub.

"Not bad at all," Liv assured him, hovering indecisively a moment longer before she mustered sufficient courage to shut the bathroom door and remain on the same side of it as Joe Harrington. She leaned against the sink, luxuriating in her opportunity to study him. Study, ha, she thought. Study implied a dispassionate, objective examination that was completely impossible for her. She was melting where she stood. Joe had stopped examining the grout and was staring at her, his expression unreadable. She licked her lips quickly and asked, "Has the itching stopped?"

"There are itches and then there are itches," came the reply. "My chicken pox don't itch any longer." He stretched and flexed his muscles as he rose slowly to his feet giving Liv a good look at what still did itch. She closed her eyes and groped for a towel, flinging it in his direction as soon as she found one.

"Dry me." It was a challenge, a dare, the first glimpse of the baiting, teasing Joe she'd had since the first blister had appeared.

"You sound like Theo."

"I don't feel like Theo." He was holding the towel out to her as he stood and dripped puddles onto Mrs. Carvalho's shiny tile floor.

He didn't look like Theo either, and Liv most definitely did not feel like his mother. There was a world of difference in drying off a small, soapy-clean little boy, and running a towel over the well-muscled back and firm buttocks of Joe Harrington. She sucked her breath in sharply as she drew the soft beige terry towel down his arms, being careful not to rub too hard and break any new blisters. Her hands smoothed the towel across his flat stomach, aching to stray below, to trace the line of damp hair that arrowed below his navel toward his groin. As if she had, she felt him draw in his breath as a shudder ran through him.

"This is not stopping the itching," he said shakily and bit down on his lower lip as she dropped to her knees and began to dry his legs.

"It was your idea," she said softly even as she delighted in doing it. She had been dying to touch him for so long. She bent her head and concentrated on drying his feet. Her hair brushed against his bare thigh.

"Liv." He sounded strangled.

She ran the towel lightly up the inside of his leg. "Yes."

His fingers clenched in her hair. The towel went back down again. And up. "What're you doing?"

"Drying you."

"Torturing me," he groaned.

"Do you want me to stop?"

"No, yes...I don't know." He hauled her to her feet abruptly, wrapping his arms around her. The towel slithered to the floor unheeded as she felt the hardness of his arousal through the thin cotton of her slacks. His breathing was a ragged echo of her own as they clung together, and waves of desire coursed through her. "How I want you," he whispered, and his hands moved to cup her buttocks and press her against him even more tightly. Then, with a shuddering sigh, he dropped his head into the curve of her shoulder and muttered, "We'd better stop." He lifted his head and gave her a rueful grin. "Famous last words, huh?"

Liv held on to him, afraid that if she let go she would topple over. Her legs were mush beneath her. "Stop?" she echoed shakily.

He shrugged helplessly. "I haven't heard the latest medical opinion of making love with chicken pox. Have you?"

His hands slid up her spine and teased their way along the line of her bra strap beneath her navy T-shirt.

"No," she allowed. Were there medical opinions on such things?

"And I don't relish calling up some unsuspecting Viennese doctor and asking," Joe went on, still grinning. "Especially not with my command of German!"

"You speak German very well," Liv replied.

"Not *that* well. Besides, I might not ask that question even in English."

"Joe Harrington? Embarrassed?"

Joe said a rude word, but Liv saw the flush spread across his skin even against his dark tan. He bent and picked up the towel, hastily knotting it around his hips. Liv grinned.

"You don't have a tan line," she remarked.

"So?" It was a growl, but he hitched the towel up higher on his hips and ignored her, studying with disgust his stubbled cheeks in the moisture-beaded mirror over the sink.

"Do you sunbathe in the nude?" she pressed.

"What of it?" But he looked decidedly uncomfortable.

"Just curious," Liv said, still smiling. "When you blush, you blush all over. Did you know that?"

Joe flung the comb he had been using onto the floor. "For heaven's sake," he exploded. He yanked the door open and disappeared into the bedroom, leaving Liv in the bathroom giggling softly. "Just wait," he threatened over his shoulder. "Just you wait."

It seemed, Liv thought as she had a bath of her own, as if she had been waiting forever. It had taken every ounce of courage she possessed to throw her strict middle-class upbringing to the winds and come to Vienna with him. She hadn't expected him to ravish her, of course; but she had made up her mind that fully sharing her love with him was the only course to take. It was the only way to express what she felt for him, what she hoped he might possibly feel for her. Did he? It was hard to say. From the looks he gave her, from his comments, from the protective instinct she sensed emanating from him, she suspected he might. But Joe Harrington was unlike any other man she had ever met. With him, who knew?

THE WEEK WAS NOTHING like the one he had planned—the chicken pox had seen to that. And in its way it confused Joe more than ever, for he had hoped that once he and Liv had spent some uninterrupted time together sight-seeing and dating, he might better figure out her role in his life. At one time he thought he might possibly, by stretching things a bit, pigeonhole her as he had the other women he had known. Of course she was a friend as well as being physically attractive to him and that made it harder. But after this week he didn't know what to do with her at all.

He plucked irritably at the cool sheet and stared at the shaft of sunlight on the empty bed across the room where she had slept each night. She was such an amazing woman—so caring, so giving, so unlike all the women he had shared rooms with before. He couldn't begin to conjure up a vision of Linda Lucas, for example, sponging down his feverish, pox-covered body, bringing him apple juice or cherry juice all through the day and night, and drying his body so skillfully and sensuously that he went almost mad with desire, completely oblivious for a time to the wretched picture he must have made. Linda Lucas would have run a mile. But Liv acted as though he was every bit as attractive as he ever was.

Liv, he thought, was crazy. She must have been to come to Vienna with him! His mouth curved into a smile as he thought about her. Liv shouting at him when he was late for their first interview, her cheeks aflame with color and her gray eyes a stormy sea. Liv's voice, soft and musical, weary sometimes, when they'd talked late at night on the phone. Liv cooking supper. Liv running on the lakeshore. Liv tucking a child into bed. Liv's hand on his knee, her fresh daisy scent, her cool lips on his fevered brow. He felt a shudder of need course through him, amazed at the way she had insinuated herself into so many corners of his life. Even now she had only been out for an hour or so and he was missing her. He rolled onto his stomach and tried to sleep again, but it was no use. He had had more than enough rest the past few days. It wasn't rest he needed now. Then he heard the front door open and felt a stab of eagerness. He called out.

"Where've you been?"

Liv poked her head into the bedroom and gave him a smile that caused his toes to curl. "Shopping. I went to the bakery and bought rolls, and to the supermarket and got wurst and cheese. Do you know how hard it is not only not to speak German but not to speak grams and kilos either. Do you think Marv would like an article on that?" She plopped down on the bed across from him and stretched her arms above her head, twisting like a cat settling down for a nap. "My stupidity overwhelms me," she exclaimed.

It wasn't her stupidity that was overwhelming Joe. "I think Marv will be delighted with anything you write," he said, forcing himself out of bed. It was easier to think of other things than putting his arms around her and loving her if he was vertical.

Liv lifted a quizzical brow. "Anything?" she asked in a speculative voice. "How about 'I SHARED A ROOM WITH JOE HARRINGTON'?"

Joe grinned and tossed a pillow at her. "Watch your step, my dear. The week is almost over," he whispered in his best villainous voice and twirled the end of a fake mustache. "Nothing can save you then."

Liv had no desire to be saved and she suspected that he knew it. So she was none too pleased when their self-imposed quarantine was in its last day and the phone rang. It was Uli asking for Joe.

"They're *not* coming back today, are they?" she hissed at him as he listened to Uli.

Joe shook his head. "No," he mouthed. Then, "Who?" she heard him ask Uli. He sat up straight on the sofa as if surprised. "Who told her I was here?"

Her? Live felt her stomach plummet. "Her" was undoubtedly one of Joe's beautiful fast-lane friends, whoever she was.

"Of course I'll talk to her," Joe was saying and Liv unabashedly eavesdropped. "But—" he ran a hand through his hair, lifting it in brown spikes all over his head "—what does she want?" he asked, then grinned at Uli's reply. "Besides that," he said, flicking a quick teasing glance at Liv. She scowled and looked away immediately, studying a photo of Uli in his soccer uniform, with all the concentration of a research scientist about to isolate a cancer-causing virus. "Okay," she heard Joe say. "Thanks for the warning."

He hung up and she knew he was looking at her, but she couldn't return his gaze. For several weeks, ever since she had acknowledged to herself that she loved him, she had been living in a dream world—a two-person universe—existing on hopes, dreams and fanciful ideas about an idyllic future for the two of them, all predicated on her love. Now she had to face reality, had to face Joe's other world, even when it intruded in the form of a phone call.

"Guess who's coming to lunch," Joe said, a forced lightness in his voice. He cocked his head and grinned. "Veronique Moreau," he answered his own question.

Liv wanted to stuff the tablecloth into his smiling face. "Should I know her?" she asked with a studied artlessness that she knew didn't fool him for a minute.

"I imagine you've heard of her." Joe's tongue was in his cheek.

Liv had. Everyone but ostriches had. And had seen her, too—all of her. Her face and, more important, her body, had graced the cover of every fashion and glamour magazine in the world over the past two years. She had co-starred with Joe in an adventure film several years earlier, but as far as Liv could remember, her name had never been linked to his romantically. But, she acknowledged bitterly, considering the extent of his conquests, it could have been an oversight.

"Ah, yes," she said still studying Uli's patrician profile. "You Tarzan, her Jane. That Veronique?" It was catty, but she couldn't stop herself, and it was better than clawing the furniture—or Joe's beaming face—which was what she felt like doing.

Joe's grin widened. "The very one. Jealous?"

"No," Liv spat.

"Good, 'cause she'll be here in an hour, Uli says."

"Fine, I'll take the opportunity to go out and do some shopping."

"Don't you want to meet her?"

"I imagine she'll have eyes only for you," Liv said tartly. "Besides, I've seen very little of Vienna and we leave tomorrow. I think I'll do a bit of sight-seeing." She had no intention of sitting in Mrs. Carvalho's living room like a lump of coal while Joe charmed Veronique Moreau. And she didn't doubt that he would, either. She knew him well enough now to know that he could do it without even trying. The only unsusceptible woman was a dead one, and at last glance, Veronique Moreau was anything but that.

Liv stepped past him and went through to the bedroom, opening the closet to find the dress she had hung there. "Excuse me," she said sharply when she turned, dress in hand, to bump right into his chest, "but I am dressing in here. Will you kindly wait outside?"

Joe's eyebrows lifted speculatively, but he didn't comment, just smirked, while Liv herded him backward through the door and shut it firmly in his face. He might want to entertain his French floozy in nothing more than Uli's well-worn bathrobe, but she had no intention of meeting Veronique Moreau, however briefly, in nothing better than cotton slacks and her navy T-shirt.

She took a quick bath and slipped into the bright blue-and-green dress she had brought with her. It was a vibrant print, a sort of gauzy, East-Indian creation, which she had bought last spring in Chicago and which contrasted nicely with the fairness of her hair and brought out the delicacy of her features and the blue highlights in her gray eyes. Not bad, she decided, as she took one last glance in the steamy mirror. But definitely not Veronique Moreau.

When she opened the door to the bedroom she heard Joe's voice in the living room, followed by what could only be described as low, sexy feminine laughter. She even laughs in French, Liv thought, and grabbing her purse, she lifted her head with more self-confidence than she felt, and marched into the living room.

"This is Olivia," Joe was saying to the most gorgeous woman Liv had ever seen. She wished she had stayed in slacks and a T-shirt. Then it wouldn't have looked as though she'd tried—and failed. But she managed a tight smile, which was returned in blinding kilowatts by the striking brunette seated on the sofa next to Joe.

"Hello, dear," the actress said, her eyes skating over Liv with a wariness and curiosity that made Liv think that Veronique was sizing her up, rather like a skater would probe a pond for thin ice. "Joe has been telling me of your sterling devotion. You must have been frightfully bored."

Liv bit her tongue before she could retort, "Bored? With Joe Harrington?" Instead she nodded a bit lamely. "Not really," she allowed as soon as she found her voice. "But I will be glad to get a little sight-seeing in before we leave. So if you'll excuse me...." She shrugged into her raincoat and opened the front door. "Nice to have met you, Miss Moreau."

"And you, dear." But Veronique was already looking back at Joe, Olivia and her sterling devotion already banished from her mind.

"When will you be back?" Joe demanded, following her to the door.

Liv shrugged. "Who knows? I'm sure you and Miss Moreau will have plenty to keep you occupied," she said, wishing she felt more satisfaction as she shut the door firmly in his face.

She wished she could have shut him as easily out of her mind. But he shadowed her the whole day. She could feel him peering over her shoulder in the toy store on Mariahilferstrasse, making suggestions about presents for the boys and Jennifer as effectively as if he'd been with her. He seemed to share her *Sachertorte* at the small sidewalk café, and he dogged her footsteps through an art exhibit in a side gallery at the Opera House, until finally she knew that, try as she might, she was not going to succeed in escaping him.

But knowing it didn't stop her from trying. Liv trudged up and down endless streets in the drizzle, lurked in the underground Opernpassage until she was sure someone would have her arrested for loitering, and stood on the street corner at the end of Uli's block absorbing the rain for so long that she thought it possible that the neighbor might come to think of her as just another bit of local sculpture. But finally, shortly past ten that night, she could wait no longer. At last there was no light on in the living room of the flat, so she thought Joe might have gone to bed. She hoped so. She had no desire to see him, to hear about his lovely afternoon with Veronique or, worse, not to hear about it but be met by awkward, embarrassed silences instead.

She let herself into the downstairs hallway and, shutting the main door heavily, sprinting for the steps, remembering that Uli told her there would be light for two minutes after she opened the door. If she didn't make it to her flat by then, she would have to creep along, feeling her way up the walls to find another button and get another two minutes. So she raced as fast as she could, her feet slipping in her damp shoes. Out of breath, she had just inserted the key in Mrs. Carvalho's door when the lights went out.

"Damn," she muttered, but at least she was home free. No need to grope now. She turned the key and eased the door open, slipping into the entryway, which was as black as the hall she just left.

"Do you know what time it is?" a hard voice rasped in her ear.

"Oh!" Her head jerked up and collided with his jaw. "You frightened the wits out of me! I thought you'd be asleep."

"With you out roaming the streets of Vienna alone?"

She could feel his breath on her neck, and although he wasn't touching her, he might as well have been. She had never been more aware of him. And was that anger in his voice? Anger? After he had spent all afternoon with the sexiest French actress this side of the Seine?

"Where have you been?" he snarled, flipping on the light and dragging her after him into the living room as if she were a piece of furniture.

"Shopping. Doing a bit more research for Marv's articles." She tried to jerk her arm away, but he wouldn't let go.

"Till ten-thirty at night?" He sounded outraged.

"I had a lot to see," she said defensively. "Why?" She tried to inject a note of calmness into her voice that she was far from feeling. "You weren't really worried, were you?" How had he had the time?

"Damn right I was!" he exploded. "You were gone for hours!"

"I thought I left you quite well occupied," she said, unable to keep the spite out of her voice.

"Hardly. Veronique left," he said in flat tones, "not long after you did as a matter of fact. She was here to deliver another pitch from Luther. He sent her to see if I'd do the Steve Scott flick if she were the leading lady." He sounded thoroughly annoyed and Liv couldn't contain a surge of gladness.

"And would you?" she ventured.

"What the hell do you think?" he demanded raggedly. "I want to do Pío and Elena. I don't want to act any more for a while—if ever. Besides, don't think she'd do it with me. She thinks chicken pox are disgusting. She thinks I'll be scarred for life, that my career as a leading man is over." His voice shook, but whether with fury or with something else, Liv didn't know. "You'd think I had smallpox, not chicken pox," he mumbled.

"Joe." Liv put her hand on his arm, suddenly singing inside, wanting only to love him and reassure him, forgetting completely that she had been cursing him all day long. His day had been nothing like she had imagined—he must have sat alone and brooded for hours while she walked around and did the same. Oh, was she a fool! Her fingers curled around his forearm.

"You'd better get changed," he said gruffly, shrugging her arm off. "You'll get pneumonia, otherwise."

Helpless, baffled, she watched as he turned and stalked out of the room. The bedroom door shut behind her and she was alone. Confused, she stood and dripped on the Oriental carpet, wondering where his anger had gone and, even more important, what emotion had replaced it.

Shutting off the light, she opened the door to the bedroom and went in, glancing over at his still form huddled in the dark beneath the eiderdown. Joe made no sound at all, so she gathered up her gown and robe and disappeared into the bathroom without breaking the silence.

They ought to be falling into one another's arms right now. Why weren't they? She shook her head wearily, puzzled. Lying back in the tub, soaking in neck-deep frothy water, she wondered what to do next, but no answers appeared. The long, hot soak was soothing as far as it went, but she was no nearer understanding Joe now than she had been when she began. Sighing she got out, drying off and then brushing her hair, putting off the moment when she would have to return to the room they shared. He might be asleep, she thought. But when she tiptoed back in, she knew she was hoping to find him sitting up, wanting to talk to her. But he hadn't moved. The lump under the eiderdown was as inert as it had been before. Sighing she slipped under her own comforter and lay unmoving as her eyes adjusted to the darkness of the room.

The rain beat a steady tattoo on the windowpane, and she thought how appropriate it sounded, damp and dismal like the feelings growing inside her. Tomorrow they would go home. Home to what? She felt a dull ache begin somewhere behind her eyes, tears pricking. But she held them back, forcing herself to swallow hard, blinking for all she was worth. She needed to look about the room, not cry, to memorize the black shapes and shadows, to store up images and memories so that she could take them out and see them again when Vienna, and possibly Joe Harrington, were only a part of her past. She bit her lip.

Was it over between them? Had her foolish excursion until all hours of the night, while he sat here and fumed, finished something that she now felt had barely even started? What else could she think? She had known great joy when she had discovered that he had spent the day alone, that he had been worried about her, angry at her. But her joy had turned to pain when, inexplicably, he had turned away. Why? She frowned into the darkness, puzzled, wondering.

"Liv?" It was almost a whisper, so soft that if a car had been passing in the rain-slicked street below, she never would have heard him. But she did, and her eyes flew to the figure across the room as he shifted in the darkness.

"What?"

"I... I'm sorry. I shouldn't have yelled at you."

Yell away, she thought. She rolled onto her side and stared across the shadowy room at him, seeing only the shaggy outline of his hair and the bare arm propping him up. "It doesn't matter," she said, fingers clenching around her comforter.

For a moment she thought he would lie down and go to sleep, but then he sighed. "It's been quite a week. I'm sorry for that, too."

"Don't be." It had been a wonderful week in its way—just the two of them together.

"It wasn't what I'd planned at all," he said ruefully and sat up, swinging his legs over the side of the bed. "There were so many places I wanted to take you, to show you...." His voice drifted off into an aching void that pained her and she shook her head, about to deny again that it mattered. But suddenly he stood up, hesitated a second, and then crossed the room, sinking down to sit on the edge of her bed. Instinctively, pulses hammering, heart racing, she inched over to give him room beside her. "Did you have a good time today?" he asked somewhat wistfully.

"Um, yes," she croaked, her leg sliding against his as his weight depressed the edge of the bed. "But I wish you had been with me," she added. Her hand crept out from beneath the comforter, daring to move close to his bare thigh but not touching it.

"Not like this, you wouldn't," he said, rubbing a week's growth of brown beard.

"I like your werewolf look," she said, smiling. "Anyway, it's your company I value, not your handsome face."

He smiled then. She could see the curve of his cheek change in the profile view she had, and his hand found hers, squeezing it gently, then tracing delicate patterns on the sensitive inside of her wrist. She felt a shiver of anticipation run through her. "Veronique would have run screaming if I'd touched her," he said softly.

"I'm not Veronique." Another time Liv would have bristled at the comparison, but tonight Veronique was of no more significance than the leaky faucet back home. This was the night she had waited for; this was the man she loved. She drew his fingers to her lips and kissed them one by one, delighted to feel him shudder against her.

"No, thank goodness, you're not," he murmured and closed his eyes. Her lashes fluttered against his hand as she drew it against her cheek and then kissed the palm of it, darting out her tongue to tease its warmth. He sucked in his breath sharply and his fingers trembled. "I imagined all sorts of awful things when you didn't come back," he said raggedly. "You hurt. You gone. You...." He shuddered again. "I thought you weren't coming back."

She reached for him then, pulling his head down, finding his lips with her own, and the tight rein of control that he had hung onto all week snapped completely. He kissed her with a hunger that astonished her, his lips hard and demanding, his tongue seeking, probing, tasting, his hands drawing her up against him so that she could feel the heavy thudding of his heart. The blood pounded like white water through her veins.

"Liv! Oh, Liv!" he mumbled against her cheek, his beard brushing her face softly, smooth one way, rough the other. "This week's been torture! Hell, for months it's been torture! Please, Liv—" But whatever he was going to say was never spoken, and the feverish, desperate kisses began again, and Liv was drowning along with him. There was no one to save her now.

He slid into the bed alongside her, their bodies touching from toes to mouths, hardness and softness melting together, seeking a unity too long denied. For a fleeting instant Liv remembered Tom's telling her that she wasn't the passionate sort and thought, he should see me now. But her giggle was muffled in the warmth of Joe's lips.

"What is it?" he muttered.

She replied, "Nothing," and was overjoyed to realize that it was true. Tom was over, past. What he thought totally ceased to matter. What mattered was Joe, only Joe. Now and forever, Joe. And she rolled over onto him, pressing him into the sheets, feathering kisses across his chest.

"What are you doing?" he gasped, catching her face between his hands.

"Kissing your scabs." She grinned at him in the moonlight that peeked suddenly through a break in the clouds as the rain stopped. "I think if I do a thorough job of it, I just might cover your whole body."

"You might," he growled, grinning back. "But don't expect me to last that long." But he didn't object further, lying back and letting her have her way a while longer, watching her with a kind of glazed astonishment on his face, and she remembered that Veronique wouldn't have touched him. She smiled, her tongue slipping between her lips to trace a circle around his navel and then dip inside.

His strong arms suddenly engulfed her, pulling her up against his chest and then tugging the nightgown over her head, so that she lay naked against him. Gently, skillfully, his hands molded her to him, smoothing down her back and over the curve of her hip, running lightly up the inner sides of her thighs, so that she ground her hips against his, aching for him, her desire as strong as his. Her fingers slipped inside the waistband of his shorts, and she lifted herself to her knees above him, sliding the shorts down over his narrow hips and strong thighs. Joe kicked them away impatiently and pulled her down again, rolling her over and lying on his side against her. His right hand came up to cup her breast, to stroke it to a taut peak before his lips came down to caress it with liquid softness. Liv tossed her head, burning, needing, aching.

"Do you know what it's like to envy a bunch of little kids?" he groaned, his mouth still planting kisses on both breasts.

"What?"

"Your kids. They'd known you for years, hugged you, kissed you. Cripes, at my house Jennifer even slept with you," he muttered. He got to his knees, hands still moving over her, memorizing her body. Then he bent his head, showering her abdomen with kisses, his hands going before him, smoothing the way, increasing her anticipation, her readiness, sending flames of desire shooting through her.

"Joe!" She tugged at his hair, her fingers twining in the dark, unruly locks, dragging him up against her, needing his warmth, his passion, his love. "Joe, please. . . ."

"Mmm." His hot breath caressed her ear as he lifted himself slightly, then gently lowered, fitting between her thighs as Liv welcomed him, drawing him down, urging him on. She was gripped in a wild, tempestuous delight, an ecstasy that knew no name, and her arms and legs tightened around him, fitting to his rhythm, mindless of everything but Joe now. She knew neither past nor future—only this—that this loving was the proper, the deepest, expression of what she felt for him. She loved him wholly and completely, holding nothing back. Her back arched, stars blazed, spirits soared and they became one together.

Weakened, spent, yet whole at last, Liv tasted the salty perspiration on Joe's shoulder, felt his galloping heart next to her own and smiled. A sense of completeness, of inevitability overwhelmed her. She had shown him her deepest feelings; she had given him her love. Her hand drifted down his sweat-dampened back, stroking the smooth skin and rough scabs, loving them all. "I love you, Joe," she whispered and settled easily onto her side, curving her back into his chest and wrapping his arms around to hold against her. She felt his cheek against her hair. "I love you," she murmured again, sleepiness overcoming her. "I do." And her eyes flickered shut and she slept, content and at peace in his arms.

It was Joe who lay, eyes open, for the remainder of the night.

Chapter Eleven

The bright morning sun said it all. Liv hummed as she set out the cups and sliced the bread, her movements quick and deft, her lips curved into the smile she'd been wearing since she'd awakened an hour before.

The temptation to lie in bed and watch Joe sleep had been almost overwhelming. She loved the strong line of his jaw, now blurred with a week's worth of beard, the slight irregularity of the bridge of his nose where he'd broken it playing football as a boy, the soft mahogany hair that drifted across his forehead, more red than brown in the sunlight shining on it. It was an indulgence that she couldn't completely deny herself. Too soon she would be bolting out of bed in the morning, hustling the kids off to school, and such luxuries would be as remote as Madison seemed now. So she had watched him, trying to synchronize her breathing with the deep evenness of his, tracing with her eyes the groove in his cheek, the tiny lines from laughter and hard living that fanned out around his eyes. And then, resolutely, she had slipped from the bed without waking him. Noting the dark shadows under his eyes and deciding to let him sleep as long as she could, she took a shower and fixed herself some breakfast. Then she fixed Joe's breakfast, too.

She had been fixing him breakfast for days, but this morning it meant more, took on a new significance. It was a small task, but done for the man she loved, the man who knew now without a doubt how much she loved him. She poured herself a cup of coffee and added milk, stirring it absently as she sat in the dining room in the warm sunshine and remembered with even greater interior warmth their lovemaking of the night before.

"Hi. Pour me a cup, will you?" Joe appeared in the doorway, hair uncombed and eyes bleary, but already dressed in gray slacks and buttoning up a long-sleeved, pale blue oxford-cloth shirt. He was barefoot and disgruntled looking, and Liv smiled at him as she poured the coffee. She handed it to him, longing to reach up and kiss his cheek, actually moved to do it, but he said, "Thanks," and took a long swallow, vanishing again into the bedroom as he did so. She heard him rummaging around in his suitcase, and moments later he reappeared, knotting a regimental striped tie around his collar.

"Hadn't you better be getting ready to leave?" he asked.

Liv felt her brows draw together as she frowned. Where were the good-morning kiss and the smile she had been expecting? As if he could read her mind, he suddenly bent down and kissed her hard and quick, then stood up and began buttering a slice of rye, saying, "When we get back to Madison you can move your stuff into my place and put yours up for rent."

"What?" She stared, a funny, hollow feeling growing where she had felt comfortably full of breakfast just moments before.

He flicked her a quick glance, then concentrated on the bread. "I said—"

"I heard what you said," Liv told him, feelings of dread building. "What did you mean?"

Joe stopped buttering the bread. "Move in with me. Live with me. Cohabit." His voice was calm, matter-of-fact, but he was holding the knife in a death grip, and Liv felt suddenly cold, as if the sun had gone behind a cloud. She dropped a piece of bread into the toaster, not really wanting it, but needing something to do.

"I can't," she said finally.

He looked at her then. Stared, his brows drawn down in a dark line, his eyes hard and grim like dull jade. "Why?"

Why? How could she answer that? "Because, because...I thought...." How did you say, "I thought we'd get married? I thought you'd be my husband and I'd be your wife and we'd live happily ever after"? She closed her eyes briefly, groping for the words which seemed to slip further out of reach.

"You said you loved me," Joe reminded her. He was leaning against Mrs. Carvalho's dark walnut buffet, looking fierce and menacing with a backdrop of delicate tea cups and porcelain horses.

"I do. I do love you." There was no point in denying it now, even though every rational thought told her to, told her to cover her weaknesses and retreat, defending herself however she could.

"Well, then...." He was looking annoyed, his fingers busy destroying the bread on his plate, crumbling it into little mounds and moving them around distractedly.

"First of all, I won't do it because of the kids. My kids know that I think what Tom did was wrong. I won't turn around now and do the same thing, too. And I won't have them subjected to more gossip. Goodness knows, having Tom for a father brought enough of that." She knew she was making a bad job of it, stumbling, breathless, her voice jerky, not saying the things that mattered the most.

"The kids like me," Joe argued.

"That's not the point! They deserve a stable life, a—"

"They were stable with us while they had chicken pox!"

"For two weeks. How long do you want to live with me? Two weeks? Two months? Two years?" She was shaking and clenched her hands in her lap, hoping he wouldn't notice.

"Who knows? Forever, maybe."

"Maybe?" Scorn dripped from her voice and she knew it. The knife slammed down on Joe's plate. The toast popped up, burned.

"Maybe. Nothing's certain. You ought to know that!" His voice rose as he loomed over her. "I suppose you want me to propose," he growled, his dark head bent over the plate in his hand.

"I suppose I do," she said quietly.

Neither of them spoke; the silence stretched like a mine field between them, each step fraught with potential for disaster. Liv held her breath, her sunny day suddenly banked with thunderclouds. She heard a distant rumble and was surprised to realize that it was only a passing truck.

"Marriage is a trap, a cage," he said finally, each word driving a nail into her heart. "It's a convention that has destroyed more relationships than I care to count."

"Lots of marriages last," Liv argued. "My parents' marriage has."

"So has my parents'," Joe said heavily. "They're the best example of what I'm talking about that I can think of."

Liv was puzzled. "What do you mean?"

"My father married my mother because it was the thing to do; it was expected. They've rubbed along together for forty-six years, and neither one of them has done a spontaneous, interesting thing in the thirty-six years I've known them. Maybe they never have; I wouldn't be surprised. Their marriage is dead, lifeless, a shell. Nothing like what I had with you last night." He looked up from his plate and she could see the seriousness in his gaze, and she wanted to deny everything he was saying, but she, too, knew of marriages like that. And how could she convince him that a marriage between the two of them would be any different?

"For years I avoided anything that remotely resembled what they had," he went on. "I had plenty of affairs, as you well know, but I never once asked a woman to live with me, not even for two days."

Liv swallowed hard, her mouth tasting of burned toast. "I'm sorry," she said into her napkin. "I still can't do it. I love you too much."

It was Joe's turn to stare. "Come again?"

She twisted her napkin around her fingers. "It would hurt too much," she began slowly, picking her way through the mine field. "I don't want anything less than all of you, just as I would give you all of myself."

"I gave you all of me last night!"

"Your body," she corrected.

"Yes, what's wrong with that?"

"Nothing. It's just not enough. I want a commitment. I want you—as husband, as father. Till death do us part."

It sounded like a sentence, not a benediction, but Liv folded her hands and bowed her head, waiting for the storm to break.

"The plane leaves in less than two hours," Joe said, picking up his plate and carrying it out to the kitchen. "You'd better get packed."

ALL THE WAY BACK to Madison she waited for a miracle—the smile that never came, the words that were so loudly unspoken that they reverberated in her head. But she waited in vain. The issue was decided; the case was closed. Joe was polite, attentive, and as distant as if she had left him standing in the Wien-Schwechat Airport instead of sitting with his pale blue, knife-creased sleeve brushing hers.

She remembered the chasm that had opened at her feet the night that Tom had announced that he wanted a divorce and knew that it was nothing compared to the emotional Grand Canyon before her now. But there was nothing she could do to close it. He had made his offer, his compromise that was, she admitted, more than he had ever offered anyone else. But she could not accept it, would not accept it. And that was that.

She had the satisfaction, grim and useless though it was, of knowing at least that she had tried. She had loved him, had given him her all, and Joe Harrington could never say he hadn't known. There were no sins of omission to be held over her head in this relationship. But sometimes, no matter what one did, it wasn't enough.

Liv shut her eyes and tipped her seat back, feigning sleep, wishing it would overtake her and obliterate the black fog of depression that surrounded her. Four more hours to O'Hare, a short hop to Madison. Home before nightfall. She squeezed her eyes tighter, refusing to let the threatening tears leak out. Home. But a home without Joe. And what kind of a home was that?

A welcoming one, if nothing else. Frantic babbling, hugging, kissing, shouting greeted them at the airport. Blond heads and brown ones bobbed around Ellie, then broke loose as small bodies hurled themselves on both Liv and Joe, nearly knocking them to the ground.

"Didja have fun?"

"What did you bring home?"

"How come you grew a beard, Joe?"

"Wait'll you see what Frances bought for your room, Ma!"

None of them noticed her pale cheeks and haunted eyes. No one commented on Joe's edginess and haunted look. Only Ellie stared—and stared—and knew. Liv could tell by her compressed lips, sad face and the resignation that had replaced her initial welcoming smile.

"Shall we go, then?" Ellie asked and began to lead the way toward the baggage claim area, but Joe shook his head and hung back.

"I have to go on," he said.

"What?" Liv's and Ellie's voices joined in chorus.

"To L.A.," he said hastily. "I have to get back to L.A."

"Now?" There was only Ellie's voice, sharp and incredulous, this time.

"Uh-huh," he patted his jacket pocket which seemed to have a sheaf of paper in it. "Meeting Luther about a contract," he explained, edging away.

Ellie just stared.

"But Joe," Ben said, "You just got here!" All the kids looked crestfallen, Liv noticed. Damn, why couldn't they just dislike him? It would be so much easier to believe that she was absolutely doing the right thing if she knew they didn't like him, if she was sure they wouldn't want her to live with him.

Joe shrugged, looking decidedly uncomfortable under their stares. "I'm sorry," he said to Ben. "I really do have to go."

"When are you comin' back?" Theo demanded.

"I don't know."

Never, Liv could have answered for him. She almost offered to pack up his things at the house and send them along to him, but why make it any easier for him than it already was?

"You gotta come to my game," Noel told him. "We're in the championships. It's two weeks from Sunday." Joe had attended more of Noel's ball games than Tom ever had, Liv knew. It had thrilled the boy that someone as busy as Joe was so interested. And now he wouldn't be there for that either. *My fault,* Liv thought, but knew she couldn't change her mind now. Nor did she want to. But it didn't seem fair that doing the right thing was always so hard!

"I'll try," Joe promised, and Liv looked to see if he had his fingers crossed, but his hand was stuck in his pants pocket, so she couldn't tell. Most likely they were. She doubted, once he'd got back aboard a plane, that they'd ever see Joe Harrington in Madison again. "If I don't make it, send me a card and tell me the score," Joe told Noel.

"Come on," Ellie said to the kids, hustling them toward the luggage turnaround. "Let's get the suitcases and give your mother a chance to say goodbye to Joe."

Liv grimaced, wanting to turn and run, following her children away from the biggest heartbreak in her life. But she couldn't move. She was rooted to the spot, devouring him, soaking up last impressions like a thirsty daisy in the rain. His tie was crooked, and a tiny scab was peeling off by the outside corner of his left eye. He ran a finger beneath his collar, then stuck his hand back in his pocket and stared at her as well. Was there nothing left to say?

She heard the last boarding call for the return flight to O'Hare and knew that he heard it, too, but neither of them moved. Eyes fenced, parried, memorized. Loved. Then she heard his voice, very low. "If you ever change your mind...."

Her teeth sunk into her lower lip, drawing blood. "I won't," she told him, sadness piercing her. "Goodbye, Joe."

He nodded slowly, his hand coming up out of his pocket to brush lightly along the curve of her cheek, his eyes as sad as her own. His lips came down, touching hers briefly, and the pain of longing welled up inside her, overpowering her, consuming her. She blinked, and blinked again. And he was gone.

WHAT FRANCES HAD bought for her bedroom was a two-foot by three-foot poster of Steve Scott at his cocky handsomeness, and after Liv had finished exclaiming over it, listening to what had happened in her absence and telling abbreviated enthusiastic accounts of a week in an apartment with Joe and five hundred chicken pox, she thought there ought to be Academy Awards given for performances in real life.

"It's just jet lag," she excused herself whenever she dropped the thread of the conversation, whenever the kids asked why she was staring off into space, chewing on her fingernail or wiping a stray tear from her eye.

"Let your mother sleep," Ellie counseled. "You'll have plenty of time to talk to her in the morning. I'll stay over tonight and ride herd on your crew," she told Liv. "Then you can get some rest." Before Liv could thank her, Ellie hustled everyone out of the bedroom, leaving Liv staring up at Joe on the wall, larger than life and twice as seductive.

She pulled the pillow over her head and sobbed her heart out.

In the morning she thought, *I've been here before; I know the terrain. I can make it through again.* It was not unlike the feeling she had had after Tom left. The same emptiness, the pain, the moving about as though she had lead weights on her feet and a sack over her head. But, before, she had had anger and the near-hatred of Tom for his faithlessess to sustain her. Now she felt no hatred, no anger, only weariness and a bone-deep sadness as she contemplated months, years, a whole lifetime, without Joe.

One day at a time, she told herself as she got out of bed, rejecting her oldest, most comfortable pair of jeans and a T-shirt as being a cop-out. If she let herself dress like a slob she would feel like a slob. And heaven knew she didn't need that. She took pains with her hair, twisting it up on the back of her head and braiding it so that she looked sophisticated and proper. If anyone had a right to look proper, she did! She stared hard at the Steve Scott poster and reconsidered her first impulse, which had been to tear it down, rip it to shreds and feed it to the rabbit. There would be the problem of explaining her actions to the children, of course, but more than that, if she left it up she would get desensitized sooner. Like being innoculated against allergies. Exposure to the allergy-causing substance over time, in controlled dosage, was supposed to cure. *Well,* she thought, bending to tie her tennis shoes, *I hope it works because if anyone needs a cure now, it's me.*

"Skunk, isn't he?" Ellie said flatly as she scrambled some eggs for Liv and thrust them in front of her, commanding, "Eat. I will not allow you to pine away because of that miserable bastard."

"Ellie!" Liv said, shocked, "he's your brother!"

"And getting heavier by the minute," Ellie retorted. "I think I'll trade him in." She poured Liv a cup of coffee and refilled her own cup. "Dare I ask what happened?"

"Only if you promise not to put it in a play."

"I promise. I don't write tragedies anyway. And by the look of you, that's what this one is."

"He did offer to let me move in with him," Liv said, wondering why she was defending him, for heaven's sake.

"Big of him," Ellie snorted. "I suppose he'd let you iron his shirts if you asked him nicely."

"Well, maybe," Liv said, a smile twitching her lips. She felt as though her face might crack, as though it had been years since she had smiled although it was really only yesterday. "He's afraid of marriage, I think," she said slowly. She didn't say, "He's doesn't love me," because, even though he hadn't actually said it, she thought he really did. He just didn't think in those terms. Or hadn't for years, anyway.

"He needs his head examined," Ellie muttered. She jumped up and rummaged under the sink, dragging out a pail and filling it with water.

"What are you doing?" Liv asked through a mouthful of surprisingly tasty eggs.

"Washing the floor," Ellie spat, tossing one of Joe's old undershirts into the hot, foamy water. "I need to do something strenuous, like wringing his neck. And since he isn't here, this is my only alternative. I'll pretend I'm drowning him instead."

PANIC.

"'S too bright!"

Fear.

"Shut the light off!"

Flight.

"It's the sun, you idiot! Sit up and drink this." Mike McPherson's voice grated in Joe's ear, and an arm came around his shoulders, hauling him to a sitting position. There were storm troopers on maneuvers in his head. A glass was thrust under his nose against his lips and tipped. Obediently he opened his mouth, swallowed, gagged, choked, spat.

"What is that?" he croaked, coughing. "Are you trying to kill me?"

"Don't ask," Mike said dryly. "As for killing you, I think you're doing quite a good enough job trying to kill yourself." He tipped the glass again and wouldn't stop until Joe had drained half the liquid in it. Then Mike let him slide back down against the crumpled sheets, where he lay moaning, eyes screwed tightly shut. "There, that should do it."

"Do what?" Joe wasn't sure he wanted to know. His consciousness was like a shattered mirror, pieces reflecting tiny impressions, sensations, a glimmering of reality, nothing more. And, like the jagged edges of a broken mirror, they hurt, each one cutting into his brain like a knife.

"Turn you into a reasonable facsimile of yourself," Mike replied. "And when you can open your eyes, I think I'd like some answers."

"So would I," Joe mumbled. *I'd even like some questions.* At the moment his universe didn't extend beyond the confines of his own throbbing head. His eyeballs seemed to have rusted. Moving them was an excruciating ordeal, as if he hadn't used them in years. He lifted a heavy hand and touched the lids, wondering if he would have to pry them open. His hand brushed against the softness of his bearded cheek, and his forehead wrinkled, perplexed. A beard? Then a bit of the mirror came into focus and he groaned, remembering.

"I'd leave you to your misery," Mike said, "but your darling niece is having a swimming party here this afternoon, and I don't want you wandering out into the middle of it. I don't think you're up to it." Joe could tell he was grinning just from the sound of his voice. "And I doubt if her guests are either."

"I don't even know what I'm doing here," Joe said plaintively as he experimentally wiggled an eyebrow. Even that hurt. "I can't remember a thing about it."

"I know. I brought you."

"What... how...." He struggled, trying to fit the pieces together, but they wouldn't come.

"First I want some answers," Mike said, and Joe got one eye open long enough to see concern on his brother-in-law's face. "I'll tell you how you got here when you tell me how you ended up out cold on Linda Lucas's living-room floor, while I thought you were still in Vienna—or at least Madison—with a very respectable lady."

It all came back with a crash. The lying awake all night, Liv's body curled warmly into his own, her "I love you" echoing in his ears for hours, her kisses, his scabs, his offer, her rejection. Then more hours on an airplane than he believed possible, followed by booze he didn't need, a phone call to Linda Lucas and.... His mind reeled. He wanted to vomit. He wanted to cry.

"That bad?" Mike asked, his voice gentler than Joe had ever heard it, no doubt in response to the emotions he saw on Joe's face.

Bad? Worse. Worst. Joe nodded infinitesimally, shutting his eyes again, wishing for more of the blessed oblivion he'd just emerged from. Painful as it was, it couldn't hurt more than this.

"Want to talk about it?"

"Can't." How could he tell anyone what had happened, explain his panic, his fears, the feelings that knowing she loved him had aroused in him. It didn't make sense. It wasn't reasonable, he didn't suppose. But it was real. He'd felt it.

Mike thrust the glass at him. "Finish this and get dressed. I'm taking you down to the boat. That way no one will stumble over you here by mistake."

"Boat?" The very thought nauseated him.

"Docked," Mike promised with a grin. "As a refuge, not for a sail. Don't panic."

But Joe knew the advice had come too late. He already had panicked, and now he had to live with it. He struggled up, swinging his legs over the edge of the bed as though he were a hundred-year-old man. He held his head in his hands. Mike pressed his glasses on him and Joe scowled up at him.

"You look like an owl," Mike told him. "The beard does wonders. I couldn't imagine it when Linda called, but I think I kind of like it."

"She called you?" Joe was beginning to get an idea of how he'd got here now. He remembered going to Linda's drunk, done in from jet lag, chicken pox, and the thought of a future without Liv. But then everything went blank.

"Oh, yes," Mike agreed. "Most interesting phone call of the day. Frantic female voice squealing, 'Joe Harrington's full of hair and scabs, and he's just passed out on my living-room floor!'" Mike laughed. "Talk about intriguing. Hurry up, will you? I'll wait in the kitchen. Don't take forever."

Why not, Joe wondered as he hauled himself to his feet, weaving unsteadily as he tried to stick one foot into his pants. What else did he have to do with his forever? What good was a forever without Liv?

LIV THOUGHT she could write a book just filled with the clichés she was collecting that were supposed to help her get over her affair with Joe Harrington. The most often heard was "Time heals all," and if she heard it one more time she thought that nothing would heal the person she murdered for having said it. People tiptoed around her at work as though she was the bereaved widow of a fifty-year marriage. They all cast her sympathetic glances when they thought she wasn't looking and began talking loudly about their geraniums or grandchildren or how the Brewers were doing and the Cubs weren't, so that they wouldn't inadvertently say anything that would upset her more. She thought she would go insane. But short of calling a press conference and announcing that it was no big deal, that Joe Harrington habitually walked out of women's lives and she had had no right to expect him not to walk out of hers, she didn't know what to do.

"It'll be a nine-day wonder," Frances promised her, smiling confidently over her knitting.

Liv looked up from the feature she was writing on pick-your-own apple orchards for the mid-September Sunday edition and scowled. "It's already going on fourteen," she reminded her friend.

Frances looked at her as though she disapproved of the truth, but then brightened considerably. "Well, it certainly has made Tom sit up and take notice. You have to admit that."

Liv did. Tom, having taken an offer to move his practice to Phoenix, was dropping by regularly now. Ostensibly he was there to spend time with the kids before leaving, but he spent most of his visits lurking in the kitchen, watching Liv stir the spaghetti sauce or make pudding, and saying things like "You'd love Phoenix this time of year." He never mentioned Joe to her, though Ben had said that his father had expressed pleasure when he learned that Joe Harrington seemed to have forgotten that Madison—and Liv—existed anymore.

Liv, for her part, was wishing she could forget him. She didn't cry herself to sleep at night anymore, and she could stare at her Steve Scott poster for upwards of four minutes without having her pulse race. But her feelings for Joe were nowhere near as dead as she wished they were, nowhere near as dead as her feelings for Tom.

Tom could come and go as he pleased for all she cared. She scarcely even noticed. And all his hints about them all moving to Phoenix and starting over together—Trudy now having gone the way of the previous eight or ten other women in his life—went in one ear and out the other. She sat next to him at Noel's championship baseball game and never felt a thing. Except regret that Joe had not been there.

She had held out a tiny, flickering hope, scarcely even admitting it to herself, that he might be there. He had known how important the game was to Noel. But she had spent more time watching the stands than the game, and she knew, positively and completely, that while the game had come and gone, Joe had not.

But it wasn't until Frances bustled in with her gossip magazine the following Friday that Liv's hopes well and truly died. Frances kept the magazine away from her, reading it like a teenager with a dirty book, stashing it between the covers of the weekly TV guide, but her gasps and cluckings couldn't be ignored. When she went out to lunch with George, Liv's curiosity could be contained no longer.

How far I've sunk, she thought as she rummaged furtively through Frances's desk drawer. And how much further she fell when she opened it to see a splashy two-page article on the latest Steve Scott film, now in the works, and pictures of a smiling Luther Nelson, his arms around the two co-stars, Joe Harrington and Veronique Moreau.

When she got home that night there was a postcard of a turquoise bay on Grand Cayman, West Indies. "Here researching next possible comedy," Ellie had written. "Gave up on my movie star-divorcée play. Some plots are too far-fetched even for me."

"Amen," Liv said to the rabbit, last hope buried, and thumped the pot of spaghetti sauce on the stove to reheat it for supper.

Chapter Twelve

The infamous contract for the next Steve Scott film had been burning a hole first in Joe's pocket and then in his bedside table for two and a half weeks, ever since Veronique had pressed it on him that afternoon in Vienna. And Luther had been burning a hole in his ear for just as long. The low pressure tactics of suggestions, hints, bribes and a visit to Madison had got Luther Nelson nowhere. Now he was hauling out the big guns—Veronique Moreau, a contract promising casting veto, script control and a percentage of the gross, a cut of subsidiary profits and so on. And Joe, at first hanging onto a future of writing and directing, of Pío and Elena and Liv knew, having lost Liv, that he was slipping, that he might at any minute give in.

Luther knew it, too. That was why he planted the article in the magazines. A fait accompli announced to the press would be harder to deny, and Joe, faced with denying it because it simply wasn't true, wasn't even sure that he wanted to.

Maybe, he thought glumly as he rolled over onto his back and let the hot September sun of southern California bake him an even darker brown, his future lay with Steve Scott after all. Maybe his ideas of writing and directing the love-and-war story of Pío and Elena were nothing more than dreams. Like Liv.

She still had the power to spear him, to make him forget where he was and what he was saying, if even for a moment her face flickered into his mind or a woman walked by with a walk like hers or blond hair that caught in the breeze in a Liv-like way. Even now he could see her against the red of his sunbaked eyelids. Damn her anyway. She had no business getting under his skin this way. He ought to be able to pick up and forget her in a minute. Heaven knew, all the others had been easy enough to forget. And the string of beauties he had wined and dined since coming back to L.A. should have had some effect.

But Liv wasn't wearing off at all. He saw her everywhere he went, day and night. She was in his thoughts, in his memories, even in his bed—her phantom caresses driving him mad. He shifted uncomfortably on the hot, sticky cushion of the lounge, all too aware of the effect that merely thinking about her was having on him. A cold dip in the pool wouldn't be amiss right now. He sprang to his feet and dived in, letting the shock of the unheated pool water do what his firmest resolutions couldn't.

"Luther was on the phone," Tim Gates told him when he dragged himself up on the pool's edge forty laps later. "Says he wants you and Veronique for a press conference tomorrow."

"To give credence to his premature story?" Joe asked sarcastically, annoyed but grudgingly admiring of Luther's persistence.

"Of course," Tim grinned. "It's not a bad idea, really. You were a great Steve Scott. This other whim of yours—this writing business—might not succeed, you know," he added tentatively. He dropped easily into one of the lounges around Joe's naturally-landscaped pool and tugged his Lacoste shirt over his head. Then, lying back, he began to sort slowly through an inch-high stack of mail.

"I know," Joe said slowly, deep breaths heaving his chest as he dripped onto the Spanish tile and wished that he were still under the water swimming. No one asked anything of people under water. But once you got out—watch out, he thought. Luther was waiting the moment he stuck his head up. And Tim. And heaven knew how many other interested parties who thought that their livelihoods might be threatened if Joe Harrington refused to be Steve Scott one more time. Liv didn't think so, he remembered. She didn't seem to care what he did, as long as he wanted to do it. She encouraged his writing, his non-acting desires. Damn, there he was, thinking about her again. "Toss me a towel," he growled at Tim. "I'll let Luther know later."

"Right," Tim said, handing him a chocolate-brown bath towel. "Here." He thrust a picture postcard into Joe's hand. "The rest of this is business, but you might like to have a personal note of your own."

There was a lake on the postcard, blue and inviting. Like Lake Mendota, he thought with a sudden yearning as he flipped it over. It was Lake Mendota. He swallowed hard, his hands suddenly trembling. God, let it be from Liv! His eyes quickly scanned down to the signature. Noel.

"Sorry you couldn't be at my game. I know you were probably too busy. We won 8-5. I hit a triple. I wish you could of come but that's okay. Mom and Dad were there," he read silently. He stood stock still, water dripping from his hair, smudging the words before his eyes. Mom and Dad? He felt as though the breath were being squeezed out of him, as if he were suffocating, smothering. "Mom and Dad were there?" he mumbled, rereading. "No," he said aloud. "No."

"Huh?" Tim looked up, puzzled. "What's wrong?"

"N-nothing. Nothing." Everything. Did that mean what he thought it meant? Liv and Tom? Liv was back together with Tom? No, she couldn't be. He wouldn't let her. Liv was his now, not Tom's. His. Always. Forever. His.

He loped up the steps through the garden to the house, going through the chrome-and-glass living room and down the elegant hallway to the rust-and-cream master bedroom, where he opened the top drawer of his bedside table and took out the picture of Liv. This was the first time he had allowed himself to look at it since he had come back. But now he needed to, desperately. His hands were shaking, his mouth dry. "No," he muttered and sank down on the bed, heedless of the damp towel around his hips, his mind totally consumed by the woman in the grainy black-and-white photo, nose-to-nose with the zoning commissioner, making her point.

"You can't, Liv," he whispered, dropping back on the bed, staring up at the worn clipping he held in his hands. "You can't. I love you."

And at that moment he knew that he did.

He closed his eyes, his throat tightening as he remembered her words in Vienna, "I want a commitment. I want you—as husband, as father. Till death do us part." And suddenly he knew what he should have known for weeks, that that was what he wanted, too. He wanted all of Liv—her love, her commitment, her children, for all time. He did not want to share her with other men—not with Tom, not with anyone.

He groped around on the bed, finding Noel's postcard and reading it again. And again. Maybe they weren't together. It was a big ball park, after all. Noel didn't say they came together, just that they were both there. Joe sucked in his breath and sat up, reaching for the phone. It wasn't too late yet. You hope, he reminded himself as he dialed.

"I want to book a flight on the next plane to Madison," he told the travel agent who answered. "No," he said firmly, answering her question, "One way."

"But what'll I tell Luther?" Tim wailed as Joe strode up and down his room throwing shirts and pants into his suitcases as fast as he could yank them out of drawers or pull them off hangers.

"Whatever you like. 'No' for a start. Use your imagination from there. Only for the moment, keep him away from Madison and out of my life! I don't know if I can make a go of it just writing and directing, but I intend to give it a try. I don't know if Liv will have me, but I intend to ask." He paused, turning to face Tim, his arms full of unfolded shirt. "Once I told Liv that marriage was a trap, but if there's a bigger trap than being Steve Scott with an endless procession of floozies, I don't know what it is." He crammed the assortment of clothes into the last suitcase and banged it shut.

"Luther will argue," Tim pointed out, arguing himself. "You know he will."

He would, too. Joe's eyes fell on the contract still smoldering on the bedside table. "Give him this, then," he snapped, ripping the contract down the middle. "Let it speak for itself."

"But—" Tim was aghast.

"No buts. Call me a taxi, will you? My plane leaves L.A. International in less than two hours. I don't have a minute to spare."

"I'll drive you," Tim said hastily, finally convinced that now, at least, was not the time to argue further. But it didn't stop him from saying as he dropped Joe off at the terminal, "I still think you've lost your mind."

Or found it, Joe thought, once he was on his way, first to Denver and then, after a brief change of planes, to Madison. He had plenty of time en route to consider the ramifications of his instantaneous decision, to know that it was the right one because he loved her, and to worry that it was already too late. What if, somehow, Tom had come to his senses first and Liv, despairing of Joe ever returning to his, had accepted Tom back?

Stop it, he advised himself. Don't think that way. Be positive. So he was, stopping on his way to her house in his rented Buick only long enough to pick up a magnum of champagne. He could feel his pulse accelerate, his heart quicken as he drove past the supermarket where she shopped, past Noel's school and the ball park, glimpsing the lake in the distance, and finally turning the corner of Liv's street.

He pulled over to the curb where he could see Liv's small frame house four doors down, and rested his head on the steering wheel, taking deep breaths to steady himself. He heard a door bang and looked up. Several bodies hurtled down the steps and sorted themselves out, tossing a football back and forth. Blond, Noel. Dark, Ben. Pigtails, Jennifer. And a tall man with thick, dark hair. He waved Ben back for a pass and turned to throw. Joe's stomach clenched. Tom.

"No," he muttered, shaken to the core. "Please, no." But he couldn't deny the sight before his eyes. He closed them, pained. The children's shouts and thudding feet echoed around his head, but all he really heard was the shattering of his own broken dreams.

He slumped in the seat, considering. There was the possibility, of course, that they hadn't remarried yet, that Tom wasn't definitely a permanent fixture in her life once more. He knew it would take Liv a while to come to trust Tom again. He could just get out of the car and walk up the sidewalk and challenge Tom's right to be there, his right to have again the woman he had once thrown away.

The woman I threw away too, Joe remembered miserably. He had even less right than Tom to come back and demand entrance to her life again. Still, it was tempting!

He needed her warmth, her love. He needed— Stop it, he commanded himself. Think about what Liv needs for a change. Liv needed a man who would appreciate her, love her, be a father to her children. "Me," he said aloud, but an inner voice mocked him. "Tom," it insisted. "He is after all their real father. He probably loves her, too."

Joe shook his head, wanting to deny it, but he knew it wasn't possible. Tom's reaction when he found out that Liv was going to Vienna with him had effectively scotched that. He was as jealous as Othello. No, there was no use telling himself that Tom didn't care any longer. It just wasn't true. He straightened up in the seat and let out a long, shuddering breath.

Be noble, Harrington, he told himself. *For once, do the right thing. Turn around and go away. Liv and the kids need Tom far more than they need you.* His hand hovered for a moment over the ignition key, then with shaky resolution, he turned the key and the engine sprang to life. He backed quickly down the street, not looking again at Liv's house or the children. His eyes were blurring, but he didn't want to think why. And he never saw the small blond-haired girl standing on the curb, staring at him as he drove away.

Tonight he would sleep in the lakeside house, he decided as he sped off into the sunset. Tomorrow was another day. Steve Scott would be proud, he thought with wry self-mockery. But if there was comfort in knowing that, it was small and almost worse than no comfort at all.

OLIVIA FINISHED wiping off the dinner table and flicked off the light in the kitchen. Just like old times, she thought heavily—the seven of them around the dinner table. But no matter how familiar it seemed, she knew that things had irrevocably changed. She could eat with Tom, make small talk with him, but she couldn't love him whether he wanted her love now or not. She'd had him for dinner only because the kids had wanted it.

"He's leaving Monday, Ma," Noel said.

"It's the last time we'll ever...." Stephen had pleaded.

And she hadn't had the heart to say no. And what would it hurt? Not her. Tom couldn't hurt her any more. So she had made a traditional pot roast, potatoes, carrots, green beans and fruit salad sort of Sunday meal, and they had waded through it with no major catastrophes. Now Liv was counting the minutes until it was over.

It had been hard trying not to pretend that it was Joe at the head of the table, hard, too, remembering that he was out of her life forever and that tomorrow it would be Noel's blond head she would see across the Formica tabletop.

"Guess what. I just saw Joe," Jennifer announced, banging into the kitchen and beaming at her mother.

Liv stared. "Joe? Where?" The roast beef whirled in her stomach.

"Down the street jus' now. Sittin' in a car. Then he left. He looked kinda funny."

Liv nearly knocked Jennifer over as she bolted to the living room windows to peer out.

"He's already gone," Jennifer said. "I tol' you that."

Joe? Back? "Are you sure?" Liv demanded.

"'Course I'm sure. I know Joe." Jennifer looked indignant. "Wanta come play ball now?"

"I...I don't think so." Jennifer vanished back outside and Liv sank into the tweedy overstuffed chair by the window, dazed and disoriented. Her mind skittered out of control. What had he wanted? Had he seen Tom? Why had he left again without even coming in?

Call him, she told herself. Tell him Jennifer said he came by. And then what? She snorted at her clammy hands and lurching stomach. She could not call him on the phone. She had to see him. Now. Tonight. As soon as Tom left she would go. With luck he would be at his house overnight at least.

But Tom was in no hurry to leave. He played ball with the kids until dark, then came in and played Scrabble with Noel and gin rummy with the younger boys, while Liv chivvied Jennifer off to a bath and bed. By the time she had all the boys but Noel bedded down, she thought she would go mad. Her mind was totally consumed by Joe.

She came downstairs, hoping to find Noel alone doing his homework and willing to baby-sit. Instead she found Tom, still on the couch, stocking-clad feet on the coffee table, totally absorbed in a movie on TV.

Leave, she thought, rummaging through her mending basket and beginning to patch Theo's corduroy jeans with a ferocity that surprised even her. Go home. Go to Phoenix. Go to another woman. Just leave.

"Remember when we saw this in Chicago?" Tom asked.

"Hmm? No." She took another stitch and glanced up at the screen, not having bothered to look before. Joe Harrington, ten years younger, was kissing a gorgeous blonde. Liv shut her eyes.

"Sure you do. We had dinner in Water Tower Place. And you told me I was better looking than him." Tom was smirking as he watched the screen.

Liv thrust the needle through the pants again, eyes still shut. Joe's voice, warm and slightly hoarse, spoke words of love to the stunning blonde. Was he still in town? Would she find him? Oh Tom, for heaven's sake, leave! She opened her eyes, knotted the thread and bit it off. "Finished," she said and stood up, moving purposefully toward the television and shutting it off. "Good night," she said.

Tom blinked, then reluctantly hauled himself to his feet. "Good night?" he asked.

"It's late," Liv explained, edging him toward the door. "I'm a working woman and I need my sleep. Besides, you'll want to get an early start for Phoenix tomorrow." She had thought she could wait him out, but now she knew she couldn't. Not after seeing five minutes of that movie. If she could be jealous of a woman in a ten-year-old movie, she had to get busy right now straightening out her life.

"Liv, couldn't we just—"

"No, Tom. We couldn't. Good night," she said firmly. "Good luck in Phoenix. The kids will call to say goodbye before you go." And by that time she had him on the porch. She smiled and shut the door on his back.

"Noel!" she shouted. "Noel! Baby-sit, will you? I'm going to Joe's!"

Noel poked his head out of the kitchen, lifting the radio earphones off his head. "Now?" he glanced at his mother, then at his watch and back at his mother again. "It's eleven-forty-five. Now?" he repeated.

"Now."

There were no lights on in Joe's house when she drove up, but a light-colored Buick was parked in the driveway so she decided her guess was right. He was probably inside, asleep. Should she leave it till tomorrow morning? She chewed her lip indecisively, then knew with absolute clarity that she couldn't. Even if he stared at her as though she was insane for banging on his door in the middle of the night and asking him why he was back, she had to do it. She had to know.

But her banging roused no one, not even when she thumped so loudly that she was sure the neighbors a hundred yards away could hear her. Liv shifted uncomfortably in the cool autumn air and wondered what to do now. Maybe he had gone down to the lake to walk in the moonlight. She smiled, thinking, oh, you romantic!

But she stuffed her hands in the pockets of her jeans and walked down to look at the lake. There was no one as far as she could see along the shore. The silvery moonlight cast fingers of light across the water, and she could pick out scruffy pine trees, several rocks and a small willow. But no Joe. It seemed so peaceful, so serene, so unlike her inner agitation. Maybe if she climbed up into the tree house she could see more. She'd never been there, but the kids had exclaimed about the view. She'd had no desire to see it herself. It was beastly high and seemed to be swaying now in the wind. Maybe climbing it wasn't such a good idea after all.

She walked back to it and tested the first rung of Joe's homemade ladder with her foot. It seemed sturdy enough.

Then what was that creaking she heard? Wind? She gripped one of the rungs with her hands, feeling suddenly as though she ought to go home after all. What could she see from up there anyway? Then she heard the creaking again. Muffled thumps. A groan. Not the wind, Liv decided, her heart lurching.

"Joe?" she called tentatively. Surely not. Who would climb up a tree in the middle of the night? "Joe?"

Another moan. More creaking.

She started climbing now, her hands damp on the rough wood, her torso drenched with a sweat of nervous apprehension, as much the result of climbing the tree as of confronting Joe. She poked her head up through the trap door in the floor of the tree house and looked around. "Joe?"

"Uhhh," he mumbled behind her. She hauled herself into the structure, scrabbling about on the floor, knees shaking. He was huddled in the far corner, knees pulled up to his chest, his dark head leaning against his knees.

"Joe?" She stood and tripped over something large. It rolled and made a clinking sound when it hit the tree house wall. "Good Lord," she murmured. She groped for it on her hands and knees, knowing by instinct—and smell—that it was a now-empty liquor bottle she held in her hands. "What on earth have you done?" she demanded, lifting his face in her hands.

He didn't seem to focus on her. "Whasit to you?" he asked roughly. "*You're* not s'posed to be here," he added when he saw who it was. He put his hands to his head as if to hold it on. "This isn't the way it was s'posed to be at all," he said plaintively like a small boy.

"Huh?"

"How can I tell you you love me and, and...no, I you...and marry...hell," he muttered. "I'm too drunk." His head slipped down again and he was asleep.

"Joe!" She shook him. "Joe!"

"Lemme sleep," he pleaded.

"We've got to get you down!" Marry? Did he say, marry? Love? I love him? Or he loves me? Stop it, she admonished herself. He's drunk out of his mind. He won't remember a bit of it in the morning. "Come on, Joe," she begged, trying to put her arms around him and drag him to the ladder. "We've got to get down."

"No," he mumbled, curling further into the corner. "Can't."

And she realized that he was more perceptive drunk than she was sober. In the shape he was in, he was treed for the duration. She chewed her nails in frustration. What could she do with a drunk man twenty-five feet up in a maple tree?

The answer wasn't all that hard to figure out. She had to go back down and call Frances, getting here to come and spend the rest of the night with the kids, gather up some blankets, and climb back up the tree and keep him warm for the rest of the night. She wasn't going to let him freeze to death now. Not when words like *love* and *marriage* were falling from his lips!

She thought afterward that there was a distinctly funny side to the whole scene, if only she'd been able to see it rather than participate in it. As it was, she spent the better part of half an hour inching her way back down the tree, rounding up the blankets and asking Frances to watch the kids.

"I'm staying up with a sick friend," she told Frances, not daring to mention whom, and Frances, Good Samaritan that she was, said she'd put on her robe and drive right over. Liv only hoped Noel had the sense not to say where she'd gone. But there was nothing she could do about that now. Now she had to head back to the tree where Joe slept like a babe.

"I'm back," she announced brethlessly, and was met by unconscious snores. "I should leave you to get pneumonia, you stupid pig," she groused at him with a sort of rough affection. But she dragged him instead onto one of the blankets and lay down next to him, pulling the heavy quilt from his bed over both of them. He didn't wake up, but the heat of her body attracted him, anyway, and he turned, burrowing into her, his cold arms going around her in a viselike grip. His champagne-scented breath, the only warm thing about him, fanned her cheek, and she shifted her body trying to get comfortable on the hard wooden floor and thought how much she loved him, how much she needed to feel him against her like this again.

"You insufferable wretch," she scolded, tears running down her cheeks as she stroked the tangled softness of his hair. "How could you do this to me? What sort of man mumbles words like love and marriage and then falls asleep?" She bit him gently on the jaw, and his head turned instinctively and his lips caught hers in a long, drugging kiss.

What have I done? she wondered. *How can I have fallen in love with a man so practiced that he can make love, dead drunk, in his sleep?*

FEATHER-LIGHT KISSES brushed her lips. She was in Vienna, waking up on Sunday morning, stretching, purring, and Joe was kissing her, murmuring in her ear, loving her. She'd had the dream before. A dozen times. More. And the ache when she opened her eyes to an empty bed was devastating. Cool, firm lips traced her jawline, nuzzled her earlobe. A cold nose caressed her hair. That was a new touch. She didn't remember dreaming the nose before. She opened her eyes, expecting the nose to vanish, the lips to disappear. A pair of bewildered jade-green eyes with a dark fringe of lashes stared into her own.

"What are you doing here?" he rasped, his voice filled with incredulity and uncertainty.

It was a new ending, at least. But she wondered if it was any more promising than the old one. He could have looked more welcoming. She propped herself up on her elbows so that her eyes were on a level with his. "Saving you from yourself, apparently," she told him, unsure of how much of last night she was supposed to know. "Whatever were you doing up here, drinking yourself into oblivion? On champagne, no less?"

The green gaze wavered, fell, then slowly rose to meet hers again. "I thought you, Tom...I saw...." He couldn't get it out. His eyelids flickered, then dropped, hooding his gaze.

"No."

"No?" He looked up again, a flame flaring to life in the eyes that now bored into hers. "No?" he asked again.

She shook her head, praying that the spark meant something. But once before, in Vienna, she had seen that spark too and, remembering, she held her breath and waited. He didn't speak for what seemed an eternity. Then, "I-love-you-will-you-marry-me?"

He said it so fast she wasn't sure she heard him at all. Her heart leaped, but her brow furrowed and, wanting to be sure, she asked, "What?"

"God," he growled, hunching his shoulders, a tide of red creeping above the collar of his thin jacket, "You're as bad at this as I am. You're supposed to say, 'yes,' or 'darling, of course,' or 'when?'" He shifted his weight onto one arm so that he bent over her, his mouth twisting. "Or I suppose you could say, 'no.'" He looked vulnerable and uncertain. His right hand moved up to caress her hair, but then, as if fearing he had no right to do so, he dropped it quickly to the quilt. "Well," he muttered. "Do you have an answer?"

"I thought you'd never ask!" She sat up suddenly, launching herself at him, flinging her arms around his neck in such an outburst of joy that she knocked him flat on the tree house floor.

"I take it the answer is yes," he said, grinning.

"Yes!" She bent over him, brushing her lips teasingly across his. But the teasing didn't last, couldn't, and it exploded instantly into a full-blown passion that enveloped them both. This time there was none of the gentleness of their Vienna love. Joe rolled her over, tugging at her clothes with the same feverish anticipation with which she was attacking his. Buttons popped, zippers rasped, bodies clung. He murmured to her in aching, broken whispers of the love he felt that he had so long misunderstood and then tried to deny. But Liv heard almost none of it, her ears were filled only with a raging passion, a roaring desire. Explanations meant nothing now. He was here, he was hers, and gripping him tightly with arms of surprising strength, she opened to him and the two became one.

"Oh, Liv," he muttered, his heart beating like a tympan against her breasts. "What have you done to me?"

"Loved you." She smiled, her own heart just now beginning to steady and slow. Her hand went up to stroke his hair and ear, and she tilted her head sideways, pulling back from him slightly to study his profile. He was clean-shaven again, with just a day's worth of sandpapery beard, handsome as ever, and when he grinned down at her, the tiny chicken pox scar next to his left eye crinkled into another engaging dimple. "Leave it to you," she teased, "to turn chicken pox to an advantage."

"Think so?" he looked enormously pleased, and she remembered that Veronique had said he'd never be the same again.

"What about Veronique and the Steve Scott film?" she asked suddenly.

"It's not on. Never has been." He told her about Luther's pressure tactics and his leak of the story to the gossip magazines. "You saw it?"

"Oh yes. That's when I thought all hope was gone."

"It nearly was," he admitted. "It seemed the path of least resistance, doing Steve Scott. I was ready to, I think. Then I got Noel's card."

Liv shook her head. "What card?"

"Telling me about his game. Remember, I told him that if I couldn't come he should send me a card with the score on it. He did. Also mentioned that you and Tom were there. I felt as if I'd been stoned. The very thought of you and Tom was all it took to crystallize my thinking. I knew then that I loved you, that I didn't want anyone else near you. Ever. I caught the next plane back to Madison, determined not to let him have you."

"So what happened? I mean, you came over last night and—"

"How did you know that?"

"Jennifer saw you."

"Oh. Well, I saw her and the boys. And Tom. I thought he was really back for good then." She saw a look of despair flash in his eyes as he remembered. "I thought I was really too late. And what was I going to do? Strap on a gun and challenge him to a duel? If he'd come to his senses sooner than I did, I figured it was nobler to leave. To try to forget you. I didn't deserve you, anyway."

Liv rolled her eyes. "You are an idiot. How could you think I still loved Tom after what he did? After what I did, making love to you?" She looked at him with all the love she felt there in her eyes for him to see, and he shook his head, smiling, kissing her, his own eyes flaming with a brightness that danced like the sunlight in the leaves rustling gently above their heads. Liv rolled over onto her back so that she lay side by side with Joe under the quilt, looking up at the green turning to gold above them. He grinned and said, "I've never made love in a tree house before." He turned his head and looked at her with warmth and gentleness in his face. "Have you?"

"Hardly." Liv laughed, then grew serious as she thought about all the places Joe had probably made love, even if he had missed tree houses until now. "Will I be enough for you, Joe?"

He frowned. "You mean, will there be other women besides you?"

"Yes." She didn't want to ask, but she had to, had to know if he'd considered it.

"No. I tried that already." He grimaced. "After I left you in Madison and went back to L.A., I told myself I could forget you. I was wrong. I loved no woman after you." He kissed the tip of her nose gently. "I'll never want to, I promise. I know now that it wasn't love I was after with them, anyway. It was challenge, coupled with needing to forget you. But I couldn't forget you. And now I've got you. Besides, just recently I discovered that you're all the challenge I'll ever need."

"I love you," Liv whispered, stroking an errant lock of hair off his forehead and following her fingers with her lips.

"And I love you." He sat up, his bare back dappled with sun as he groped in the blankets for the champagne bottle. "This was supposed to be for us to celebrate our future with," he said ruefully, tipping it upside down and letting the last drops spill out. "Shall I get dressed and go buy us another?"

Liv shook her head. "No thanks," she murmured, running her hands down the length of his spine till he shivered. "I think you should lie back down and prove how much you love me some more. And then when I'm convinced, we can climb down from our little love nest and drink a toast to our marriage as we mean to go on."

"Huh?"

She tugged him back under the quilt and wrapped her arms around him. "I mean, why bother with champagne when right in the kitchen here we have enough grape Kool-Aid to float a ship on!"

THE SEDUCTIVE KISS and warm breath touched Liv's ear just as a pair of hard arms went around her and pulled her back into her husband's arms. She started, then relaxed, loving the feel of his lean, hard length against her, relishing the kisses that continued down the edge of her jaw until suddenly they stopped.

"What's that slop you're mashing?" he demanded.

"Banana," she told him, turning in his arms and kissing him soundly on the lips before she stepped back to wave a forkful under his nose. "Want some?"

"Yuck." Joe wrinkled his nose. "Nick eats that? I thought he was a smart baby."

"He is," Liv agreed. "Takes after his mother."

Joe glared. "All Harrington. Spitting image of his father, everyone says."

"In looks, maybe," Liv conceded. "And personality. Who else has a two-month-old Casanova for a son?"

"Keep picking on me, and I won't tell you what I've planned for tonight," Joe mumbled into her hair.

"Tonight?"

"Our first anniversary. Or had you forgotten?" he teased.

"Of course not. But I thought you might have had enough to do recently, what with finishing up the screenplay and preparing to direct it, convincing Luther to produce it and arranging locations in Spain, to spend time planning anything else."

"I told you, I love a challenge," Joe grinned, kissing her nose. "That's why I married you."

"That's why, is it?" she asked tartly, turning back to the banana.

"Of course. And because I thought it was the easiest way to give my father a half-dozen grandchildren. Besides, I love you."

She dropped the fork with a clatter and turned, the banana forgotten. "I love you, too. More each day if possible."

"Good. You can start proving it right now." He spun her around again and untied the apron around her waist.

"But I've got to feed Nick," she protested. Aprons were a necessity with Nick. "And then I've got to pick up Ben at scouts and Stephen at cello, and Jennifer is—"

Joe shook his head. "Nope."

"Nope?"

"Nope."

"Are you trading Steve Scott for Gary Cooper these days?" Liv asked, but Joe didn't answer, just took her by the shoulders and steered her into the living room of the architect's house that was now permanently theirs. "Joe..." she began again, but then she looked up to see Arthur Harrington sitting on the couch, his youngest grandson regarding him in cross-eyed awe as he bounced up and down.

"Hello, my dear," Arthur's wife, Louise, said brightly from her seat by the bookcase, as though they had just popped in from next door.

"What on earth are you doing here?" Liv asked, stunned. "I thought you'd had enough of us to last till Thanksgiving at least." They had seen Joe's parents only last month at a lake in Minnesota. She thought the chaos of that week, joyful though it had been, would satisfy them for quite a while. Obviously she was wrong.

"They're baby-sitting for the weekend," Joe told her.

"All the way from Sioux City?" Liv sputtered.

"Absolutely," Arthur Harrington said firmly. "A man can't see too much of his grandchildren."

Joe looked at Liv and rolled his eyes. "Humor him," he told her. "It'll work in our favor, I promise you. We're spending a weekend at the Sheraton, just you and I. Undisturbed." He reached behind the chair where his mother was sitting and pulled out an overnight bag he had already packed. "Come along, my love," he said, taking her arm.

"But...." Liv stared at him in wonder, then looked at his parents, who beamed and urged her out. Shrugging she bent to give Nick a quick kiss. Then, marveling at the resourcefulness of the man she had married, she followed him, still bemused, out the door. "I can't believe they're really going to take care of the kids," she said as he helped her into the car.

Joe grinned. "Believe it. My father would walk across the Sahara for you and those kids." He bent over and kissed her lingeringly on the mouth before going around and getting in on the driver's side. "He considers marrying you the smartest thing I ever did." He touched her cheek tenderly, the love of a lifetime there for her to see in his eyes. "He was right, Liv," he said softly. "It was."